THE
HANGED MAN

A MYSTERY IN FIN-DE-SIÈCLE PARIS

GARY INBINDER

PEGASUS CRIME
NEW YORK LONDON

THE HANGED MAN

Pegasus Books Ltd.
148 W 37th Street, 13th Floor
New York, NY 10018

First Pegasus Books cloth edition August 2016

Interior design by Maria Fernandez

This is a work of fiction. Names, characters, places and incidents either are the product of the author's imagination or are used fictitiously.

ISBN: 978-1-68177-164-9

10 9 8 7 6 5 4 3 2 1

Printed in the United States of America
Distributed by W. W. Norton & Company, Inc.

In memory of my sister,
Carole, who told me fantastic stories

Frères humains, qui après nous vivez,
N'ayez les cœurs contre nous endurcis,
Car, si pitié de nous pauvres avez,
Dieu en aura plus tôt de vous mercis.
——François Villon, *Ballade des pendus*

PARIS

JULY 24, 1890

THE SUICIDE BRIDGE

A burst of sunshine pierced a cloud bar, spotlighting the crime scene. A landscape appeared within the boundaries of the metropolis, an Eden for the urban masses. A focal point of this pastorale, a single-arched masonry footbridge, led to the Temple of Sybil, the classical belvedere perched on a rocky promontory that rewarded the visitor with a panoramic view of Montmartre.

Sultry winds stirred leafy elms, gingkoes, beeches, and shrubbery; rustling branches reflected on the smooth, olive-colored surface of an artificial lake spanned by the high bridge. A flight of cawing crows circled overhead. A uniformed man, standing in the center of the bridge's planked walkway, hurled pebbles in the general direction of the scavengers.

"Damned rooks," muttered Sergeant Rodin. "I hope they haven't torn him up too badly." The sergeant frowned beneath his immense red moustache. He hooked his thumbs in the broad leather belt encircling his beefy midsection, turned his head, and addressed his next remark to Inspector Achille Lefebvre. "It'll be a shame if the birds have gotten to the face, Monsieur. Assuming we find no papers on him, it could make identifying him that much harder."

A guard making his early morning rounds had discovered the body hanging by its neck from two meters of stout rope fastened securely to the bridge's iron railing. Now, two police officers were carefully lifting the corpse by a cord looped under its armpits and around its chest.

Inspector Lefebvre kept his eyes fixed on the men raising the body. "I doubt he's been hanging long enough for the crows to have made a feast. Identification papers would help, but I don't rely on the dead for such conscientious assistance," he replied. Then, turning to his friend with a wry smile, he added, "But there are always clues, Sergeant."

Rodin laughed. "Well, Monsieur Lefebvre, if there are clues, you're the one to find them."

The police officers were in the process of hauling the body over the railing. One let his line slip, causing the body to drop to one side and swing precariously. The other man swore and groaned with the added effort of keeping the dangling corpse from plummeting into the lake.

"Careful, boys," Rodin shouted. "Don't want to break anything that's not already broken." The admonition worked; the grunting policemen soon regained control of their burden.

The photographer, Gilles, approached Achille and Rodin. He was a handsome young fellow who could approach even the most grisly crime scene with the jaunty air of a *flâneur*. "My equipment's set up," he told the two men. "There's plenty of light for some good exposures before we cart him off to the morgue." He lifted his straw boater, gazed up at the brightening sky, and mopped his forehead with a handkerchief. "It's going to be a warm one, don't you think?"

"A regular scorcher," Rodin replied. "I'd like to be out by the seashore and stay there till September."

Gilles looked to Achille. "What do you say, Inspector? Nice time for a holiday by the sea?"

Achille grimaced. He had promised his wife a romantic holiday at Trouville and had already made arrangements, but as he watched the policemen maneuver the corpse over the railing and down to the planking, he feared that the dead man might interfere with his vacation. "I'm afraid this job will keep us busy for a while, my friend."

Gilles sighed. "Somehow, I knew you'd say that, Monsieur." He looked again at the body and shook his head sadly. "Why did the poor bastard come all the way up here to hang himself, when he could have more easily done it at home? The attraction of this place for those looking to kill themselves is usually the twenty-two-meter leap."

Achille gave Rodin a knowing, sidelong glance before answering. "It's a good thing you're such a fine photographer, Gilles. You'll never be a detective. Why assume it's a suicide?"

Gilles gave a perplexed stare in reply.

Achille smiled and clapped his shoulder. "All we've got so far is a dead body hanging from a bridge in the Parc des Buttes-Chaumont. It could be suicide, homicide, even a macabre prank; perhaps something associated with the Butte. The place has quite a history, you know. The Montfaucon gibbet stood at the summit for centuries. It figured in Villon's *Ballade des pendus* and Victor Hugo's *Notre Dame de Paris*. The army took some of their Communard prisoners up here, shot them, and dumped the bodies in the old lime pits."

Achille pondered the bloody uprising following France's defeat in the Franco-Prussian War, the Communard insurgents who had declared a new government that lasted less than two months. It was certainly a historic place, perhaps even a haunted one.

"At any rate," he continued after a moment, "we'll know more after the pathologist makes his examination of the remains."

"Monsieur Lefebvre, I've found something—a couple of things, actually." Achille's assistant, Inspector Legros, knelt by the body and gestured to his superior, as if to emphasize the importance of his discovery.

Achille nodded and excused himself. On the way to investigate the body, he encountered the two policemen who had lifted the corpse. Puffing and mopping their sweaty brows, they seemed to be making a show of their recent exertions.

"Excuse me, Inspector," said the sweatier of the two, "but would you mind if we took a break?"

"I've no objection, but check with your sergeant first. And please don't wander off."

The policeman smiled. "Thank you, Monsieur." Suddenly reinvigorated, he and his companion took off in Rodin's direction.

Achille approached the corpse. Legros looked up and seemed about to speak, but Achille silenced him with a wave of his hand. He wanted to get his own first impression, unprejudiced by the assumptions of his assistant.

The birds had pecked here and there, but, thankfully, the damage to the man's features was minimal. Except for a few avian scratches, the pale, bloodless flesh was smooth and clear. His eyes were closed, and the gaunt face bore a serene expression that gave the illusion of eternal sleep. Obviously, the man hadn't strangled. Achille was familiar with the faces of strangulation victims, the mottled skin, bulging eyes, and black, protruding tongue, all evidence of their agonizing departure.

But he would not waste time speculating as to the cause of death; that was a job for the medical examiner. Achille was a skilled practitioner of

M. Bertillon's portrait *parlé*; his eye had been trained to act like a photographer's lens, his memory a fast photographic plate. He concerned himself with taking note of the facts: *a man of medium build and average height and weight; age forty to fifty years; medium brown hair and full beard; streaks of gray; receding hairline; long, straight nose, fleshy at the tip; slightly protruding ears, long lobes; no distinguishing scars, moles, ulcers, carbuncles, etc.*

But more than the photographer and his camera, Achille observed the corpse from the perspective of a true artist. Like his acquaintance, M. de Toulouse-Lautrec, Achille had attended dissections and lectures at the morgue. He understood the bone structure, the muscles, nerves and sinews, veins and arteries, the complex anatomical totality of the dead face confronting him.

Pursuant to his instructions, the policemen had not disturbed the noose; he wanted to leave that to the pathologist. The skill used in tying and placing the knot could provide an important clue. *Fracture of the vertebrae and compression of the arteries causing unconsciousness, followed by asphyxiation and death.* That was a quick and dirty assessment; he'd learn more from the doctor at the morgue, later that day.

Prior to the hanging, someone had removed the collar and necktie to make way for the noose. He made a mental note to have the area searched to see if they could be found. The nondescript dark brown suit was neither cheap nor expensive, and lacked any obvious patches, holes, or other signs of wear. The black leather boots had been polished recently; there was little wear on the heels and soles. *The shoes would have been muddied if he'd gone off the footpath. Leaves or dirt might have clung to his clothing. There might be tears if a sleeve had caught on a branch.*

Having made these quick, initial observations, Achille concentrated on one of the items that had caught his assistant's attention. There was a note pinned to the breast of the dead man's jacket. Adjusting the pince-nez balanced on the bridge of his aquiline nose, Achille hunkered down next to Legros to get a better look.

"Is this note one of the interesting 'things' to which you referred?"

"Yes, Monsieur; it's in a foreign script, as you can see. A suicide note, perhaps?"

Achille smiled, and turned to Legros. "Is perception reality, Étienne?"

Legros eyed his superior with a puzzled frown. "Pardon me, Monsieur. I don't understand."

Achille shrugged and heaved a little sigh. "It's a note pinned to a dead man's jacket. As of now, neither you nor I know who wrote it, when, where, or to what purpose." He rose to his feet and made a gesture pointing to one end of the footbridge. "This bridge, M. Legros, is a means of getting from point A to point B, and it's supported by an arch. Think of it as analogous to our investigation. We are at point A, just beginning to cross the lake on our way to a destination, over there, the Temple of Sybil." Achille made another illustrative gesture.

"Now consider each clue, each relevant bit of evidence we discover, as a stone in the arch. To reach our objective, we must first build the bridge. Omit one block and the whole thing will collapse and tumble twenty-two meters into the water below. Moreover, we are not winged creatures who may take flights of fancy over the lake, skipping the laborious task of erecting our sturdy bridge."

Having made his point, Achille turned his attention back to the note. "The script is indeed foreign; it's Cyrillic, used in writing Russian, Bulgarian, Serbian, and other Slavonic languages."

Legros smiled broadly. "Yes, M. Lefebvre, and now you'll see why the other item I discovered is of particular interest." Legros rose and stood next to Achille. He took a pair of tweezers from his breast pocket, opened an evidence bag, retrieved a cigarette butt, and held it up for Achille's inspection. "It's a Sobranie, isn't it?"

Achille recognized the distinctive paper and cardboard-tube filter. "Where did you find this?"

Legros pointed. "Over there, on the planking next to the railing where the rope was fastened. I've marked the spot with chalk."

Achille eyed the cigarette butt with a skeptical squint. "Did you find anything else on the individual's person, or in close proximity? Identity papers or passport, watch, rings, billfold, photographs, tickets—perhaps a packet, cigarette case, or match box?"

Legros frowned and shook his head. "No, Monsieur."

Achille muttered under his breath, *"Merde!"* After a moment, he pursued. "So, Étienne, you think a note in Cyrillic script and a half-smoked Sobranie equals one dead Russian?" Before Legros could reply, Achille turned toward Gilles and Rodin, who were engaged in an animated debate concerning the relative merits of dancers at the Moulin Rouge and the Folies Bergère. "Say, Gilles, bring your camera over here, if you please. Sergeant Rodin, you might also find this of some interest."

The photographer and the sergeant joined Achille and Legros. "Gilles," said Lefebvre, "I want photographs of the corpse with the note. When you've taken the pictures, M. Legros will remove the note." He turned to his assistant. "Carefully, Étienne, I don't want your fingerprints on the paper."

Gilles interjected, "Ah, Monsieur, I anticipate another of your forensic experiments. Do you want me to check the note for latent prints, using the Coulier method?"

"Yes, Gilles, and I want a good, sharp photograph of the document for my expert translator. The original, of course, must be carefully preserved in evidence."

"But of course, Monsieur." Gilles nodded the affirmative with a wry smile, indicating that he knew the Lefebvre manner and did not need to be reminded.

"You know, Inspector," Rodin broke in, "I was certain Chief Bertillon would incorporate fingerprinting into his identification method following your stunning success in the Virginie Ménard case."

Achille turned to Rodin. He appreciated the comment, since he believed that it was prompted by sincere admiration for his detective skills, rather than mere flattery. "Thank you, Sergeant. For the moment,

M. Bertillon considers his anthropometric system sufficient, though he does not forbid my using fingerprinting on an ad hoc basis." In fact, Achille had been gravely disappointed by Bertillon and the prefect's rejection of his plan to incorporate fingerprinting into their identification system, an innovation that would have put the Sûreté ahead of all the world's police agencies in the new science of forensics. At least Achille had the consolation of knowing that his own chief, M. Féraud, and the *juge d'instruction*, Magistrate Leblanc, had backed him to the hilt.

Achille left his companions to walk slowly up the bridge in the direction of Temple Island. The others went about their business and didn't disturb him; they knew his habits and moods. He was thinking about the case.

At the end of the bridge, Achille turned to his left and leaned against the railing. Pulling down the brim of his black bowler to shade his eyes from the sun, he scanned the area: the dense green- and gold-hued foliage on the muddy banks; the murky, olive-drab surface of the placid lake; and the sunbeams streaming through chinks in the cloudy sky. He wiped sweat from his neatly bearded cheeks with a handkerchief and brushed away the buzzing flies that had swarmed near the corpse. After a moment's contemplation, he gestured for Legros to join him.

"Do you see the incongruity of the situation, Étienne?"

Legros was accustomed to his superior's cryptic remarks, and gave his standard response: "Pardon, Monsieur?"

Achille made a sweeping gesture that encompassed the scene. "Look around you, Étienne. Isn't it lovely? And whom do we have to thank for this charming Rousseauian retreat in the midst of our bustling metropolis? Why, none other than the late Emperor and his prefect, Baron Haussmann. Yet many Parisians who enjoy this park as a place of recreation would condemn the Empire as a cesspool of corruption. So we have the incongruity of what many would consider a great good arising from what they might also condemn as an insufferable evil.

"But then, who, viewing from our present perspective, would deny the pristine beauty of this place? Yet, a thousand years ago, a great battle was fought on the bald summit, when Count Odo saved Paris from the marauding Vikings. Imagine all the hacked, dismembered, bloated corpses rotting in the sun, picked at by vermin. Think of the stench——"

"If you please, Monsieur Lefebvre, I'd rather not," Legros interrupted. "After all, our next stop is the Morgue."

Achille laughed. "You're right, Étienne. I've a tendency to prattle about such things. I suppose that's why the 'old boys' on the force call me the 'Professor.' I'll come to the point—look to the incongruities. A body hanging from this scenic bridge is like a pile of horseshit in front of the fancy shops on the Rue de la Paix, and we're the sanitary workers who must clean up before some elegant lady steps in it.

"Please take out your pencil and notebook, and we'll begin our list of things to do. We must determine who the victim was, as well as the time, place, and manner of his death. How, when, and under what circumstances did he enter the park and end up hanging from this bridge? Perhaps you noticed the relatively clean state of his shoes and clothing. He couldn't have spent much time off the beaten path. And the collar and necktie are missing, though I doubt he entered the park without them—a well-dressed man going about Paris without a collar and necktie would have been quite conspicuous. We'll need to conduct a search for the missing apparel. That's your job, Étienne, and Rodin and his men will assist you. And start looking for witnesses. Question the guard who found the body, and other park employees who might have seen the victim.

"I'll go to the Morgue on the meat wagon with the attendant, then check the records department. I'll get the note translated, follow up with Gilles on the photographs and fingerprint test, and attempt to locate the tobacconists who sell Sobranies. At the end of each day, we'll write up our reports for the chief. Any questions?"

Legros had a question, but he expressed it silently in his penetrating gaze, a narrowing of the eyes and a twist of the mouth beneath his neatly trimmed brown moustache, as though he'd bitten into an apple and discovered a worm. After being lectured by the "Professor" about unfounded assumptions and leaps of faith, he questioned whether his mentor was practicing what he preached. Achille appeared to be transforming a routine suicide, a case easily closed, into a full-blown homicide investigation. But the pupil lacked the self-confidence to question the master. "No, Monsieur," he said finally.

"Very well, Étienne. Let's get on with it."

⁓∞⁓

The hanged man lay supine on the "butcher's block," a bloodstained oak table deep within the bowels of the great Morgue on the Île de la Cité. Here, unidentified bodies, many of them fished out of the nearby Seine, were autopsied and embalmed prior to being placed on steel slabs in the refrigeration room. There they remained in cubicles behind immense plate-glass windows for public display. The intended purpose of this morbid exhibition was identification, though the Morgue also functioned as a popular theater of the macabre.

Cabinets filled with surgical instruments and chemicals lined the drably painted walls; anatomical charts hung from an easel near the dissection table. A blaze of intense white light streamed from gas mantles, and was amplified by a large reflector, highlighting the naked cadaver like an actor in a spotlight. Doctor Cortot, the pathologist, had removed the noose, examined the markings on the neck, and palpated the cervical vertebrae.

"A neat hangman's fracture, M. Lefebvre," he observed, lifting the head to show Achille. "If this had been an execution, I'd say the executioner had done his job well."

"So the man didn't strangle?"

"No, Inspector. He died of asphyxiation, after being rendered unconscious by the fracture and compression that cut off the blood flow to the brain. The rope was strong and pre-stretched, the knot expertly tied and correctly placed, the drop calculated accurately for a man of his height and weight."

"Do suicides typically hang themselves in this manner?"

The pathologist rested the head back on the table, wiped his hands with a towel, and looked up at Achille with a twisted smile. "In my experience, they do not. They bungle it badly, and suffer as a result. I can think of several better means to an end. I'm ready to certify hanging as the cause of death, probable suicide. As for the time of occurrence, based on the condition of the body, I'd say within the last twenty-four hours."

Achille sighed. *If only dead men could speak*, he thought. His eyes scanned the corpse, as if for the last time. Under the strong, concentrated light, he noticed some marks on the wrists. Achille bent over to get a better look. "What do you make of these bruises and abrasions?"

Cortot adjusted his spectacles and walked around the table to stand beside Achille. He examined the marks on the wrists. "I noticed these, Inspector, but I concentrated on the neck injuries to determine the cause of death. The marks are recent." The pathologist paused and looked to Achille. "I doubt he would have tied his own hands before killing himself. Was he bound when you found him hanging from the bridge?"

"He was not."

Cortot thought for a moment. Then he stated with authority, "I'm changing my opinion, Inspector, not as to the cause of death, but as to the person—or persons—involved. I'm afraid, without further evidence, that must remain undetermined."

Achille frowned and nodded his agreement. The doctor had confirmed his suspicions, but Achille was uncertain if that confirmation pleased him. "Thank you, Doctor. There's one more thing before I go. I want to finger-print the corpse, and I've brought equipment with me for that purpose."

The pathologist raised his eyebrows at the novelty of Achille's request. "Fingerprint a corpse? I know you had some success with fingerprinting in the Ménard case, but isn't this somewhat . . . irregular?"

Achille shrugged. "It's an experiment in forensic science, Doctor. I have authority from chiefs Féraud and Bertillon; you may check with them if you are concerned."

The pathologist responded with a bemused smile. "No, that's quite all right, Monsieur Lefebvre. Please proceed with your experiment. I'm at your service."

"Thank you, Dr. Cortot. As always, I appreciate your medical expertise and cooperation."

⁓

The Pont Neuf had spanned the Seine for three centuries, linking the Left Bank and the Right Bank to the Île de la Cité. Achille walked from his office on the Quai des Orfèvres to the long, stone-arched section of the bridge that crossed over to the Right Bank. From there, it was not more than a ten-minute walk to his apartment on a quiet, tree-lined avenue.

In truth, the apartment belonged to his mother-in-law, Madame Berthier. Achille paid Madame a nominal rent that permitted the Lefebvre family to enjoy greater comfort than they could have managed on an inspector's salary. Achille had a reputation for scrupulous honesty, and was generally respected and well-liked by his peers. But his agreeable, bourgeois domestic arrangements had given rise to an unkind intimation that having married well, Achille could afford to be honest.

Halfway across the bridge, Achille stopped, leaned against the balustrade, and lit a cigarette. He lifted his bowler and mopped his brow. Then he took a moment to gaze in the direction of the dark, shadowy bastions of officialdom—police headquarters, the Palais de Justice, the Conciergerie, and the Morgue—that comprised the hub of his working life. From this ancient, central location extended the Magistrate's Sword, reproducing itself in a multiplicity of sharp little blades poking and prodding their way through all points of the metropolis, and beyond.

The natural darkness of the hour was made softer by artificial light, emanating from thousands of gas lamps and new electric bulbs. So much light, it outshone the stars. *Has a false light made the city safer and more secure?* he wondered.

A throbbing of engines and a blaze of electric illumination announced a *bateau-mouche* chugging its way under the arches and up the river past the island. He watched the boat for a while, its propellers churning a white wake on the dark, still surface of the Seine. *Why couldn't the poor bastard have jumped off this bridge, like so many other routine suicides? Was it suicide? Murder? Or something else?*

Paris had a relatively low murder rate for a city of two and a half million, and most detectives liked routine cases. Something nice and easy, like a man who comes home from work, finds his wife in the arms of her lover, and kills them both in a fit of jealous rage. Achille had built his reputation on cracking the hard cases, the ones no one else wanted. Yet even he didn't want this one. *If only there hadn't been those marks on his wrists.* He could have turned the file over to Legros and gone off on his holiday with a clear conscience. But there was more to the conundrum than the evidence of bound wrists; there was the note; the Sobranie; the absence of any other personal items; the time, place, and manner of death; the totality of the circumstances. What if the iodine-fuming test brought out fingerprints that didn't match those he had taken from the corpse? And the note could raise more questions without providing answers.

Achille flicked his half-smoked cigarette away and watched as the tiny, glowing red tip disappeared into the darkness below. He muttered, "*Mon Dieu*, what a case."

◈

"I'm sorry I'm so late, my dear. I hope you received my message?" He bent down and kissed Adele's cheek. *How soft and warm she is*, he thought. *And such a delightful fragrance.* At that moment, he longed for three things: a bath, a cognac, and his accustomed place in bed beside his young wife.

"Indeed I did," she replied with just a hint of disappointment in her voice. "A new case, I assume. And as usual, you missed an excellent supper. I trust you made do with a sandwich?"

"Yes, I picked up something at the café-bar and took it back to the office. I'm reporting to Féraud first thing in the morning." He paused for a moment, then said, "The little ones are asleep, I suppose?"

Adele laughed softly. "Yes, thank goodness. Have you any idea of the time?"

He sighed and scanned the shadowy entry hall for signs of his mother-in-law. "Has your mother retired for the evening?"

"Yes, Achille, she has."

At least the dragon's in her lair, he thought. "I'm sorry I missed her."

She smiled at his polite fib. Then she noticed the condition of his shirtfront. "You're awfully damp. Why don't you get into the bathtub? When you're ready, I'll wash your back, and you can tell me about your new case."

He smiled and took her by the hand. "You're an angel. Sometimes I wonder what I've done to deserve you."

2

GIVE HIM ENOUGH ROPE

A fly buzzed around the green-shaded oil lamp on Chief Féraud's cluttered mahogany desk. The chief glanced up from Achille's report; his sharp brown eyes followed the insect's circuit around the lamp's smoking chimney. A hand lashed out and grasped the fly. A pathetic buzz emanated from the clenched fist.

"Gotcha, you little bastard." The fist tightened like a vise; the faint whining ceased. The chief leaned to his right, picked a scrap of paper from his wire wastebasket, and wiped the fly's remains off his palm. Having disposed of the pest, he returned to his perusal of the hanged man's file.

The dial on the wall clock read five-fifteen. The dusty shades were drawn down, covering the grimy windows that faced out onto the quay two stories below. There was little activity at this early hour; the only sound penetrating the tightly shuttered windows was the monotonous chugging of a tugboat towing a barge upriver. The pre-dawn hour was a good time to work, undisturbed by outside distractions and untroubled by the summer heat.

Féraud closed the file and laid it down on top of a pile of others. Leaning back in his chair, the chief hooked his thumbs in his vest pockets and stared for a moment at Achille, who sat stiffly upright on the other side of the desk. "Well, my boy, you think this might be a homicide?"

"It's possible, Chief," Achille replied cautiously. "The circumstances are suspicious, and there are the bruises and abrasions on the wrists, evidence that the individual had been bound. At any rate, I'll know more by the end of the day."

The chief nodded his agreement. "What's your plan?"

"Regarding identification, the morning papers will report the discovery of the hanged man, the location of the incident, and a brief description of the body. He's on display in the Morgue, and the attendants will keep an eye open for anyone showing an unusual interest in the corpse. An initial review of records didn't turn up anything, but with some additional information, especially the translation of the note, I should be able to narrow things down.

"Legros, with the aid of Sergeant Rodin and a couple of his men, is conducting a search of the area around the bridge. In addition, Legros is questioning park employees and concessionaires to see if he can turn up witnesses, or leads. I've placed a map of the park in the file. There are several ways in, besides the main entrance. A couple of these entrances would be close to the bridge, and less conspicuous. If this is a homicide, it's possible the individual was lured to the spot for a rendezvous."

"It's possible," the chief agreed.

"I'm going up to Gilles's studio in Montmartre to collect the photographs and get the results of the Coulier test on the note. If the prints on the note don't match the ones I collected from the cadaver, that, along with the other evidence, may rule out suicide."

The chief closed his eyes and fiddled for a moment with the ruby-eyed death's-head charm on his watch chain. Presently, he put his hands on the desk and stared directly at Achille. "Maybe he was illiterate, and had someone write the note for him?"

Achille frowned. "Yes, that's possible. I'll know more when I get the translation. I'm taking it to Mme Nazimova. She has a bookstore on the Boulevard St. Michel near the Sorbonne. She's good with all the Slavonic languages. I've used her before; she's discreet and reliable."

Féraud glanced down at his hands and mumbled, "Nazimova—Nazimova," as if trying to recall the name. Then he looked back at Achille with an enlightened gleam in his eye. "She's one of the Russian émigrés who came here via Switzerland back in '81."

The chief's reference to Nazimova's political background troubled Achille. Perhaps it would have been more prudent to suggest another translator. "That's correct, Chief," he said cautiously. "She and her late husband came here as political refugees. Of course, if you'd rather I use someone else—"

"No, that won't be necessary," Féraud broke in. For a moment, he rested his chin on his hand, stroked his thick black moustache, and marked Achille with a gimlet eye. "She may be under surveillance, but that could be to our purpose."

"Do you think she's being watched by the political brigade?"

Féraud raised his eyebrows. "But of course. Who else do you think would have her under surveillance?"

Achille almost blurted out, "The Okhrana." They were the Russian secret police, which ran a network of agents from its headquarters in the Russian Embassy on the Rue de Grenelle. The Okhrana spied on Russian émigrés with the cooperation of the prefecture's political brigade and the unofficial sanction of the French government.

Instead of directly referring to the Russians, Achille decided to broach the subject obliquely by mentioning his old partner, Rousseau. After twenty years on the force, Rousseau had resigned in disgrace following his questionable actions in the Ménard case. He'd subsequently obtained a position in the political section, where he had gained credit for deploying his broad network of snoops and snitches on behalf of superiors who ignored Rousseau's extrajudicial methods. Moreover, rumor had it that Rousseau worked directly for the Russian bureau chief.

"If she's being watched, isn't it likely one of Rousseau's men would be shadowing her?"

Féraud grinned and gave a little snort, a knowing laugh through the nostrils. "Oh, I'd say it's more than likely; it's a certainty." For an instant, the chief's keen eyes studied his protégé's features for a reaction. Then he observed, "Achille, you're stiff as a soldier on parade. Sit back and relax." He glanced up at the clock and then opened a desk drawer and retrieved a cigar box. "We've time for a smoke and a friendly chat. You'll appreciate these, I'm sure. The finest clear Havana, a gift from a generous friend."

Achille smiled. "Thank you, Chief. I'll save mine for after dinner."

"Ah, there's nothing like ending the day with cognac and a good cigar. So you shall have two; smoke one with me now, and save the other for later."

"That's very kind of you."

"Not at all, Inspector." Féraud sliced the end off a cigar with his miniature desktop guillotine and handed the neatly decapitated Havana along with its unclipped companion to Achille. They lit up and each took a few satisfying puffs. "Yes," the chief remarked, "this is a real gentleman's smoke." Féraud exhaled and blew a couple of rings, watching them drift toward the ceiling. Then he set the cigar down in a brass ashtray. "Now, getting back to the case. Let's say our unidentified hanged man turns out to be a Russian émigré. What will you do?"

Achille took his cigar from his lips and leaned over to knock a bit of ash into Féraud's tray. Then he sat back in his chair and looked the chief squarely in the eye. "I'd turn the file over to the political brigade, let Rousseau and his pals handle it."

The chief smiled broadly. "Yes, my boy, that would be very proper—according to the book. Were I in your position, that's exactly what I would have said. Get the damned file off my desk, that's what I'd do, especially if I had a nice seaside holiday with my young wife to look forward to." Achille frowned, about to protest, but Féraud cut him off. "Believe me, that's no criticism. The brigade knows I'm planning for my retirement this year, and you're my picked successor. When the prefect asked who my best detective was, I gave him your name without hesitation.

"But there's more to this job than detective work—much more. There's administration, public relations, and politics. Our brigade runs on money, and that must be appropriated by the legislature. The prefect goes begging to the legislators for every precious franc and centime. As for me, I must ensure that we receive our fair share of the pie, and not just a few crumbs from the crust.

"Now, there are plenty of plodders in the brigade. They handle the routine cases, put in their time, and collect their pensions in due course. But you, my boy, are a thoroughbred, destined for great things. The press and the public have noticed your work; you're well-regarded in high places. That's why you get the cases no one else wants. Because when you crack the case, it brings credit to the brigade, and along with that credit come the appropriations we need to run efficiently and, hopefully, to expand our operations. And remember, it's all done for the public good."

"But what about the political brigade?" Achille interjected. "We can't poach on their preserve."

"Ah, I was coming to that. Tell me truthfully; do you harbor a grudge against Rousseau?"

Achille recalled Rousseau's obstructionist attitude and performance in their last case. Whether through negligence or by design, Rousseau had botched his end of the investigation, making Achille's job more difficult. But Achille knew that the chief wanted to promote an atmosphere of collegial cooperation between the criminal investigation division and the political branch—at least, up to a point. He answered carefully. "I'm willing to let bygones be bygones, as long as it's in the best interest of the service."

Féraud smiled and nodded his approval. "I knew you'd see it that way. Now, here's how I want you to proceed—for the time being, stick with the case. If it turns out that the hanged man is a political émigré, it's most likely Mme Nazimova knew him. Don't tell her anything about the case. Ask her to translate the note, and see how she reacts. You may tell her what's already in the public record, and be sure to show her the victim's photograph. If she identifies him, find out what she knows.

"One of Rousseau's snoops is probably keeping an eye on Nazimova's shop, and your former partner will have files on all the Russian émigrés. Contact him and tell him you're willing to work with him, exchange information, and so forth. Shake hands on it, for old times' sake. After all, it's to your mutual benefit. You have your methods and he has his, but we're all playing on the same team—for the good of France."

Achille smiled and accepted the situation with the ostensible enthusiasm of a career public servant.

Achille took a tram to Gilles's studio on the Boulevard de Clichy. Dressed in a light summer suit and straw boater, he rode on top in the open air to avoid the stuffiness and sour smell of the closed passenger compartment below. As the large draft horses plodded along, he yearned for the day when the line would become electrified. The anticipated advancement in metropolitan transportation would improve speed and efficiency, cut down on the piles of horse dung and puddles of piss with their attendant swarms of disease-spreading flies, and relieve the poor animals from the torment of hauling such heavy loads.

To pass the time—and be less conspicuous—Achille concealed his face behind a copy of *Le Petit Journal*. While ostensibly concentrating on the latest installment of a detective novel, he surreptitiously observed his fellow passengers: a couple of chattering young women, perhaps shop-girls, and an old man with a long white beard, who was dressed in a shabby suit, his wizened head crowned with a battered bowler hat.

According to Bertillon, there were three points the detective should concentrate upon for his verbal portrait: the lips, the ears, and the shape of the skull. The contour of these features remained constant from cradle to grave. A suspect could pad his nostrils to change the shape of the nose, use tinted glasses to cover his eyes, shave a beard or moustache or add false facial hair, or use dye—or a wig—to change hair color. A young man could make himself look old, or vice versa; he might disguise himself to look like a woman, or a woman could transform herself into a man.

Using Bertillon's method, Achille could get an accurate *portrait parlé* of his fellow passengers without much trouble. But in the serial-ized novel, the detective was tailing after a young woman through the dark, twisting streets of Montmartre. The suspect in the story wore a broad-brimmed hat and a veil; for all the detective knew, she could have been a he. *How could he determine the correct form of her ears, lips, or skull under such circumstances?* Achille shook his head, annoyed with the fiction, and sighed.

The clopping of the horses' hooves ceased, the brakes squealed, the bell clanged; they had arrived at the tramway stop near Marshal Moncey's statue in the Place de Clichy. Achille folded his newspaper, rose from his seat, and walked down the winding exit stairs to the pavement. At street level, he crossed the busy intersection in the direction of the large, four-story office block that housed Gilles's studio. Achille entered the foyer, his footsteps echoing on the checkerboard marble floor as he walked briskly to the stairway. Bright, warm rays of sun streamed down from a skylight high above the fourth-floor landing, where the photographer's studio was located. Achille bounded upstairs, two steps at a time, anxious to see how the photographs had come out, and most particularly concerned about the results of the fingerprint test.

Gilles greeted his friend with his customary cheerfulness. "Good day, Inspector, and a lovely day it is. Sunny, clear, and not as bloody hot and humid anymore."

Achille took a moment to catch his breath. Then he asked, "Did the prints come out all right?"

"Champing at the bit, eh? Well, I won't keep you in suspense. Everything came out splendidly; I think you'll be pleased." Gilles beckoned, leading Achille to a long workbench at the back of the studio near the darkroom. Achille noticed what appeared to be a large parcel wrapped in brown paper, seemingly displayed on the bench in such a conspicuous manner as to pique his curiosity.

Achille smiled knowingly and pointed toward the object. "I suppose you're going to tell me what's in that package. Is it another one of your gadgets? The latest American Kodak, perhaps?"

Gilles laughed. "This, my friend, is something of my own devising: a camera disguised to look like a parcel." Gilles turned the camera around so Achille could see the concealed lens, the shutter buttons, and the knob that could be rotated to change the plates. "It contains enough dry plates for twelve exposures. Might come in handy in your line of work, don't you think?"

Achille lifted the camera to examine it more closely and get the feel of it. "It's a bit bulky to carry around all day, even with the handle. I suppose you'd aim it like this?" Achille pointed it in Gilles's direction.

"That's right, Inspector. And I tried to keep the weight to a minimum."

"Hmmm . . . all right. But I assume you'd need good weather, plenty of light. And the detective would need to consider the range, and focus—"

"They could be trained," Gilles broke in with a frown. "I could train them."

Achille nodded and returned the camera to the workbench. "It's a good idea, Gilles. I'll keep it in mind. Now let's take a look at the photographs."

Gilles had expected more enthusiasm for his camera, but he didn't express his disappointment. He retrieved a large envelope from a nearby file cabinet, blew off some dust, and handed it to Achille. "You'll see I got a sharp image of three fingers from the back of the document. I'm afraid the thumb prints on the obverse near the writing are a bit blurred."

Achille took out his magnifying glass, then reached into his jacket pocket and removed the card containing the hanged man's fingerprints. He set the card next to the photograph on the end of the workbench that was lit brilliantly by sunshine streaming through the large skylight. After a few minutes' scrutiny, Achille said, "Look, Gilles, you can see a distinct difference in the whorl and loop pattern."

The photographer bent over and peered through the magnifier. Achille used a pencil as a pointer to highlight the discrepancy. Presently, Gilles nodded his agreement and returned the glass. "Yes, Inspector, I see the difference. So, what does it mean?"

"It means someone other than the deceased got his or her hands on this note, and it wasn't the police. Rodin's done a good job training his men in that regard."

"So, what's next, Inspector?"

Achille packed up the photographs and tucked them into his jacket pockets. Then he announced, "I'm off to headquarters to deposit the evidence; then, I'll take copies of your photographs to an expert translator in the Latin Quarter. And I must meet with Legros to see what he's turned up, if anything." He smiled and held out his hand. "You've done excellent work, as always, my friend. And I really do like your concealed camera. I'll talk to Féraud about it when I get a chance. But for now, I'm afraid I'm preoccupied with this case."

Gilles shook hands warmly and returned the smile. "I understand, my friend. And good luck, though I doubt you'll need it."

Achille shook his head and remarked wistfully, "With this one, I fear I'll need all the help I can get."

∾

It was a short walk from headquarters across the Pont Saint-Michel and up the boulevard past the monumental fountain to Madame Nazimova's shop. Achille habitually enjoyed this stroll—his favorite café-bar was nearby—but his mind was too focused on his case to notice the familiar sights. Nor was he much concerned with the milling crowd in the Place Saint-Michel; they were mostly tourists this time of year, the students having gone off on holiday.

On such ostensibly informal excursions from his official world on the Île de la Cité, he tried to blend in with the crowd. He hoped his light-colored summer suit, the straw hat worn at a jaunty angle, a copy of *Le Petit Journal*, and an affable manner would camouflage the sign that his profession had permanently hung around his neck: "Beware the Cop."

The jingling shop bell on Madame Nazimova's door announced his arrival. He entered the dusty warren of narrow aisles and towering bookshelves stacked halfway to the ceiling. A high-pitched voice squeaked from the shadowy recess behind the stacks. "Good afternoon, Monsieur Lefebvre. Are you here to see Madame?"

Achille smiled and peered in the direction of the greeting. "Good afternoon, Marie. Yes, I have some business with Madame. I hope she's available?"

The shop assistant emerged from her shelter, a mousy miniature in grisaille. "She's in the back taking tea, Monsieur. Please wait here; I'll just be a moment."

While waiting for Madame Nazimova, Achille amused himself by thumbing through a leather-bound volume of Paul de Kock's *La Pucelle de Belleville*. He shook his head and smiled at the marked price. *The illustrations and binding are much better than de Kock's scribbling*, he thought. *Only tourists would pay good money for such outmoded rubbish.*

"Madame will see you now, Monsieur."

Achille replaced the volume and walked to a curtained-off room in the back of the shop. Marie drew back the *portière* and announced Achille. She gave him a quizzical, sidelong glance before returning to her duties.

Madame Nazimova sat at a round tea table in the center of the small chamber. She was a bird-like woman of indeterminate age, dressed in a well-worn russet silk frock. Her curious, light blue eyes stared at him through steel-rimmed glasses. "Forgive me for not rising, M. Lefebvre. A touch of rheumatism, I'm afraid; surprising in such lovely weather."

Achille lifted his hat, smiled, and made a slight bow. "Please don't go to any trouble, Madame," he replied. "I trust you are otherwise well?"

"As well as can be expected, Monsieur." She gestured to an empty chair and place setting. "Marie has set a place for you. I'd be honored if you would join me for tea."

"That's most kind of you, Madame." Achille sat and immediately searched for a place to hang his hat. The little room, with its faded rose wallpaper and mildewed scent, was bare of furniture except for the table and two chairs.

She noticed his confusion and offered a solution. "Please set your hat on the table, Inspector."

Achille placed his boater on the white linen tablecloth, next to a tarnished samovar. She served him tea; he accepted a slice of lemon, but declined her offer of milk and sugar. Then she called his attention to a plate of madeleines. "You must try one of these, M. Lefebvre. They're fresh from the local bakery."

Achille refused the tea cookie. "No, thank you, Madame. I just ate, and I'm quite full." In fact, he was quite hungry, and the madeleines were tempting. He had survived all morning on coffee and cigarettes, but there was still plenty of work ahead. He was anxious to get down to business and move on, but he would be polite. On the other hand, he would not prolong the tea ceremony. After a few minutes of small talk, Mme Nazimova must have sensed Achille's impatience in his terse statements, darting eyes, and drumming fingers.

"I enjoy your company, M. Lefebvre, but I assume you're here on official business rather than social. Do you have something that requires translation?"

Achille smiled with relief. "Yes, Madame. I've a very short document written in Cyrillic characters. I'll pay the usual rate, if you'll be so kind as to provide a receipt for my expenses."

Madame adjusted her glasses and held out her hand. "If you please, Inspector."

Achille retrieved the photograph from his jacket pocket and handed it to Madame. She examined the note for a moment, returned it to Achille, and regarded him with a blank stare. The blankness of her expression transmitted a mixed message: Either she was indifferent to the contents of the note, or she was concealing her true feelings by affecting a lack of interest. "The message is written in modern Russian," she said in a flat monotone that matched her facial expression. "It's a verse from the Bible, Matthew 27:5: 'And he cast down the pieces of silver in the temple, and departed, and went and hanged himself.'"

Achille confronted her studied emptiness with a critical eye. *The hanged man was Judas, but whom did he betray, and why? She knows something, and she's holding it back.* His questioning frown transformed quickly into a disarming smile. "Thank you, Madame. This information is helpful, and I believe you might be of further assistance in my investigation. I'm trying to identify a man found hanging from a bridge in the Parc des Buttes-Chaumont, and I'd like you to look at a photograph. But I must warn you, it's somewhat unpleasant."

A faint smile played along her bloodless lips. "I'm used to the face of death, Inspector. And I'm pleased to cooperate with the police." She scrutinized the photograph of the dead man taken on the bridge, with the noose still looped round his throat and the note pinned to his jacket. "Lev Dmitryevich," she muttered. She handed back the photograph and looked at Achille with eyes like windows with the blinds drawn—he could get nothing from them.

"Who was he, Madame?" he asked in a quiet, sympathetic voice.

After a moment, she said, "Lev Dmitryevich Kadyshev. He and my late husband met at the university in St. Petersburg; they studied medicine together. We left Russia for Switzerland about the same time, in 1881, and remained in contact when we immigrated to Paris. But I haven't seen him since my husband died, more than a year ago." She paused before asking, "But I assume you have a dossier on him?"

Achille supposed Rousseau had a file, but he wanted Nazimova to believe he already had the information, or could easily obtain it. On the other hand, he needed to locate Kadyshev's residence immediately. "Yes, Madame, but I must confirm his present address. It's a matter of some urgency, as I'm sure you'll appreciate."

She eyed him warily for an instant before answering. "As far as I know, he still rents—pardon me, rented—a room in a house on the Rue des Saules, near the vineyard on the Butte."

Achille took out his pencil and notepad. "Thank you, Madame." Looking up from his note he added, "Do you know his occupation or place of work?"

"Well, Inspector, as I said, it's been more than a year. At any rate, since he couldn't practice medicine in France, he worked in an apothecary shop on the Place du Tertre across from the new town hall. Is that helpful?"

Achille smiled and returned the notepad and pencil to his breast pocket. "Thank you, Madame, and I won't trouble you further—today. You've indeed been very helpful, but please understand that I may return for more questioning."

"I understand perfectly, Inspector. One might assume Kadyshev was under surveillance—to a greater or lesser extent, we all are. However, being constantly watched can get on one's nerves. One longs to be free. Then, who is free in this world? Perhaps death is the only true liberation."

Achille nodded politely, but he had no time for gloomy philosophy. He bid Madame good day, dashed out of the shop, and walked rapidly up the boulevard and across the bridge. As soon as he reached his office, he telephoned the police station in Belleville with a message for Legros and Rodin: "Urgent. Have discovered victim's name and residence. Break off search and meet me at the Montmartre station. Lefebvre."

⌘

"Inspector Legros, over here—I've found something!"

Legros and Rodin were standing on the path leading to the bridge. They supervised a detail of three policemen searching an area approximately ten meters from the site of the hanging. Having spent most of the day looking for evidence without success, the policeman's summons was a welcome interruption.

The men walked to a shady clearing a few meters from the footpath, where they came upon the young policeman, flushed with excitement and pointing toward his discovery. "It's a man's necktie and collar lying in the grass at the foot of that tree."

Legros crouched to examine the objects resting in a clump of grass between the thick, gnarled roots of a tall elm. He took out his evidence bag, put on a pair of gloves, and lifted the tie to get a better look. "Average quality silk, cut neatly with a razor or sharp knife," he said to no one in particular. He deposited the necktie in the bag and turned his attention to the collar. "Appears to have been ripped off; the buttons popped. One's over there in the grass." He got up and turned to Rodin. "Let's continue searching this area. And I want to send a message to Inspector Lefebvre."

"Right, Inspector," the sergeant replied. Rodin scanned the area for a moment, then pointed and exclaimed, "Look, over there, in the bushes."

Legros focused on the undergrowth near the elm. He noticed a white object. Hunkering down, he parted the foliage and retrieved a linen handkerchief. He dropped the evidence in his bag, and continued his search. A dark, familiar shape caught his eye. Reaching into the tangled underbrush, he retrieved a small, uncorked brown bottle. Legros sniffed the bottleneck.

His eyes widened with recognition of a faint, cloying odor, like overripe fruit. "Chloroform?"

Legros's speculation was interrupted by a red-faced, panting gendarme. The man took a moment to catch his breath and then handed an envelope to Rodin. "Sergeant—M. Legros, I have an urgent message from Inspector Lefebvre."

∽

Kadyshev had rented a room in a yellow-painted, four-story residence on the Rue des Saules across from the vineyard that had recently been decimated by phylloxera. This quiet neighborhood, known for its rural charm, had acquired a somber aspect, perched high above the city near the Butte's summit and close to the rising white walls of Sacré-Coeur. The once-thriving vineyard had become a graveyard of the grape, its abundant vines had withered and grown moribund, denuded of their broad green leaves and succulent fruit.

The arrival of three policemen on her doorstep shocked Mme Arnaud, the concierge. She knew Sergeant Rodin well and expressed her anxiety to him directly. "One of my tenants, murdered, M. Rodin? Such a thing is unthinkable. It will give the house a bad name."

Rodin's familiarity and solicitous demeanor calmed her. Achille thought it best to question Mme Arnaud in Rodin's presence, trusting Legros to conduct a thorough preliminary search of Kadyshev's room. The concierge led the policemen into her tightly shuttered sitting room, where she settled her ample skirts onto a velvet-upholstered settee and offered Achille and Rodin a pair of lumpy, stiff leather chairs. After a tense moment, a tinkling silver bell and a plaintive meow initiated conversation. Achille was greeted by a cat rubbing its muzzle against his pant leg.

Mme Arnaud's eyes widened in surprise and a network of wrinkles spread across her face in reaction to the prodigious sight. "This is impossible, M. Lefebvre. Cyrano hates strangers. To be honest, he doesn't much like people he knows, including me, not to mention other cats. But he absolutely loathes strange humans."

Madame's wonder magnified when Achille scratched the old Siamese behind his ear. Cyrano responded by springing onto Achille's lap, curling into a ball, and purring blithely while casually flipping his tail against Achille's thigh.

"I guess I have a way with cats, Mme Arnaud," Achille remarked. He didn't add that cats had a way with him, too. If he didn't get on with his questioning, his eyes would begin to water, his throat would scratch, and he might be seized by a fit of sneezing.

Rodin viewed the interchange among cat, concierge, and detective with a knowing grin. Good relations with a concierge could prove invaluable in police work. The ubiquitous Parisian gatekeepers tended to be more knowledgeable and reliable than the best-paid informers, at least when it came to the comings and goings of their tenants.

"My dear Mme Arnaud," Rodin said, "in addition to his remarkable affinity for cats, M. Lefebvre is one of France's most distinguished detectives. I vouch for him without reservation."

The old woman smiled fondly at Achille. "Since both Cyrano and my old friend Sergeant Rodin hold you in such high regard, I shall, of course, do whatever I can to assist in your investigation."

Achille smiled, thanked her, and began his polite interrogation. He continued gently stroking Cyrano's neck and back, as if by doing so he could further ingratiate himself with both the cat and its mistress. "Mme Arnaud, how long have you known M. Kadyshev?"

She narrowed her eyes, pursed her lips, and thought a moment. "I believe he first came here by way of Geneva, back in the fall of 1881. Of course, I have a record of the exact date. That was the year of the Tsar's assassination. Many Russians came here back then."

"Can you tell me what sort of gentleman he was? I mean, his habits, customs, and general demeanor. Did he have many friends, or was he the sort who kept to himself?"

"Well now, he was an educated gentleman; he had a medical degree from his own country, but he wasn't qualified to practice here so he worked as an apothecary at a shop in the square. I'd say in most regards he was an ideal tenant—neat, quiet, and always paid the rent on time. And he was polite, but not friendly, if you know what I mean. A solitary fellow, and rather gloomy—but I have no reason to complain of him."

Achille thought, *Speak well of the dead or not at all.* "I see. Can you recall any friends or acquaintances of his—male or female?"

Madame sighed. "There were no women, which might seem odd. He was a decent-looking man and seemed healthy enough. He dressed well for a man of his class and occupation, but he wasn't a pansy. I know that sort, not that I have any particular prejudice against them. At any rate, in all the years he was here I can recall only two male acquaintances, both of them Russian."

"Do you know their names?"

"Yes, there was a M. Nazimov. He was a doctor by profession, like M. Kadyshev. A thin, pale gentleman as I recall, and he coughed a good deal. He might have been consumptive. Anyway, he hasn't been here in years."

Achille assumed that she referred to Mme Nazimova's husband; the information squared with what Nazimova had told him about their relationship with Kadyshev. "And the other man?"

"Ah, that would be M. Boguslavsky—what names these people have. He visited quite frequently, as recently as last week. I think he's a chemist. A loud man, not as polite as M. Kadyshev, and he smokes like an old stove."

Achille immediately recalled the Sobranie. "Excuse me, Madame. Did this man smoke a pipe or a cigar?"

"No, Inspector, he smoked cigarettes, one right after the other. And he dropped the butts on the landing, the stairway, in the entrance hall, or anywhere else he pleased."

"Do you remember anything different or unusual about the cigarettes he smoked?"

"Yes, they were long with cardboard tips, the kind Russians smoke. Heaven knows I've had to pick up enough of them."

"Can you give me a more detailed description of M. Boguslavsky? His approximate age, height, weight, and build, and color of skin, hair, beard, and eyes? Or any unusual distinguishing features—scars, deformities, and so forth?"

"Oh, he's a bear, taller than you by a couple of centimeters, and stocky. I'd say he's in his forties; he has a full brown beard that comes down well below his collar and he's balding on top, but no gray. Big brown eyes and a gruff manner. And he does have a nasty scar above the beard on his left cheek. Might have got it dueling, which wouldn't surprise me; he's that sort of man."

"This is very helpful information, Madame. You said you believe he's a chemist. Do you know where he's employed?"

She shook her head. "No, M. Lefebvre, I'm afraid not. You might ask over at the café near the apothecary shop. He and M. Kadyshev used to go there for coffee and to play chess. And, I assume, to talk politics."

The mention of politics piqued Achille's interest. "Politics—did you ever overhear any of their discussions?"

Mme Arnaud flushed a bit and laughed nervously. "Well, Monsieur, I don't eavesdrop. But I have overheard them, on occasion, speaking in a mixture of French and Russian, and I could make out some of it. Stuff about workers and peasants, oppressors and tyrants, strikes, revolution, that sort of thing."

She paused a moment, glanced at her old friend Rodin, and then looked back at Achille with a grim frown. "You know, M. Lefebvre, many of us up here still have bitter memories of 1871. I remember an old priest, Abbé Laurent, a kindly gentleman who always cared for the sick and the poor, and never harmed anyone. He was one of the hostages shot by the mob on the Rue Haxo. No, Inspector, I want nothing to do with that sort of 'politics.'"

Achille understood perfectly. Across the political spectrum, Parisians had painful memories of the Commune. Asking questions about what had occurred, especially during the Bloody Week, was like probing an old wound that had never completely healed. "Madame, we'll need to question your other two tenants. I understand they're both presently at work?"

"Yes. Messrs. Jacquot and Lebel. But I assure you, they had nothing to do with the Russians."

"I understand, Madame. It's just a matter of routine."

A knock on the parlor door interrupted them. "Pardon me, Madame; that must be my associate, Inspector Legros." Achille placed Cyrano down gently on the carpet, leaving the cat staring up at his new friend with wistful blue eyes, his tail curled into a question mark. Achille walked to the entrance with the cat padding alongside. When the door opened, Cyrano let out a low growl and dashed into the hall, having spotted a mouse scampering along the skirting board.

"Excuse me, Inspector, I'm sorry to interrupt. But I've found some items of interest upstairs."

Achille smiled. "Not to worry, Étienne, I'm finished down here." He turned back toward Mme Arnaud. "Thank you again, Madame. You have my card. If you have any questions or any further information of interest, please don't hesitate to contact me. You may also get a message to me or M. Legros through Sergeant Rodin."

Madame replied, "I'll certainly do that, M. Lefebvre." She then turned to her old friend Rodin and engaged him in local gossip, a variety of topics including Russians, radicals, and the tragic aftermath of the phylloxera infestation, most particularly the plight of the unemployed vintners and the sharp rise in the cost of *vin ordinaire*.

Upon entering Kadyshev's sparsely furnished room, Achille was struck by its tidiness. From the neatly made cot to the orderly rows of books on a shelf, everything seemed almost too perfectly arranged.

Aside from the bed, the only furnishings were a small round table with a half-empty bottle of vodka and two glasses on top, three plain wooden chairs, and a marble-topped washstand with porcelain basin, pitcher, and shaving mirror. A scrupulously cleansed chamber pot occupied a cabinet beneath the washstand, and a rack held what appeared to be recently laundered washcloths and towels. A mahogany armoire was the most prominent item in the room, and it contained a presentable wardrobe for a man of Kadyshev's social status and profession. Achille noticed two plaster busts decorating the bookshelf, one of Jean-Jacques Rousseau and the other of Karl Marx. *Someone was certainly making a political statement*, he thought.

"Did you find any letters, papers, photographs, or other personal effects?"

"No, Inspector. That's odd, isn't it?"

Achille shook his head. "Not odd if someone was here before us and cleaned the place out."

"But wouldn't the concierge have known if anyone had been here?"

Achille muttered, "Not necessarily." He pointed toward the open window. "The air's surprisingly fresh. Was that window open when you entered?"

"Yes, Inspector, it was. I assumed Kadyshev had left it open. Or perhaps the concierge opened it?"

Achille shook his head. "It wasn't Mme Arnaud. She told Rodin she hadn't entered the room since Kadyshev was last here." Achille walked to the window, looked down, and noticed paint chips on the sill. He felt for gouges, running his hand along the rough underside of the sash. Achille removed his hat, raised the sash, leaned out the window, and examined the exterior.

Anticipating Achille's discovery, Legros joined him. "It was forced, M. Lefebvre?"

"Yes, of course," Achille replied. Still leaning out the window, he craned his neck to look up at the guttering and eaves. Then he glanced over in the direction of the drainpipe and beyond, to the narrow airshaft separating this building from the next. A warm breeze ruffled his hair; sparrows flitted by, then perched on the gutter and chattered; a one-horse cart rumbled up the cobblestone pavement four stories below.

Finished with his inspection, he pulled back from the window and dusted off his jacket front and sleeves. Then he turned to Legros. "This was the expert work of a cat burglar. Do you remember Jojo, the acrobatic clown at the Circus Fernando?"

"Indeed I do, Inspector. You sent him up for a nice long holiday in *Le Bagne.*"

"Well, whoever did this was as good as Jojo." Without another word, he walked over to the table. Legros followed. Taking a large magnifying glass from his breast pocket, Achille examined the bottle and glasses. "I suppose this is what caught your eye?"

"Yes, you can see the prints quite clearly."

Achille nodded and put away his glass. He looked at Legros with a wry smile. "Another forensic experiment. Too bad we have no method for transferring them at the scene. At any rate, we'll take the glasses and bottle into evidence and see what we can do with them in the laboratory to enhance the prints." For a moment, he glanced at the threadbare rug beneath the table, and then scanned the bare wooden floor and skirting board. Achille shook his head. "I don't suppose you found any cigarette butts?"

"No, Inspector."

"He smoked like an old stove," Achille muttered. *And he was careless about the butts, even perhaps at the crime scene.*

"Pardon, M. Lefebvre. Are you referring to Kadyshev?"

"No, Étienne. We need to track down a Russian named Boguslavsky. I want to question him as soon as possible. He may be a chemist by profession, and Mme Arnaud gave me a good description. Ask about him at the café in the square; he used to hang out there with Kadyshev. I'll check M. Bertillon's records and I may have another source as well."

"Is that all, Inspector?"

Achille grinned sardonically. "Isn't that enough?"

3

HEAVEN AND HELL

Inspector Lefebvre's cubbyhole office was as well known in the brigade for its uniformity and efficient organization as was the chief's for its individuality and casual disarray. Rousseau had a running joke with the "old boys": "I'm afraid to touch anything in the Professor's office. I might leave germs—and incriminating fingerprints."

Achille had set up an easel in the small space between his desk and the opposite wall, from which hung a map of the park; the crime scene and the area of the search were circled and marked with pins. Féraud rested his backside on Achille's desk, cup and saucer in hand. While sipping his morning coffee, the chief concentrated on the map, and Achille gave him an update on the status of the investigation.

"Here's where Legros and his detail discovered the necktie, collar, handkerchief, and chloroform bottle." Achille indicated the location with a pointer. "The evidence we've gathered thus far has given me an idea of how the crime was committed, and of the perpetrators' motives."

Féraud put down the cup and saucer, walked a couple of steps to the map, and peered at the highlighted areas as though he were visualizing the crime. "And what have you deduced from the evidence obtained thus far?" he asked without turning to look at Achille.

"The park is open to the public until ten on weekdays in the summer, which is around sunset in July. I believe the victim went to the park for a meeting with a person, or persons, who were known to him. The best time for the perpetrators would have been near closing; shadowy, and not many people about.

"Without a witness, we can't establish which entrance he used, but that's not of immediate importance. If he were familiar with the park, or had good directions, he might have used the entrance closest to the bridge. Otherwise, he probably would have entered the main gate on the Place Armand Carrel.

"The victim was a man of average height and weight. I believe his killers were either two, or perhaps three, strong individuals."

Féraud turned his eyes from the map to Achille. "Why two or three?"

"It would have taken a minimum of two strong individuals to subdue the victim, chloroform him and bind his wrists, carry him to the bridge, secure the rope, hoist him over the railing, and, finally, drop him. Let's say three, for a job like that. More than three would have been risky for the perpetrators; you don't want too many inside witnesses."

Féraud nodded and turned his attention back to the map. "Please continue."

"The perpetrators used a sharp knife or razor to cut the victim's necktie; I believe they used the same to cut the ligature binding his wrists before they dropped him."

"Why tie him up when he was already knocked out with chloroform?"

"He might have come to and struggled. They had to work quickly and flee the scene before the gates closed."

"Is Legros looking for the ligature?"

"Yes. It may have fallen along the bank near a pathway. But it might have gone into the lake, in which case it's not likely to be found."

"What about the motive? You said Mme Nazimova identified the victim?"

Achille nodded. "Based on her identification, we believe the victim was Lev Dmitryevich Kadyshev, a Russian émigré. Legros, Rodin, and I questioned Kadyshev's concierge and searched his room. We have a person of interest, Boguslavsky, another Russian émigré. We're looking for him; if we don't locate him soon, I want to put out an all-points bulletin to bring him in for questioning. And there's evidence that someone broke into Kadyshev's room through a window and removed his personal effects. The job appears to have been the work of an expert cat burglar, and considering the neatness of the room, the thief must have known what he wanted and where to look for it.

"As for motive, the note pinned to the corpse quotes a passage from the Bible in reference to Judas—his betrayal of Christ for money and subsequent suicide by hanging. Therefore, it appears the hanging was an act of revenge against an informer, which raises some troubling questions concerning the political brigade's activities, most particularly the involvement of Rousseau."

Féraud looked at Achille with a tolerant frown. "Speak your mind. What's troubling you about Rousseau and the political brigade?"

Achille looked directly at his chief and answered firmly. "I have reason to believe Kadyshev was under surveillance. The murder was carried out in a public park, in a manner intended to send a warning. But who were they warning, and why? I might know more after I meet with Rousseau."

Féraud stroked his mustache meditatively, his eyes fixed on Achille. "You've set up a meeting with him to discuss the case?"

"Yes, Chief. We're meeting at the Sainte-Chapelle this morning, before it opens to the public."

The chief smiled. "That's quite an interesting place for such a rendez-vous. At any rate, I'm sure you'll have some pointed questions for our old friend and colleague."

Achille did not read too much into Féraud's tone of voice and wry smile. But the chief's expression, coupled with his veiled reference to "pointed questions," was insinuating. It was as though Féraud had said, *You're a big boy; deal with it.*

Achille replied laconically, "Yes, Chief, I will."

∽∾

Achille's tricolor badge had gained him admittance to a place once reserved for kings, queens, and their courtiers. He stood in the nave of the Sainte-Chapelle; facing the chevet, he craned his neck and gazed upward as the first light of dawn filtered in through a vast expanse of towering stained glass. The predominantly blue- and red-glazed biblical pictorials glittered like multifaceted gemstones. Rows of graceful piers framed the glass; they towered like ancient trees, their uppermost parts supporting the vault of a starry heaven.

Let there be light. He thought of the first creative words of Genesis, the heavenly command that imposed order on a chaotic void. Saint Louis, the great crusader, had decreed the building of a chapel to serve as a giant reliquary, housing the spurious relics so prized by medieval kings as symbols of their divine right to rule: splinters of the True Cross; a fragment of the crown of thorns; a piece of the spear that pierced Christ's side. Trumped-up mementoes of the Passion displayed in a royal jewel box.

The king's chapel had been built in the Rayonnant Style: radiant, brilliant, beautiful. The Jesuits had taught him about physical beauty from the perspective of St. Thomas Aquinas, King Louis's thirteenth-century contemporary. According to Aquinas, the beautiful gave immediate pleasure when perceived, and radiance was one of its intrinsic qualities.

The sunlit stained glass windows had radiance in abundance; the upper chapel shimmered and floated within a warm flood of reflected and refracted light. But at that moment, alone in the silent chapel, he thought that nothing on earth could compare to the light in Adele's eyes. He longed for that singular look when he knew, with absolute certainty, that she loved him. Even if God existed, Achille could not touch Him, but he could embrace his wife's warm flesh, feel the softness of her lips against his mouth. He could see their combined images in their children. Her loving light, something radiant yet tangibly human, could guide him through this investigation with its twists and turns like a dark Montmartre back alley. But he could not discuss the case with her. No, he must rely on Rousseau for enlightenment, his former partner who knew all about the chaotic underworld of criminals and terrorists.

"Praying, Professor?"

The familiar voice startled him. It seemed to come from the void. He flinched like a cat, and then turned around to face Rousseau.

"You seem a bit on edge," the man said. "Well, that's to be expected. We live in a dangerous world."

Achille contemplated the massive frame, small, round head, and porcine eyes. He seemed out of place in the graceful chapel. He was more like the Gothic Grotesques carved in stone that decorated the grimy outer walls of the great cathedrals. Achille was above average height and very fit, a skilled oarsman, a master of savate, and unafraid of a brawl. But Rousseau was a force of nature, a legend in the brigade and on the streets. Years earlier, he had been ambushed in a Montmartre alley by four knife-wielding hoodlums. Rousseau was badly cut and lost a great deal of blood, but, fighting with only his fists and truncheon, he left two gangsters dead on the pavement. A third died the next day in hospital; a fourth had run for his life. A couple of months later, the fourth man's mutilated corpse was fished out of the Seine. No one doubted that Rousseau had put a distinctive finish to what the gangsters had foolishly begun.

Choosing to ignore Rousseau's reference to his nerves, Achille instead noted the quality of his former partner's dark gray suit. "My compliments to your tailor; you're looking very debonair. The political brigade must pay well."

Rousseau grinned broadly. "Thank you, Professor. My new job does have its rewards."

Achille guessed that Rousseau's evident prosperity was not entirely the consequence of his inspector's salary. But he prudently kept such thoughts to himself. "I congratulate you on your success. Now, pleasant as this reunion has been, I think we should get down to business. You're already aware of my investigation into the circumstances surrounding the death of a man found hanging in the Parc des Buttes-Chaumont. We believe the deceased was a Russian émigré, Lev Dmitryevich Kadyshev. Does that name mean anything to you?"

Rousseau narrowed his eyes and rubbed his clean-shaven chin as if in thought. "Kadyshev, eh? That has a familiar ring to it. I guess we do have a file on him somewhere; nothing too exciting, I'm afraid."

"You didn't have him under surveillance?" Achille asked, a hint of skepticism in his voice.

Rousseau laughed, a deep rumbling like the pedal tones on an organ. "We can't shadow every rat in the Paris sewers. Not enough resources, I'm afraid. But cracking a big case could remedy that."

Achille recalled what Féraud had said about politics, publicity, and appropriations. "I'm also looking for Kadyshev's friend, a big fellow named Boguslavsky. We believe he works as a chemist. Have you got anything on him?"

"Ah, yes, Boguslavsky; a damned anarchist. I'll pull Kadyshev's file, and Boguslavsky's, as well, and help you find him. Anything else?"

"I believe the killers brought in a cat burglar to remove evidence from Kadyshev's room. Do you know of anyone the Russians might have used to pull off a job like that?"

Rousseau nodded and grunted, "Maybe. I'll look into it."

"I'm also interested in files relating to Madame Nazimova and her late husband."

Rousseau grinned like a gargoyle. "Oh, I'm sure we have something on *them*. They were chummy with that old bitch, Louise Michel."

Louise Michel was one of the prominent Communards who had been transported to New Caledonia. Returning to France following the 1880 amnesty, she immediately became involved in anarchist plotting. Sentenced to six years imprisonment in 1883 and released after serving three, she was soon re-arrested for inciting to riot. She wasn't incarcerated for long, but upon release she lived under close surveillance and constant threat of arrest. Fearing that her political enemies were about to have her committed to an insane asylum, Michel had recently fled to London.

While he strongly disagreed with her politics, Achille admired Louise Michel for her courage, honesty, self-sacrifice, and social work among the poor. He would have never referred to her as an "old bitch," but unlike Rousseau, Achille had no bitter personal memories of the Commune.

"Very well. In addition to Kadyshev and Boguslavsky's files, please provide me with what you have on Nazimova and her late husband."

"They'll be on your desk this afternoon. Is that all?"

Achille frowned. "I don't suppose you have any suspects in this case?"

Rousseau cracked a sly smile. "Maybe Kadyshev poked his nose where it didn't belong and his anarchist pals cut it off?"

Achille stared directly into Rousseau's insinuating eyes. "Was Kadyshev one of your paid informers?"

"Listen, my friend. People in high places want us to cooperate on this case, and I'm going to follow orders like a good soldier." Rousseau's granitic expression and cool tone of voice revealed nothing. "But you work your side of the street and I'll work mine, all right? Review the files I send you, continue your investigation, and follow your leads. I'll try to find your cat burglar. I know them all, especially those who work in Montmartre. We'll put on the screws and make 'em squeal. Keep me informed, and if I turn up anything useful, I'll do the same for you. Fair enough?"

Achille disliked the way his former partner evaded a direct question. But for the time being, there was nothing he could do about it. "Fair enough, Rousseau. Shall we shake on it?"

Rousseau grinned and held out a beefy hand. "Just like old times, isn't it, Achille? I always liked working with a gentleman."

⁂

Achille spent most of the day at headquarters doing paperwork, taking a mid-afternoon break at his favorite café-bar on the Boulevard Saint-Michel for coffee and a croque monsieur. He sent a message to Adele not to delay supper for him. She knew he was on the case and could hardly be surprised at his absence, but he anticipated a few sharp words upon his return to the apartment later that evening.

He had an anxious sense of precarious immobilization, like a wasp on flypaper, waiting for the files from Rousseau. The remedy for his predicament was to attend to piles of routine work—a status report on a burglary on the Rue Caulaincourt; evidence obtained pursuant to the *juge d'instruction*'s search warrant and so forth. He chain-smoked while shuffling papers; the brass ashtray on his otherwise neatly organized desk overflowed with a hecatomb of immolated cigarettes. "Damn it," he muttered as he stubbed out the last butt in the pack.

The telephone rang just as he was rummaging in his desk drawers, searching for a fresh pack of cigarettes. He ceased this exercise in futility (he had, in fact, smoked his last pack), lifted the receiver, and held the transmitter to his lips. Legros was on the line.

"We've located Boguslavsky's residence and workplace, but he's disappeared. Gone to ground, most likely. We've put out a sweep to search for him."

Achille sighed. "I'm hardly surprised. What else?"

"A concessionaire believes he saw the victim walking up the path to the bridge on the evening of the incident about half an hour before the park closed."

"Was the victim alone?"

"Yes, Monsieur."

"Did the concessionaire notice anything unusual about the victim's demeanor?"

"Yes, he said the victim was distracted and seemed to be in a hurry. He was walking very fast and bumped into a couple who were strolling in the opposite direction."

"Good work, Étienne. Have you turned up any other evidence?"

"No, Monsieur; we're still looking for the ligature."

Achille glanced up at the wall clock; it was after seven P.M. "You may return to headquarters and complete your report. Tell Rodin to leave a good man up there. We might get lucky; perpetrators often return to the scene of the crime. And they have Boguslavsky's description. Since he's done a bunk, he's our prime suspect."

Achille hung up the phone, leaned back in his chair and thought for a moment. The concessionaire's narrative confirmed his hypothesis that the victim had been lured to the bridge for a meeting of some importance. And the late hour fit with his theory. Boguslavsky's disappearance was evidence of guilt. According to Mme Arnaud's description, Boguslavsky was strong enough to have lifted Kadyshev over the railing. He smoked Sobranies. If his fingerprints matched those on the note, the bottle, and the glasses, they had their man—or at least a conspirator who could be pressured into giving up his accomplices. Maybe they could crack the case before his planned holiday.

Achille removed his pince-nez and rubbed his tired eyes. *Where are the damned files?* He muttered a few expletives, made another futile search for cigarettes, and returned to his routine.

∞

Rousseau's files arrived by special courier shortly after nine that evening. The late delivery led Achille to observe that his former partner had taken an overly broad interpretation of "afternoon." Since his working day had begun at five A.M., he decided to pack the files in a briefcase and carry them home to review in his study.

Adele did not greet him with sharp words; rather, she gazed at him with a concerned frown that pricked his conscience. "Are you all right, Achille? You look so tired."

"I apologize for the late hour, my dear. It's this new case. I'm afraid I've got a bit more work to do before I stop for the day. Please don't wait up for me."

His wife's concerned frown transformed into a pensive, red-lipped smile. Her soft hand brushed against his bearded cheek; she stood on tiptoe and kissed him gently. "Nonsense, darling," she whispered. "I'll see you later in bed." She turned and disappeared up the shadowy hallway with a rustle of silk, leaving behind a trace of her seductive fragrance. Achille sighed and retired to his study, briefcase in hand.

An hour later, he turned down the flame on his green-shaded kerosene desk lamp, then removed his pince-nez and blinked his overworked eyes into focus. His perusal of the files had raised more questions than it had answered.

Kadyshev, Nazimov, and Boguslavsky's association began in 1869, when the three were students at the Medical Academy in Saint Petersburg. They were "Narodniks," members of the Chaikovsky Circle, a radical organization formed by Nikolai Chaikovsky. Ostensibly a literary society, the members of the circle sought to foment revolution through the printing and distribution of scientific and revolutionary material. Nazimova was also a member; she met Nazimov early in 1871 and they wed later that year.

In the early days, the Narodniks used peaceful means—the education of the peasants and workers—to achieve their revolutionary ends, but they were frustrated by the peasants' resistance and outraged by the brutality and repression of the Tsarist police. Harassed by the Okhrana, Chaikovsky left Russia in 1874. He sojourned in Kansas, living in a religious agrarian commune before returning to Europe to continue his revolutionary activities.

Kadyshev, Boguslavsky, and the Nazimovs joined the People's Will, a radical group of Narodniks. In 1881, several members of the People's Will plotted and carried out the Tsar's assassination. While there was no evidence linking Kadyshev, Boguslavsky, or the Nazimovs to the plot, they fled Russia to escape the police roundup and persecution that followed the assassination. Then, beginning in Geneva, there was an ideological split among the friends. The Nazimovs became "evolutionary," non-violent anarchists aligned with the Russian social philosopher Peter Kropotkin, and formed a friendship with the French activist Louise Michel because of their mutual interest in the education (someone, perhaps Rousseau, had noted "indoctrination" and "propaganda" in the margins of their files) of the poor and working classes.

Boguslavsky was a "revolutionary" anarchist, with an alarming interest in high explosives and electric detonators. Kadyshev was a follower of Karl Marx, which had put him at odds with the anarchists entirely.

Achille closed the files and returned them to his briefcase. The political ideologies were of interest to him only to the extent they pertained to a motive for murder. According to French law, the anarchists and Marxists had a right to their beliefs and the liberty to express them freely, as long as they didn't cross the line into criminal activity.

Kadyshev and Boguslavsky had known each other for more than two decades, and for the past nine years, despite ideological disagreements, they had met regularly to play chess and discuss politics. What had changed in their relationship? What might have caused Boguslavsky to turn on Kadyshev and participate in his murder? Where *was* Boguslavsky? What more could Achille get out of Nazimova? Could he trust Rousseau?

Achille rose from his chair, and a sudden dizziness made his legs buckle. He braced himself against the edge of the desk. While shaking his head to regain his senses, it occurred to him that working seventeen hours on coffee, cigarettes, and a croque monsieur was not such a good idea.

Achille picked his way gingerly through the dark corridor that led to the master bedroom. The hallway was little Jeanne's favorite "play place" and, despite Adele's scolding, the child persisted in leaving her toys on the runner. At times, Achille wondered if his daughter were playing a game with him by mischievously obstructing the passageway with obstacles for her near-sighted father. Bleary-eyed as he was, Achille navigated the minefield without tripping over Oscar the Duck.

A warm golden light streamed through the cracks separating door-frame from bedroom door. He knocked softly and entered. Adele was sitting up against a bolster as she read by the glow of a bedside lamp. She glanced up from her reading, smiled, and returned to her book without speaking.

Achille went straight to the armoire and changed into a clean linen nightshirt. Adele's eyes darted furtively from the page to her naked husband; after seven years of marriage, she still admired the "Professor's" lean athletic body. But when he sat on the edge of the bed, she took no notice and appeared engrossed in her book.

"What are you reading, my dear?"

"Maupassant's *The Flayed Hand*," she replied, without looking up.

Achille shook his head, smiling, and tugged at the book gently. "You shouldn't read something like that before you go to sleep. It'll give you nightmares."

Adele closed the book and set it down on the bedside table. She gazed up at him, her green eyes sparkling, her red lips parted. Placing her hands on his shoulders she whispered, "I shan't be afraid with my big, strong man in bed to protect me."

Achille was dog-tired, but he wasn't dead. He undid the ribbons of her nightgown, pulling the soft garment down over her shoulders and breasts. Leaning over, he caressed an erect pink nipple with his tongue.

A piercing cry came from the nursery. "Oh, dear, it's Olivier," she exclaimed. "He's been colicky today." Adele pushed her husband away and did up her bodice.

He took her gently by the wrist. "Please, don't go. Nanny will see to him."

She frowned; the sparkling emerald eyes grew cold as ice. "Nonsense. What do you know of these things? He wants his mother. Since you're so tired, you needn't wait up for me." She got out from under the covers, put on her slippers, and left him, aroused and unsatisfied.

Achille leaned back on the bolster and contemplated the shadows on the ceiling. *"Merde alors!"* he muttered. Then he picked up *The Flayed Hand* and flipped through a few pages. "Ah, M. Maupassant," he sighed. "Reality is much scarier than fiction."

∞

In the early morning hours, raindrops pummeled the pavement on the Boulevard de Clichy. Rousseau stepped out of the darkness and passed through the jaws of hell. The gatekeeper greeted him satanically: "Enter, and be damned."

A crooked grin creased the hulking detective's face. He lifted his bowler and shook out the brim. Rousseau examined the soggy felt hat for a moment, and then held it by his side as it continued dripping onto the floor. Looking back at the Devil of Pigalle, he said, "I was damned long before I got here, my friend."

The doorman at the Cabaret de L'Enfer, a down-on-his-luck actor costumed as a stage Mephistopheles—green tights, horns, cloven hooves—replied, "As were we all, M. Rousseau."

Rousseau grunted his agreement. He took a few steps beyond the threshold, then paused to imbibe the atmosphere. Beams of warm, colored electric light flashed through a haze of tobacco smoke and steam that hissed periodically through strategically placed jets in the walls and ceiling. To his left, three demonic fiddlers, bobbing in what appeared to be a seething iron cauldron, scratched out a waltz from Gounod's *Faust*. Above the musical racket, he heard the buzz of conversation, punctuated by the shrill giggling of whores laughing at their companions' suggestive jokes.

Crimson-painted, high relief moldings, depicting lost souls and their tormentors, writhed over the walls and ceiling. Rousseau focused his attention for a moment on an imp prodding a sinner's ass with a pitchfork, and wondered at how the imp's face resembled his own. *I might have sat for the portrait*, he thought.

Glancing past two rows of men and women seated at round tables draped in oilcloth, he noticed a devil-costumed illusionist performing one of his tricks, transforming water into wine. Alongside the magician, a demonically attired young woman tended bar. Bustling waiters dropped off orders from their guzzling customers and returned with expertly mixed concoctions with clever names. The very sight of the drinks made Rousseau thirsty.

Two young women sat at a corner table near the bar, their painted faces half-hidden beneath enormous plumed hats. Their slender throats were wrapped in pink-feathered boas, and their undernourished bodies draped in clinging crimson silk. One girl noticed Rousseau and whispered something in the direction of her companion. A small, round head popped out from the narrow space between the whores. Keen brown eyes peered through the yellowish haze. Sensual red lips, framed by a black moustache waxed imperial, greeted Rousseau with a smile of recognition.

As Rousseau approached the table, the *poules* rose and walked toward the exit, passing him on either side with eyes averted. In proximity, he noticed that neither girl appeared to be more than fourteen. He paused a moment and glanced over his shoulder at their swishing little behinds, eyeing them with a mixture of pity and contempt. Then he proceeded to the table.

The man placed his pudgy hands, covered in rings, on the tabletop and half-rose in salutation. "Good morning, M. Rousseau. I see you're a trifle damp. Please, be seated. Would you care for some refreshment? I suggest Devil's Brew and Hellfire to brace you up." The man spoke elegant Parisian French with just a hint of a foreign accent. His impeccably tailored suit would have passed muster among the most discriminating swells at the Jockey Club.

Rousseau nodded and took a chair. "Thank you, Monsieur. I need a drink."

The man snapped his fingers at a waiter loitering by the bar. "Some service, Raymond, if you please."

The imp-costumed waiter immediately sprang to life, skipping over to take their order. He gave an unctuous smile in anticipation of his patron's generous *pourboire*, then dashed off to fill the order.

The man glanced after him and then looked back at Rousseau. He leaned forward with his elbows on the table and lowered his voice. "We can speak freely, my friend. Just be careful when the waiter comes around. Now, I understand you have some information for me?"

"Yes, Monsieur." Rousseau answered in a discreet *sotto voce*. "I've turned three files over to my friend, and the bloodhound's taken the scent. He's put out a search for Boguslavsky, and he's looking for a cat burglar as well. Someone did a good job cleaning out Kadyshev's room. And I expect he'll go back to Nazimova for more questioning."

The man's eyes narrowed. He formed a steeple with his fingers, and then intertwined the digits as if in prayer. "Who do you think will get to Boguslavsky first?"

Rousseau shook his head. "I don't know. Achille's very thorough. He and Legros have developed their own network of informers in and around Paris. He'll also have police watching the railways, ports, and border crossings. And he has excellent contacts in London and Brussels, Boguslavsky's most likely destinations outside France."

"Well, we have excellent contacts in London and Brussels, too." The man started fussing with a black onyx cameo ring, twisting it around and around his finger. "As for the cat burglar and Kadyshev's room, do you think Lefebvre has any idea what's missing?"

Rousseau shook his head and snorted. "He's clever, Monsieur, but he doesn't have second sight. At any rate, I expect he'll sniff things out soon enough."

Raymond interrupted with their drinks. The man gazed up at the waiter and smiled appreciatively, but remained silent until he was out of earshot once more. "He'll get something out of Nazimova, I'm sure," he eventually continued. "It's a good thing she's under close surveillance."

Rousseau nodded and sipped his coffee and cognac.

The man smiled and stopped toying with his ring. "Inspector Lefebvre's an interesting fellow. He's in line to become the next chief of the detective's brigade. I'll want to meet him one of these days. I'm sure you can arrange that, when the time comes."

Rousseau finished his drink and wiped his lips on the back of his hand. "No problem, Monsieur."

The man sipped his drink, leaned back and hooked a thumb in his vest pocket. "I won't detain you any longer, my friend." He paused a moment, then added, "Those little girls are very friendly, and I don't mind sharing. That is, if you have nothing more pressing."

Rousseau looked over the man's shoulder. A golden-eyed demon leered at him from its wall niche. "No, thank you. I have a woman waiting for me."

The man shrugged. "As the Parisians say: *à chacun son goût.*" He extended his hand. *"Au revoir."*

4

LE TEMPS DES CERISES

At five A.M., Chief Féraud tasted his morning *café*, smiled, and smacked his lips with satisfaction. "Perfection," he sighed. The brew was hot as hell, black as mud, and strong as the biblical Samson; those were his standing orders for the clerk who was assigned the task of procuring the chief's coffee, and this morning they'd been carried out to the letter.

Thus fortified with a jolt of caffeine, the chief hunched over his desk while shuffling through routine paperwork, until he came to a manila envelope date-stamped that morning at the Morgue. He turned the screw on his oil lamp until the flaming wick flooded his cluttered desk with light. His stubby fingers eagerly tore open the flap and retrieved a sharp, expertly composed image of a guillotined head on a slab. A knock on the door interrupted the chief's scrutiny of the photo. He expected Achille, and so answered with a cheerful "Come in!"

Achille entered and took a seat opposite Féraud. His haggard face and red eyes outlined in dark circles appeared in sharp contrast to his chipper boss. Achille's weary countenance led to the chief's observation, "You're not getting enough sleep, my boy." The chief handed over the photograph. "Here's something to wake you up."

Achille rubbed his eyes and put on his pince-nez. Nodding in recognition, he said matter-of-factly, "It's Palmieri, the Corsican axe-murderer. An excellent likeness." He handed back the photo. "I suppose you're going to add it to your Rogue's Gallery?"

Féraud returned the photo to its envelope. He smiled with a sense of pride, like an old hunter about to mount his valedictory trophy on an overcrowded wall. "Yes. He might be among the last of my tenure. You'll be starting your own Rogue's Gallery soon. And you deserve much credit for Palmieri's arrest and conviction."

Achille forced a smile. He and Legros had followed a trail of evidence that had led them to a crawl space beneath the Palmieri residence, where they had exhumed Mme Palmieri's badly decomposed body parts from a vermin-infested pit. The stench, filth, and horror had remained with him, and the image of the head brought back unpleasant memories. Nevertheless, he could shrug it off. It was all part of his job; routine, compared to the Hanged Man case.

The chief rested his arms on the desktop, leaned over, and contemplated his protégé with a father's eyes. For an instant he glanced at a silver-framed desktop photograph of his own son, an officer serving in Algeria, then looked back at Achille. "I've read your report, my boy, and I'm quite pleased with your progress. But you mustn't overwork yourself. If you need assistance, don't hesitate to ask."

Achille knew what was expected of him. He had worked for Féraud long enough to know that the chief's "don't overwork yourself" line was intended as a spur to greater effort. Nevertheless, Achille was short of detectives and he would make a reasonable request for more. "Thank you, Chief. In fact, Legros and I have our hands full looking for Boguslavsky, questioning his acquaintances and co-workers, and searching his residence. And we're looking for the individual who burgled Kadyshev's room. I'd appreciate some assistance."

The benign smile transformed into a businesslike frown. "Of course, Achille; I'll see what I can do. I suppose there'll be some duplication of effort between you and Rousseau?"

"Perhaps, Chief. We're cooperating all right, but frankly, I believe we're competing to see who can get to Boguslavsky first. Have you obtained an arrest warrant?"

Féraud nodded. "Yes, but this is an unusual case. The Magistrate won't be taking an active role in the investigation, at least not at this stage. That'll be left to us—and the political brigade."

Achille's eyes widened, and he stared at the chief for a moment before speaking. He disliked procedural irregularities, but he knew that in this particular case, he couldn't push Féraud too far. "I understand, Chief. But I hope we get to the suspect first. You know what Rousseau and his thugs will do to Boguslavsky if he doesn't talk. At any rate, the sooner we bring him in, the better. There's the issue of public safety. Boguslavsky worked for a research laboratory that tests high explosives and electric detonators used in the mining industry. And Rousseau hinted at an anarchist plot, though I fear Rousseau's holding back information. That puts me at a disadvantage."

Féraud sat back in his chair, eyes closed, and fiddled with the death's-head charm on his watch chain. After a moment, he leaned forward and looked directly at Achille. "I don't think you have ever understood Rousseau. Do you know what happened to his friend Marchand?"

"I've heard the story, Chief. Marchand was one of the policemen taken prisoner by the Communards and was killed in the final days when the Versailles army was advancing on the Butte."

Féraud nodded. "That's common knowledge in the brigade, but there's more to it than that. Rousseau and Marchand grew up together in

Belleville. They ran with the same gang, a couple of tough little monkeys. Marchand looked up to Rousseau, more like a kid brother than a friend. When Rousseau decided to go straight and join the force, Marchand joined up with him. That pissed off their former pals. But Rousseau had quite a reputation on the streets; the gangsters feared him more than they hated him, and that salutary fear extended to his best pal.

"Marchand married and had a couple of kids; Rousseau had his woman, Louise. He rose through the ranks and joined the detective's brigade. That's when I met him. Then the War came, followed by the Siege and the Commune. The National Guard uniform was the only one respected on the streets. Rousseau was already in plainclothes, and wisely went to ground. He tried to persuade Marchand and his family to go into hiding with him. He figured they could hold out until the army restored order in Paris."

"Pardon me, Chief," Achille interjected, "this much Rousseau has already told me."

Féraud frowned and shook his head. "There's more, things he's told no one—except me. Marchand thought he could keep his job under the Commune and remained at his post until an old enemy denounced him as a spy for the Versailles government. The charge was false, but the Communards took him prisoner anyway. Following a drumhead court-martial, Marchand was found guilty and sentenced to death. Rousseau saw his best friend, his 'little brother,' die at the hands of a mob. They were bad shots; the volley was sloppy, hit and miss. They wanted to save their lead for the barricades, so rather than give him a *coup de grâce*, they beat Marchand with rifle butts and stuck him with bayonets. Then they dragged the mutilated corpse through the streets and hung it from a lamppost.

"After the Versailles army stormed the barricades and retook the Butte, Rousseau denounced the Communards who had murdered his friend. He took pleasure in watching the executions. And for as long as I've known him, he's always set something aside from his salary for Marchand's widow and the children."

"I had no idea, Chief. This explains much about Rousseau."

Féraud nodded in agreement. "You know the song 'Le Temps des cerises'? It was popular in the sixties, and they still sing it at the café-concerts. When I was young, it was a nostalgic song about Paris in the spring and the cherry blossoms. But it took on a new meaning after the Commune—now, they look back to a Golden Age that never was and long for a world that will never be. It's an illusion, but some people are so dedicated to their utopia that they'll use any means—riots, mayhem, murder—in a futile attempt to realize it.

"You were still a schoolboy in the country when Rousseau and I were patrolling the Paris streets. I respect your ideals, your concern for human rights and equal protection under the law. But you must realize that there was a time not long ago when the law broke down and anarchy ruled. The majority of our citizens appreciate the order, stability, peace, and prosperity of the past twenty years; they don't want to return to that 'Time of the Cherries.' It's our duty to serve, protect, and defend the good citizens, their lives, and their property—even if it requires an occasional bending of the rules. You understand?"

Achille thought that even the best ends rarely—if ever—justified the means, but the world was more gray than black and white. There was a difference between a practical good and a fantasy, and a moral distinction between evil and an occasional divergence from the ideal. He disliked hair-splitting, but he wouldn't let punctiliousness get in the way of doing his job. "I understand, Chief. But I'd prefer having suspects arrested and interrogated properly, rather than leaving them to Rousseau."

Féraud smiled warmly, as though Achille's reply had pleased him, and returned to his affable manner. "Of course, that goes without saying. I'm going to release a few good men from their present duties to assist you. Now, what do you have planned for the rest of the day?"

"I'm going again to Mme Nazimova. Hopefully, she'll provide more information about Boguslavsky. Then I'm meeting Gilles at his studio. He's using iodine fuming to bring out the prints on the bottle and glasses we found in Kadyshev's room. I'm also calling off the search in the park—the ligature isn't an essential piece of evidence, and I can make better use of my *limited* resources." Achille's emphasis caused a slight twitch of Féraud's moustache in response. "I'm going to send a message to Le Boudin—"

"You're bringing in the *chiffoniers*?" the chief broke in.

"Yes, Chief. They're my eyes and ears on the street, and they're loyal to me, not Rousseau. I want authority to pay them the going rate, and a bonus for good results."

Féraud eyed Achille sharply, then breathed in and out for a moment while fiddling with his watch chain. At last, he said, "All right, my boy. This is your case, and I'm backing you to the hilt. Anything else?"

"That's all for now, Chief. You'll have my report on your desk first thing tomorrow morning, as usual. Of course, if anything breaks, I'll report to you immediately."

Féraud nodded. Then he remarked, "The weekend's coming. I want you to promise me something."

Achille grinned knowingly. *Our hours at the Sûreté are midnight to midnight.*

But what Féraud said next surprised him. "Take Adele somewhere. Get your mind off the case and relax. Just make sure you stay in Paris and let me know where you are at all times."

Achille smiled gratefully. "Thank you, Chief. I'll certainly do as you suggest." But both he and the chief knew that Achille's mind would remain focused on the case until it was closed.

⌒∞⌒

The tinkling doorbell announced Achille's entry into Nazimova's shop. Marie, the shop assistant, was sweeping a little dust cloud from the floor while Madame rearranged a row of leather-bound volumes stacked on a corner shelf. The women stopped working, turned toward the door, and gazed at him apprehensively.

Achille sensed their fear immediately and tried to alleviate it with a friendly greeting. He lifted his hat and smiled. "Good morning, Mme Nazimova, Marie. I hope all's well in your realm of books?"

Nazimova answered, her face wrinkled in a worried frown. "As well as can be expected, M. Lefebvre. How may I help you?"

Achille noticed her guarded manner and reply; it reinforced his suspicion that she knew something about Boguslavsky's disappearance, perhaps more than she wanted to reveal. "I regret interrupting your work, but I have a matter I must discuss with you—in private."

Nazimova glanced at Marie for an instant, and then turned back to Achille. "Very well, M. Lefebvre. Please follow me." She led him to the same room behind the shop where she had translated the note and identified Kadyshev's post-mortem photograph. As Achille walked past Marie, he felt her piercing gray eyes on the back of his head.

Once seated at the small table, Achille wasted no time with pleasantries. "Madame, I've come here on an urgent matter. Viktor Boguslavsky is wanted for questioning in the murder of M. Kadyshev. I believe you know Boguslavsky well?"

Nazimova's face assumed the blank expression he'd noticed at their last meeting. "I *knew* him, Inspector."

Her equivocation irritated Achille. "Madame, I must warn you that withholding information from the police is a serious offense. As a Russian émigré with ties to Peter Kropotkin and Louise Michel, your situation in France is precarious."

A smile twisted through a narrow opening in her defensive mask. "Ah, Monsieur, now you question like a true policeman. Do you threaten me with deportation? Very well. I doubt I'll live much longer, but I'd rather die in Paris than Siberia. At any rate, I spoke truthfully, in the past tense. My association with M. Boguslavsky ended with my husband's death."

"Did you not attend the International Workers' Congress last year?" Achille knew that both Kadyshev and Boguslavsky had attended. Nazimova's file contained only a notation: "Suspected affiliation."

She shook her head. "No, Inspector, I did not attend. I've ended my political activities and severed my affiliations. All I want is to live here in peace."

"But you're still a follower of Kropotkin, aren't you? Doesn't your ideology require some action on your part? Aren't you obliged by your beliefs to work for the overthrow of governments that you consider oppressive and unjust?"

Nazimova's pale lips quivered; a tear started in one eye. "What I believe, Inspector—" She coughed into her hand to clear her throat before continuing. "I believe in the natural goodness of humankind. But human nature has been corrupted by materialism, greed, competition, and the authoritarian institutions that exist to protect privilege and property. But I also believe that we are by nature predominantly cooperative, and that through a process of evolution and education we can recover what's been lost. We can learn to live communally, through mutual aid and respect for each other, and this fundamental socio-economic transformation can be achieved without violence."

Le Temps des cerises, he thought. "Madame, I respect your beliefs, though I disagree with them. We live in a democratic republic according to a rule of law, and the laws protect the persons and property of our citizens. Perhaps in the future we'll evolve into something better or recover something we've lost, as you say, but for the time being, and for generations to come, this is the best we can do."

Achille leaned over the table. His eyes grew cold, his voice firm and unrelenting. "You say you've discontinued your activism and broken off your political associations; I believe you. I also believe that you would pursue your ends by peaceful means. But there are those who are not so patient. They would stop at nothing to achieve their utopian dream. Boguslavsky is such an individual, and he's an explosives expert. You know what a dynamite bomb did to the late Tsar. Perhaps there's some justification for assassinating the leader of a tyrannical state. But imagine what such a bomb would do to a crowd of innocent men, women, and children. I have a wife and two little children, Madame. I think of their torn and broken bodies, their screams, and their agony—"

Nazimova covered her face with her hands and sobbed. "No, M. Lefebvre, please stop. I don't want that. I never wanted that."

Achille slammed his fist on the table. "Then tell me what you know about Boguslavsky and his confederates, Madame! Tell me everything, before it's too late."

Marie interrupted with a timid knock on the doorjamb. "I—I'm sorry. There's a gentleman in the shop who wants the complete Victor Hugo. But he demands a twenty-percent discount. He's very insistent, Madame. He says he won't leave until he speaks to you."

Achille glared at Marie, wondering if she'd been eavesdropping.

Nazimova wiped her eyes with a handkerchief and blew her nose. Then she turned to Marie and said firmly, "Tell the gentleman I'll give him a ten-percent discount. If he doesn't like it, he may take his business elsewhere."

Marie hesitated a moment, but then replied "Yes, Madame." She glanced at Achille, turned around, and returned to the shop.

Achille waited until he could hear Marie speaking to the customer. "I regret having to press you like this," he said, "but I believe it's a matter of public safety. If you have any idea of Boguslavsky's whereabouts or can give me the names and addresses of his current friends and associates, I insist you tell me now."

She looked down at her hands and sighed. "Viktor has changed, M. Lefebvre. Years of persecution and frustration have taken their toll. He may now be as dangerous as you say." She paused for a moment before looking him in the eye. "He used to meet with a group of like-minded individuals at the Lapin Agile in Montmartre. They were still meeting at the time of the International Congress last year. I swear this is all I know." She said no more, but continued staring at him with eyes worn out from having seen too much of the world.

Rousseau has paid informers at the Lapin Agile; he could have spared me the trouble, Achille thought. He grabbed his hat and rose from the table.

"Thank you, Madame. I apologize for my persistence in questioning, but I'm only doing my duty. And I trust you appreciate the gravity of the situation."

Nazimova did not look up. She slumped in the chair with a look as though she'd been beaten physically. "Oh, yes, Inspector, I do. Good day."

He made a slight bow and exited. On his way out, he passed a stout, well-dressed gentleman, still dickering for the Hugo, now insisting on a compromise of fifteen percent. Marie crossed her arms stubbornly and held firm at ten. Achille noticed a spark of aggression smoldering in her gray eyes.

⌯∞⌯

Gilles leaned back against a cast-iron pillar in his loft studio. He folded his arms and watched patiently while Achille, magnifying glass in hand, bent over a worktable and scrutinized a group of photographs. A shaft of sunshine streaming from the immense skylight flooded the area with intense white light, leaving the remainder of the room half-hidden in purple shadow.

Achille returned the magnifier to his breast pocket and turned to face the photographer. "Good work, my friend. Two sets of fingerprints are clearly distinguishable; one matches those I took from Kadyshev's corpse, the other is as yet unidentified."

Gilles left his observation point and approached the workbench. "Do you think the unidentified prints belong to the man you're looking for— what's his name?"

Achille nodded. "Viktor Boguslavsky. Perhaps. I'll have to find him first, then bring him in and take a set of his fingerprints to make that determination. And even if the prints match, it's not dispositive, just one more link in the chain of evidence." He paused, then remarked, "We're so limited, Gilles. I long for the tools of the future. I'm afraid we're a decade away from incorporating fingerprinting into our identification system. And think what we could do with better chemical analyses of poisons and drugs, bloodstains, hair, bones, fabrics, and all the other bits and pieces we discover at a crime scene. We're hamstrung by our ignorance. We might as well be working in the Dark Ages."

Gilles smiled and gave his friend an encouraging tap on the shoulder. "It isn't as bad as all that. This is a progressive age. We're on the threshold of a new century that holds great promise, and I expect we'll both live to see it."

"I'll admit we've made progress, but we could make better use of what we've got." Achille shrugged. "The telephone, for example. Paris is behind London in that regard, not to mention the large American cities. Rapid communication is essential to police work, but we must make do with the pneumatic post, telegrams, and messengers. As for transportation in the city, the police need to move faster than the speed of a horse or bicycle. We need automobiles and airships—"

Gilles broke in with a laugh. "You sound like Jules Verne. Perhaps you should leave the Sûreté and take up the pen?"

Achille smiled wistfully. "That's not a bad idea, my friend. At least my dreams are within the realm of scientific possibility, like you and your friends' experiments with color plates and moving pictures. It's not 'Le Temps des cerises.'"

"Why do you mention that song?" Gilles gazed at his friend with a perplexed squint. "It's lovely, but very sad. I'll admit a good performance can bring a tear to my eye."

Achille frowned. "Do you assign any particular meaning to it?"

The photographer thought a moment before answering. "I know the meaning given it on the streets, in the cabarets and café-concerts. They refer to Louise Michel and the girls who tended the wounded at the barricades. Some of them took up arms and fought alongside the men. I suppose you know what the soldiers did to the women when they re-took the Butte?"

Achille looked as though he'd been forced to swallow bitter medicine. "Yes, I know. It haunts us like a ghost that can never be appeased or exorcised."

Gilles exhaled audibly. "Sometimes I think you're too philosophical to be a good detective." Then he smiled broadly and winked. "But then, you're not a good detective; you're a great one. What you need is a stiff drink or two and a day off, or a night out. You may begin here. I've a bottle just itching to be uncorked."

"No, thank you; I'm on duty and I've a long day ahead of me." He paused a moment and then asked casually, "I believe you frequent the Lapin Agile?"

"Yes, now and then. Are you thinking of going? It's an amusing place, but I wouldn't take the wife, if I were you."

"Thanks for the tip, but I'm actually interested in a group that hangs out there. I believe the man I'm looking for was one of them." He gave a *portrait parlé* of Boguslavsky before asking, "Do you recall seeing a man answering to that description?"

Gilles rubbed his chin. "No, I'm afraid I don't. But then, my friends are photographers, artists, musicians, and writers, you being a singular exception. And then, of course, there are the women. I avoid the political crowd. They're too gloomy and hostile for my taste. Sorry I can't be more helpful."

Achille shook his head, disappointed by the response but convinced that his friend would not deceive him. "Think nothing of it, Gilles." He reached into his vest pocket and checked his watch. "I must be off. I need to stop by the station and see Rodin. And I must get a message to Legros." *I also need to contact Rousseau*, he thought. He gathered the photographs and deposited them in his briefcase.

Gilles escorted Achille to the landing. They shook hands at the top of the stairway. "Good day, my friend, and best of luck with the case," Gilles said. "If I can be of any further assistance, you know where to find me."

"Thank you. Actually, Legros is searching Boguslavsky's residence. I may have more fingerprints for you."

He shook his head and smiled. "Ah, yes, more prints and iodine fumes. It's becoming one of my specialties. *À bientôt!*"

⁂

Upon his arrival at the Montmartre station, Achille was greeted by Sergeant Rodin, who handed him a message. Achille had missed Legros by less than half an hour—he'd finished searching Boguslavsky's room and had already returned to headquarters.

Returning immediately to the Quai des Orfèvres, Achille found his assistant, evidence bag in hand, puffing on a cigarette and pacing the office corridor. Seeing Achille, Legros removed the cigarette and exclaimed, "M. Lefebvre, did Rodin give you my message?"

"Of course he did. You found something significant?"

"Yes, Inspector." Legros gestured toward the office door. "If you please."

Achille opened the door and entered, followed by his eager assistant. Legros placed the bag on a corner table across from Achille's desk, put on a pair of cotton gloves, opened the flap, and carefully removed a partially burned scrap of paper.

Achille looked at the item for a moment, and then stared at Legros. "This is all that you found?"

"I'm afraid so, Monsieur. I questioned the concierge. Boguslavsky had packed his bags in the middle of the night and decamped in a hurry. The concierge was very angry, because the Russian was a week in arrears in his rent. And he left the stove going, apparently in an attempt to burn some papers. But it's summer and the chimney needed sweeping, so not everything burned completely.

"A tenant alerted the concierge when he smelled fumes on the landing. She went upstairs and knocked; when no one answered, she entered with her passkey. She immediately opened the windows and attended to the stove. She's a sharp one, that concierge, and she has a good relationship with Rodin. She smelled a rat, so she notified the police and preserved the evidence. Please examine the paper. I can make out some writing; it looks like it might be a cipher or code."

Achille borrowed Legros's gloves to handle the brown-edged, half-consumed note. He took out his magnifying glass and walked to the window for more light. While examining the note, he commented, "I see it plainly, Étienne. The letters *abfhm* followed by *'Gay/Rossignol/ramée/jour/aimee.'* This could indeed be important. It might be the key to an encryption. I believe the words are taken from a poem, but I can't place it. We need to get it photographed. I can ask old Maître François about the poem. He's discreet and has no ties to the Russians or any suspect political affiliations."

"Do you think that might be a job for the Deuxième Bureau?"

Achille shook his head and laughed mordantly. "Étienne, my friend, we already have two brigades involved in this investigation. Do you want to bring in military intelligence, as well?"

"They do have the best cryptanalysis department in Europe."

"That may be true, but remember the old saying about too many cooks. At any rate, that's for the chief to decide. We'll note your discovery in our report. You did well, Étienne."

Legros smiled with a mixture of relief and satisfaction. "Thank you, Inspector. Are you going to share this information with Rousseau?"

Achille considered his assistant, and then shook his head. "Frankly, I'm not sure what I'm going to say to Rousseau." He glanced up at the wall clock. "Which reminds me: I need to send him a message and arrange a meeting. This day is far from over."

⁘

Darkness enveloped the Sainte-Chapelle; night had fallen, covering the glittering reliquary like a deep purple baldachin. Achille and Rousseau met in the shadowy dado arcade and spoke in hushed tones, their voices modulated by the nature of their relationship, as well as a reverence for the time and place of their conversation.

"So, Professor, it seems as though you're headed up a dark, twisting alley and need your old partner to light the way. How may I help?" Rousseau's eyes glowed; candlelight delineated his granitic features in chiaroscuro.

Achille respected his former partner, but he would not be intimidated. His response was etched in sarcasm. "You *might* have helped by letting me know about Boguslavsky's chums at the Lapin Agile. Why wasn't that information included in the file?"

Rousseau didn't flinch. "Sorry about that, old man. The association is recent, but you're right. The file ought to have been updated: an oversight on our part. Is that all?"

"No, that's not all. Do you have an informer at the Lapin Agile? Have you infiltrated the anarchist cell? Are you shadowing these people? With any luck, they might lead us to Boguslavsky."

Rousseau grinned, displaying a row of large yellowish teeth. "That's three questions and a supposition. I'll take them in order. One, yes. Two, not yet. Three, of course. As for luck, we'll need that and a bit more to hook this fish and reel him in. By the way, who tipped you off to the radical circle at the Lapin Agile?"

Achille hesitated; Rousseau's grin and overall manner annoyed him; but more than that, he wanted to protect Nazimova, if he could. He decided to throw Rousseau's words back at him and see how he reacted. "As you said, old man, you work your side of the street and I'll work mine."

Rousseau's pedal-tone laughter echoed through the nave. "Very well, Professor. Have you anything else for me?"

Achille considered the cryptogram; he had already decided to play his cards close to the vest. "We might have something of interest, but it's too early to tell. Of course, I'll notify you immediately if it pans out."

"Good. Shall we call it a night?"

"Have you any leads on the cat burglar?"

Now it was Rousseau's turn to play it cagey. "We're working on it."

Achille smiled. "Very well. Good evening, Rousseau."

"Until we meet again, Professor."

They walked up the nave together, past a saluting gendarme, and out the door into the mild night. They stopped for a moment. Rousseau glanced up.

"A fine night, Achille. Even above the lights of the city, you can see the stars. They're like our quarry. The stars hide in plain sight, but sooner or later they reveal themselves."

Achille looked up and smiled at Rousseau's reflective observation. "Yes, indeed; it's very fine." He said nothing in reference to the fugitive Boguslavsky.

After a moment of stargazing, they parted and went their separate ways.

5

ROSSIGNOL

W*here am I? How long have I been here?* Viktor Boguslavsky had posed that question to himself repeatedly, obsessively, and futilely. He had no answer, not even a clue.

He sat on a rough wooden stool behind a makeshift table—a few planks across a couple of empty flour barrels. A pallet occupied a corner to his right. He had slept there, but couldn't recall for how many nights or days.

Is it night? Is it day? He didn't know. When he'd arrived at the safe house in Montmartre, they had taken everything he had not already burned—identity papers, money, ring, watch.

"Did you burn the codebook, ciphers, and formula as we instructed?" they'd asked.

"Yes, all of it," he'd replied. "I understand why you took my identity papers. You're providing me with a forged passport. But why take my watch, my ring, my cash?"

"You'll have a new identity; we'll provide everything you need. There mustn't be a trace of Viktor Boguslavsky left for the police."

They'd given him a drink to calm his nerves. After a few minutes, he'd felt ill. When he'd tried to get up to go to the lavatory, he'd become dizzy, disoriented. Then he'd collapsed, unconscious.

He'd woken on the pallet in the corner. *When was that?*

He turned his attention to a tin plate, covered to keep out mice and bugs. The plate had been left for him, by whom he did not know. He lifted the cover, broke off a wedge of moldy yellow cheese, and placed it on a slice of stale brown bread. He chewed a mouthful with a disgusted frown, and then washed it down with a cup of sour wine taken from a half-emptied bottle. *Why are they feeding me this shit? Prisoners in the Conciergerie eat better than this.*

As bad as this place was, at least it wasn't prison. Or was it? He was in a small, low-ceilinged cellar filled with dusty, empty shelves. What sort of goods might this place have once contained? He didn't venture a guess. Gray-green mold splotched the cracked, plastered walls; two ground-level windows had been boarded up; a couple of stubby candles stuck in wine bottles provided dim light; ventilation was poor and the place stank of damp, rot, and a slop bucket that he used for a privy. He did not want to think about what he'd do once the bucket was full. *Will someone at least have the decency to empty the slops?*

He heard the distant cry of a steam whistle, the chuffing and rumbling of an approaching train. The sounds grew louder, the vibration more intense until it rattled the shelves. Then it passed, and everything was silent again. *I'm near a railway line. But what does that signify? It could be anywhere. Have I already been taken across the border? Which border?*

There was one entrance, a door at the top of a rickety staircase. The door was locked day and night. When he knocked, no one answered. Even when he pounded and cursed, there was no reply.

Boguslavsky had studied medicine; he knew this place was a breeding ground for disease. *How much longer must I hide in this hole?* He turned his attention to a large black spider dangling from a web spun across the tops of two contiguous shelves. *I'm like a fly trapped in a damned web. I've done what they asked. When will someone come to free me, or at least to tell me where I go from here?*

The clicking of a door lock and the sliding of a bolt broke in on his thoughts. Boguslavsky turned toward the entrance. "At last," he muttered. "Perhaps now I'll get some answers."

❦

The dawn sky flushed crimson. Here and there, a brilliant golden flash pierced the scattering clouds. The Butte slept half-hidden in shadows, sporadically lit by street lamps, tiny points of light winding their way uphill and down like a procession of glow-worms.

On the Rue de l'Abreuvoir, a young *chiffonier* trudged upward, following the narrow street as it snaked its way toward the summit. Hunched over, he hauled a cart filled to overflowing with rags, old clothes, and odds and ends, his gleanings from hours of labor along miles of avenues, alleys, and boulevards. Puffing with exertion, he halted for a moment alongside a mossy wall. He eased back on the cart handles carefully, so as not to spill any of his treasures on the cobblestones.

He mopped his brow on a ragged sleeve, and then took a moment to admire the tranquil beauty of the scene. Here, the street was like a tree-shaded village lane, lined with vine-covered walls, wooden fences, and brightly painted two- and three-story houses.

Above the humble skyline loomed the rising dome of an unfinished Sacré-Cœur. Completion of the Basilica had been delayed for years due to political wrangling between the Left, who considered the church an affront to the Revolutionary spirit of *Liberté, Égalité, Fraternité,* and the Right, who viewed Sacré-Cœur as a symbol of their triumph over Jacobinism,

Marxism, and Anarchy. But the young *chiffonier* did not think of politics. He had spent hours scanning the pavements and gutters like a miner panning for gold, and rummaging for buried treasure in the stinking, flyblown *poubelles*. Now, for a moment he could rest his aching muscles, look up, and wonder: *How beautiful it is*.

"Good morning, Moïse."

The *chiffonier* spun around, crouched defensively and flicked out a razor with the swift agility of a tomcat baring its claws. But in an instant, his feral snarl turned to a smile of recognition. He closed the razor, rose to his normal stance, and returned the greeting.

"Good morning, M. Lefebvre. You certainly gave me a start. What are you doing up here so early in the day?"

Achille glanced around; he'd taken precautions against being shadowed, but one could never be too careful. Satisfied that they were unobserved, he said, "I want a meeting with Le Boudin, in the Zone. Can you arrange it?"

"In the Zone, Monsieur?" He eyed the well-dressed inspector critically. "You can't go looking like that."

Achille smiled. "I don't intend to, my friend. I'll go disguised, and we'll need to take precautions against surveillance. I want to meet your boss on his own ground, for security reasons. Of course, there's something in it for you." He paused for effect, then said, "You look like you could use a cigarette." Achille reached into his breast pocket and took out a silver case. "Here, take a whole pack—and the case, too."

The *chiffonier* handled the offering as though it were a holy relic. He stroked it fondly and then placed it in his pants pocket. "Thank you, Monsieur. You know, when anyone says something bad about the cops, I say 'But then there's Inspector Lefebvre.' And they reply, 'Ah, yes, Lefebvre's a good man. Always on the square.' Don't worry, Monsieur, I'll arrange the meeting without fail. I'll get a message to you this evening with the details."

"Very well, Moïse. Remember, I'm counting on you." He looked up; the sun had risen, exposing them to the full light of day. "Now, we'd better break this up before someone sees us."

The *chiffonier* nodded. "Of course, Inspector. *Au revoir.*" Moïse reached into his pocket, opened the case, took out a cigarette, and struck a match. Then he watched Achille's back until he rounded a corner and disappeared from view.

Rejuvenated by his good fortune, the *chiffonier* raised the cart handles and began his long descent to the boulevard.

⌒∞⌒

Boguslavsky rested his elbows on the crude tabletop. His greasy fingers grasped a breast of roasted chicken; his teeth tore away gobbets of crisp, golden skin, yellow fat, and tender white meat. The ravenous chemist gorged himself to the point of choking. He dropped the half-devoured hunk of fowl on its tin plate, coughed into his fist to clear his throat, and then gulped *vin ordinaire* straight from the bottle. His airway cleared of chicken meat, he then returned to his feast.

A young man attired in a fashionable bicyclist's outfit—tweed flat cap, Norfolk jacket, and plus fours—observed the Russian with smirking condescension for what he considered a pitiful display of weakness. *How can we trust a man who can't control his appetites?* Revolted by Boguslavsky's unseemly voraciousness, the young man looked down and examined his carefully manicured nails. If the Russian had not been so focused on filling his belly, he might have noticed an incongruity in the youth, his small, slender frame, fine flaxen hair, beardless cheeks, soft white skin, and effeminate gestures in sharp contrast to his hawk-like blue eyes, firmly set mouth, hard, high-pitched monotone, and supreme self-confidence.

Boguslavsky finished his meal by wiping his mouth and beard on a serviette and belching into his hand. Then he smiled sheepishly, as if apologizing for his uncivilized table manners. "I'm sorry, comrade, but you must understand my condition. I haven't had a decent meal in days. And the drug you gave me—I assume it was chloral hydrate?—made me quite ill. You must admit that the conditions in this place are deplorable, unfit for human habitation."

The young man had brought food, wine, cigarettes, soap, towels, a pitcher and washbasin, and a couple of books for the detainee's diversion. The cellar had been swept and dusted; the vermin killed, the slop bucket emptied and disinfected. *What more does he want?* the young man thought.

"We had to work fast, comrade. You were drugged for security reasons, which I trust you appreciate. As for the conditions, they are, of course, temporary, until we can relocate you. Sorry we can't put you up at the Grand Hotel."

Boguslavsky did not appreciate the sarcasm, but the look on the youth's face defied any challenge on that ground. But the Russian couldn't help lodging a protest couched in courtesy. "Of course, you've done what you can and I'm grateful. But I gave you everything you wanted. I even participated in the execution of an old friend to prove my loyalty. With all due respect, you owe me." Boguslavsky tried to soften his demand with a benign smile.

"You'll get all that's coming to you, in due course," the youth replied with an unpleasant grin. "But for now, I advocate patience."

"But, comrade," Boguslavsky persisted. "Before I went into hiding, I heard that Inspector Lefebvre was leading the investigation. By all accounts, he's a brilliant detective."

The young man shook his head; the cellar rang with shrill laughter. "You overestimate the Sûreté, my friend. Compared to the Okhrana, they're nothing but a bunch of bungling amateurs. We'll have the celebrated M. Lefebvre running around in circles, chasing his tail. You have my word on it."

Boguslavsky stared at the young man. He was struck by the way this girlish youth could inspire confidence or instill fear with a slight adjustment of attitude, a gesture, a subtle change of expression, an inflection of the voice. Finally, he replied, "Very well, comrade. I trust you implicitly."

The young man rose from his chair and dusted off his backside fastidiously. Then he took a moment to put on a pair of leather gloves before saying laconically, "Good. You'll be well attended to from now on and should have no complaints, as long as you follow instructions."

Boguslavsky nodded agreeably. "Thank you, comrade." The young man turned and was halfway up the stairs when Boguslavsky added, "Pardon me. Must the door remain locked?"

The youth glanced back over his shoulder and glared. "Yes, it's for your protection." Then he turned and left the cellar without another word.

Boguslavsky stared at the door until he heard the hard metallic snap of the bolt and the clicking of the lock. He shrugged, sighed, and returned to the table to finish his meal.

∞

Maître François occupied two rooms on the fourth floor of a mansard-roofed building on the Rue des Écoles. Achille enjoyed the walk across the bridge and along the Boul'Mich, but this particular afternoon he'd been caught in a sun shower. He sprinted down the final blocks and, upon arrival, shook himself like a poodle that had just retrieved a mallard from a river. Still dripping, Achille knocked loudly on the oak door and then listened for sounds of life within.

"All right, all right, I'm coming." A faint acknowledgement emerged from the apartment. After a minute or so, a latch clicked and the door creaked open. A pair of rheumy hazel eyes peered into the dark landing and then widened upon recognition.

"Ah, Inspector Lefebvre. You're right on time, as always. Please come in."

Achille smiled at the familiar sight of the gnomish gentleman dressed casually in a smoking jacket, velvet tasseled cap, and baggy checked trousers, which had been new and fashionable the year Louis Napoleon proclaimed himself Emperor of France. The Maître's slippered feet shuffled along the worn carpet. Bent and twisted with rheumatism, he required the aid of an ivory-handled walking stick.

Achille followed slowly as François led him through a cramped ante-room that served as study, sitting room, and bedchamber. The windows were shuttered and the place reeked of pipe smoke and the fetor of old age, particularly oppressive on the warm summer day.

They passed into the Maître's true realm, a library containing shelves stacked high to the ceiling with rare volumes, a repository of centuries of wisdom and wit. The old man offered Achille a seat, then carefully eased himself into a comfortable armchair vis-à-vis his visitor. He laid his cane across his lap, adjusted his gold-rimmed spectacles, leaned forward, and began the conversation with an observation.

"Pardon me for saying this, Inspector, but you are very wet."

Achille grinned, took a handkerchief from his breast pocket, and wiped his forehead and beard. "Yes, Maître, I was caught in a sudden downpour. Quite lovely, actually. I saw a rainbow arcing over the Seine."

The old man smiled wistfully. "Yes, these summer showers can be quite refreshing. But I don't go out anymore. In my condition, the four flights of stairs make it impossible."

Achille offered some encouragement. "Perhaps the landlord will install a lift?"

The old man laughed feebly, showing his few remaining teeth. "That's very droll, M. Lefebvre. A lift, indeed. I imagine they'll be carrying me downstairs in a box long before this establishment incorporates such a novel improvement." He coughed into a handkerchief before proceeding. "At any rate, you have something for me. May I?" He extended a palsied hand.

Achille opened his briefcase, retrieved a transcription of the crypto-gram, and handed it to the retired professor.

M. François held the item up into the light and adjusted the distance until the words came into focus. After a moment, he read aloud, *"Gay Rossignol, Gay Rossignol—"*

He returned the document. "The nightingale, like the lark, is a very poetical bird. *Rossignol* and *alouette*. The words trip from the tongue so delightfully, like birdsong. Do you have any idea, M. Lefebvre, how much verse, in how many different languages, has been written about the nightingale?"

"I wouldn't venture a guess, Maître. That's why I've come to you."

The old man smiled pensively; apparently, he was still good for something. "Perhaps today we are fortunate, Inspector, for I believe I recall the poem from which these words were taken." He lifted his cane and pointed toward a row of books on a shelf. "If you go to the stacks, you'll find Blanchemain's eight-volume edition of the complete works of Ronsard. Bring me the index, please. I regret I can no longer retrieve it without assistance."

Achille went to the shelves and returned with the book, then handed it to the old gentleman.

M. François riffled through the pages until he found what he was looking for. "Ah, yes, here it is." He glanced up at Achille. "Now, Inspector, would you be so kind as to bring me the sixth volume?"

After Achille had done as requested, the Maître opened the book to the page indicated in the index and read aloud:

> *Gay Rossignol, honneur de la ramée,*
> *Qui jour et nuict courtises ton aimée*

"'Le Rossignol,' a charming little poem." M. François closed the volume. He turned with some difficulty and looked up at Achille, who had been reading the poem by glancing over the old man's shoulder. "But I doubt you have come to me out of admiration for the father of our lyric verse."

Achille came around the chair and rewarded the Maître with a broad smile of gratitude. But the inspector could not avoid giving a grim warning in reply to what might have been an expression of curiosity.

"I'm afraid the reasons for my interest in the poem must remain secret, and I request that you not mention the purpose of my visit to anyone."

The old man shrugged. "You needn't fear on that account, Inspector. My associations are few these days. As for my friends and old acquaintances, they all reside in Père Lachaise. They tell no tales; I expect to join them presently."

Achille nodded in response to the gloomy observation, and tried to cheer up the old gentleman with an optimistic compliment. "I find your services indispensable, my dear *Maître*, so I earnestly desire that you remain with us for many years to come."

"That's very kind of you, Inspector. I trust you will now pay me at the usual rate?"

"Of course, Maître. I'll require information about this particular edition, the date of publication, printing, and so forth, and I'll need a fair copy of the poem. Since it's little more than three printed pages, if you permit, I can do the work here. Otherwise, I must take the volume to headquarters and have a clerk make the copy. If that's the case, I'll leave you a receipt and have the book returned by messenger as soon as possible."

M. François scratched his white-stubbled chin and thought a moment before answering. "I'd prefer you do the work here, Inspector. I'll gladly provide you with pen, ink, paper, and escritoire, at no extra charge."

"Thank you, Maître. I'll try not to trouble you for too long." Achille smiled at the old gentleman's cannily calculated display of generosity. "By the way, are you acquainted with Mme Nazimova, the proprietress of a bookstore not far from here, on the Boulevard Saint-Michel?"

M. François narrowed his eyes inquisitively. "I've come across the lady once or twice. Why do you ask?"

"Oh, I was just wondering if she carried this particular edition of the complete works of Ronsard in her shop."

"That's certainly possible. Why don't you inquire of her yourself?"

I doubt she'd welcome my inquiry, he thought, but said aloud, "Of course, Maître. It was just idle curiosity on my part. Now, if you please, I'd like to get started on the copying."

⁓∞⁓

Late in the afternoon, Achille sat at his desk, toiling away at the cryptogram. A knock on the door interrupted him. Leaning back in his chair, he stretched his cramped arms and yawned. "Come in," he answered.

Legros entered hesitantly. "I'm sorry to disturb you, M. Lefebvre. I've completed my report for the chief."

Achille smiled; he needed to talk to someone and welcomed the pause. "No problem, Étienne. Pull up a chair. I'm working on something that will interest you, especially since you made the discovery."

Legros deposited the report on Achille's desk and grabbed a chair with eager anticipation.

Achille removed his pince-nez, rubbed his eyes, and then reached for a pack of cigarettes. "Care for a smoke?" he offered.

"Thank you, Inspector," Legros replied sheepishly. There were only two remaining in the pack and it seemed rude to take one. But Legros was dying for a cigarette and he assumed his superior had more hidden away in his desk.

After lighting up, Achille turned the cryptogram toward his assistant and began his explanation. "You mentioned the Deuxième Bureau the other day. Did you know I was acquainted with Commandant Bazeries of the Bureau du Chiffre?"

"No, I did not."

Achille took a deep drag, exhaled, and knocked off a bit of ash into a brass tray. "We met on a case. It involved a smugglers' ring that communicated with each other in code. Most of the codes used by common criminals are basic, easy to break. But this was different. They had a clever leader and he worked out something sophisticated, so the chief brought in Bazeries and he taught me some of his tricks. I'm far from expert, but I learned enough to enable me to break the code and nab the criminals in the act. You might have read about it in the newspapers?"

Legros rested his half-smoked cigarette in the ashtray. "Yes, now I remember the case."

Achille raised his eyebrows as he recalled the sensational articles. "Féraud was very pleased; good publicity for the brigade. Anyway, they were using transposition for encryption and decryption, using the lyrics to a popular song. Boguslavsky and his confederates have chosen a poem by Ronsard."

Legros frowned. The famous name brought back memories of a schoolmaster who enjoyed beating the classics into his pupils. "Oh, yes, Ronsard. I remember him from my school days."

Achille smirked. "It appears that our quarry is an individual with a taste for the pedantic; someone who likes showing off his erudition. But more of that later." Achille pointed to the letters *abfhm*. "This is a five-letter indicator-group, which refers to the five words that Boguslavsky, or any member of the gang, could use to encrypt a message."

Achille proceeded to explain the cryptographic method in detail, including a demonstration of the encryption key and grids for encrypting and decrypting messages.

Following Achille's explanation, Legros studied the encryption key and the grids. Then he nodded his head. "Yes, it's ingenious. It must be awfully hard to crack?"

"Without the key, it's almost impossible. Only an expert like Bazeries would attempt it. But fortunately for us, Boguslavsky has left us the key. That's how I broke the smugglers' ring. First, I got hold of the key to their code. Then I intercepted a message that revealed everything we needed for a warrant: the time, place, manner, and means of a contraband shipment. We caught the whole gang red-handed on the Marseilles docks. A fair cop if ever there was one."

Legros's face beamed with admiration for his superior. "Do you think that's how we'll crack this case?"

Achille took one last drag on his cigarette before stubbing it out. He exhaled slowly, looked down, and folded his hands. Then he looked back at Legros with a sober frown. "It's possible, but I'm afraid we're up against something greater than a band of thieves. I'm developing a theory of the case, and I'm going to take you into my confidence. Some of this I haven't discussed with anyone, not even the chief. Do you understand?"

Legros nodded; his expression mirrored Achille. "I understand, Monsieur."

Achille's lips formed a wry smile. "You can drop the 'Monsieur.' We've worked together long enough to be on a first-name basis—at least in private. Anyway, this is the sort of case that could make or break us. The chief has given me a great deal of latitude, and I'm going to take it all, and perhaps a bit more. If things go wrong, I'm prepared to take the blame—all of it. On the other hand, if we succeed, I'll see to it that you get the credit you deserve. Do you follow?"

"Yes, Monsieur—Achille."

"Good. Now, let's get oriented to our present situation. In my opinion, the victim, Kadyshev, was a sacrificial pawn. Did he betray, or was he about to betray, his associates? Perhaps, perhaps not. He might have been hanged because he knew too much, or his death could have been a loyalty test, an example for the others. I've seen that before with gangs.

"Boguslavsky is also a pawn. Considering his long association with the victim, he might have been an unwilling participant in the murder. He might become expendable if his handlers think the risk of protecting him exceeds his usefulness to the organization. Regardless, he's an explosives expert, which leads me to believe that his expertise was used to make a bomb."

"A bomb?" Legros broke in. "Surely that raises the level of urgency in this case?"

"I've put my concerns in the report. The chief and the prefect must be aware of the risk. At this point, I'm not sure what more can be done." Achille saw fear in Legros's eyes, perhaps a reflection of his own anxiety about the case. He tried to remain cool and objective. "Frankly, I don't think the conspirators are ready to act. And they must be aware of all the attention they've drawn to themselves by murdering Kadyshev and harboring a fugitive.

"Getting back to Boguslavsky, assuming that they've already got what they want from him, his superiors must decide whether to save or get rid of him. I expect they'll do what they determine is most expedient.

"I believe there's someone at mid-level or at least nearer the top of the conspiracy; let's call him the knight. He might have devised the code system, planned Kadyshev's murder, and recruited Boguslavsky. He might even still be in charge of the man—assuming, of course, that Boguslavsky isn't already dead. He could even be the cat burglar who broke into Kadyshev's room and removed his papers.

"The knight is devious, ruthless, cunning, and self-confident. But his strengths harbor a weakness. Hanging Kadyshev in a public park with a note pinned to his body was an act of devilish arrogance. If I'd been in charge, I'd have done everything I could to keep the murder inconspicuous. He would have done better to make it look like an accident, a street mugging or credible suicide. And this business about Ronsard and *Le Rossignol*. Rossignol is underworld argot for a skeleton key. But historically, it's also the family name of France's most famous cryptographers." Achille paused in his narrative to ease the tension with mordant humor: "The choice of the name is part of his game."

Legros responded with a wince and nervous laughter.

Achille sighed. "Pardon me, Étienne. My wit's as weary as my eyes. At any rate, the knight's a cheeky bastard. I'm sure he has nothing but contempt for the police, and that's his weakness. Let him underestimate us; we won't make the same mistake with him. If he's so damned confident that he doesn't consider the possibility of our breaching his security, he won't bother to change the poem. So we can use the key to decrypt any messages we manage to intercept. When the time comes, we might even create our own coded message to bait them, hook them, and reel them in.

"In the smuggling case, the gang used a dead drop to mail their messages. A signal—a shuttered or un-shuttered window—indicated if something had been left at the drop, a loose stone in a wall marked with a chalked symbol. I'm betting the knight and company transmit their messages in a similar manner. But here we run into an obstacle.

"We need good, trustworthy surveillance to locate the dead drop. So far, I've been relying on Rousseau. But he's playing it cagey. It could be a simple matter of inter-service rivalry, or something else entirely. Frankly, I don't know. We worked well together until the Ménard case, but since then, things have gone sour between us. My point is this: I can't take chances. I'm going to use my own resources to get the best intelligence, independent of Rousseau and the brigade. Not every detail will go into my reports. Are you comfortable with that, Étienne?"

Legros looked fixedly at Achille. His faith in his superior remained unshaken, but he knew the Professor's reputation for going by the book. But Achille had implied that he'd use any means necessary to crack this case. Legros couldn't help wondering just how far his mentor would go.

"I'm all right with it, Achille," he declared after a tense pause. "But may I ask a question?"

"Of course."

"Are you convinced the course you've chosen in this matter is in the interest of justice, and not because of something personal between you and Rousseau?"

Achille had asked that question of himself each day since Féraud told him he'd be working with his former partner. Surely there was an element of competition in this case, but he believed he could answer honestly. "I'll proceed in the interest of justice and for the good of the people. Of that, you must have no doubt."

Legros smiled and nodded his understanding. "Thank you for taking me into your confidence." He glanced at the wall clock; the hour was late. "If that's all, I'll be on my way. But . . . but before I go, I want to apologize for taking your last cigarette."

Achille smiled and shook his head. "Don't worry, my friend. I'm sure I've another pack or two squirreled away."

There was a knock at the door. A guard entered with a scrap of paper in his hand. "A *chiffonier* left a message for you, M. Lefebvre. We tried to chase him off, but he insisted it was important and said he knew you."

Achille thanked the guard and took the message. Legros, curious as to the note's contents, remained in the office as Achille read.

"Is it important?" Legros asked.

Moïse had arranged a meeting with Le Boudin in the Zone at four A.M. the next morning. Achille folded the note and placed it in his pants pocket.

"Yes, it is," Achille answered matter-of-factly. He looked up at the clock. *I'll be lucky to get three hours' sleep.* But he smiled at Legros. "It's late, my friend. Let's go home. I'll walk out with you. On the way, I can fill you in about the message."

He grabbed his hat and jacket from the coat rack, and then extinguished the kerosene lamp on his desk. They left headquarters together and walked up the quay toward the bridge. Achille explained his agenda for the following day, as part of his overall scheme for solving the case.

◦∞◦

"Should I cancel our plans for Trouville?"

Adele did not look directly at Achille when she made her inquiry. Instead, she studied his reflection in the dressing-table mirror.

Achille sat up in bed, watching his wife as she slowly brushed her long, light brown hair. The sight of her *en déshabillé* was almost more than he could bear as he tried to reconcile sexual desire with an imperious need for sleep. At times like these, he wondered if detectives should remain celibate, like priests and monks. Moreover, he didn't have a good answer to her question.

He tried an equivocation. "Not necessarily, my dear. There's still time until our holiday. I might have the case closed by then."

Adele set her hairbrush down on the tabletop, and then lowered the lamplight. She approached their bed in a delicately sensual manner he had once compared to a blossom floating on a pond. Resting on the edge of their bed, she leaned over and stroked his cheek. "I'm sorry about the other night, darling."

He inhaled the fragrance emanating from her warm bosom. *Like a soft bed of flowers*, he thought. "You needn't apologize for being a good mother."

Adele smiled and brushed her lips gently against his. "I try to be a good mother. But I'm also a wife," she whispered.

Achille glanced at the bedside clock. *My God, it's almost midnight.* "I'm sorry, my love. I must be up and out of here by three. I promise I'll make it up to you this weekend."

Adele said nothing in reply. She turned down the bedside lamp and burrowed under the covers with her back to him. "Good night, Achille."

For an instant, he considered doing—or at least saying—something. But his thoughts turned to the four A.M. rendezvous. He rolled away from her and sighed. "Good night, my dear."

6

THE ZONE

A hansom cab rumbled along the Boulevard Ornano. An early-morning mist had turned to drizzle and then a light steady shower. Achille peered out the rain-streaked carriage window into the lamp-lit darkness. A faint reflection stared back at him. "It would have to rain," he muttered.

Leaning back on the leather seat, he reached under his stained and tattered working-man's blouse and removed his Chamelot-Delvigne revolver from its concealed belt holster. Achille flicked back the side-loading gate and slowly rotated the cylinder—click, click, click—until he had counted six brass cartridges. This routine checking of his sidearm was a distraction, repeated to alleviate his fear. He was venturing into the territory of the cutthroats and footpads who inhabited the undeveloped Zone outside the city walls.

The steady *clip-clopping* of the horse's hooves had an almost hypnotic effect. He rubbed his eyes, blinked them into focus, and tried to concentrate on his objective. But his mind drifted to diversions—for example, the relative merits of his 11mm Chamelot-Delvigne versus a top-breaking Smith & Wesson .38. His revolver was sturdy and reliable, and the 11mm black powder load packed a wallop. But the double-action trigger pull was too heavy, and the side-loading gate and ejector slow compared to the Smith & Wesson. *What difference does it make?* he thought. *If I get into a tight corner and use up my six, I'm a dead man.*

A dead man. The hazard of his profession. What would it mean to his wife and children? He relied upon his mother-in-law's generosity to supplement the meager savings he had gleaned from his inspector's salary. Moreover, he had an insurance policy. Nevertheless, his best legacy would be the memory of a husband and father who gave a good account of himself and died in the line of duty. If the worst came to the worst, that would have to suffice for Adele, little Jeanne, and the infant son who would never know his father.

He sensed that the carriage was slowing, his thought confirmed by the diminishing pace of the hoofbeats and the driver speaking gently to his horse as he tugged on the reins. The hansom came to a halt. The driver leaned forward from his rear-end perch and rapped on the trap door with the butt end of his whip. Achille looked up into the raindrops.

"This is as far as I go, Monsieur. The Porte de Clignancourt is no more than one hundred paces ahead."

Achille nodded. The cabbie turned a crank and the door swung open. Achille exited the cramped passenger compartment and stepped down to the pavement. The driver shook the reins, flicked his whip, and clicked at his horse. The horse whinnied in reply, its skittering hooves clattering on the cobblestones as the cab turned around.

The cabbie glanced down at Achille. "Good luck, Inspector." With a light snap of his whip, the cab pulled away and rolled down the boulevard.

Achille gazed after the receding image until it vanished around a corner. For an instant, a sense of isolation almost paralyzed him. Then he turned toward the gate. Raindrops shimmered in gas light. Without his spectacles to aid him, the passageway through the city wall appeared distant and blurred. *Like the gates of hell.* He wiped his bleary eyes with the back of his hand. *If I must shoot this morning, it had better be at damned close range.*

He walked slowly toward his destination, his footsteps echoing on the pavement. As he neared the Porte, he made out the vague, caped figures of two gendarmes on patrol. *I hope Legros got my message through to Rodin.* Sergeant Rodin had arranged for Achille's passage through the gate, without his having to show identification papers. Achille was not carrying his badge. If Moïse did not hold up his end of the bargain, the *zoniers* might ambush Achille, capture him and discover he was an inspector, then hold him for ransom. If it came to that, he would save one bullet for himself.

As he approached the gate, one of the officers pulled out a truncheon. When Achille had come within ten paces, the gendarme called out the guard's challenge: "Halt! Who goes there?"

"A weary traveler seeking shelter," Achille replied. Legros was to have arranged the password with Rodin. Achille wished he'd had time to confirm it.

The officer barked, "Stay where you are, and keep your hands out where we can see them." Then he motioned to his companion, a brigadier.

The brigadier stepped forward. He had gotten the message, and he recognized Achille. He nodded and said, "You may pass."

As he walked through the arched passage, Achille thanked God for Legros and Rodin.

When Achille had passed beyond earshot, the first gendarme turned to the brigadier. "He's a brave man."

The brigadier smiled grimly. "He's got guts, all right—or he's a damned fool. Anyway, if he isn't back by five, we're to notify Rodin."

The first gendarme pulled out his watch. "Less than two hours from now. I hope he makes it."

∽∞∾

Achille tramped along the muddy, unpaved military road, past the fortification's looming glacis and weed-clogged ditch. The pervading atmosphere was distinctly rural: chirring crickets, croaking frogs, and rustling branches in a stand of drenched poplars bordering the pathway. This was *terra incognita* for bourgeois Parisians, the demarcation line between the city limits and the suburban village of Saint-Ouen. Not far up the road was the strip of wasteland that Le Boudin, the uncrowned "King" of the *chiffoniers*, had claimed for his flea market. On Sundays, intrepid shoppers would pass through the gate, leaving behind the relative safety of metropolitan Paris to search for a bargain.

Achille kept his right hand near the revolver. His eyes darted around for a sign, and his ears pricked up for a signal. He flinched when an owl swooped overhead. He halted at a prearranged spot, a fork in the road near a wooden footbridge that crossed a drainage ditch, and waited a minute that seemed like an eternity. Finally, a familiar voice called out from the darkness:

"What have you brought to market?"

"A rare item for my friend, Le Boudin," he replied with a sigh of relief.

Moïse's small figure emerged from its cover amid a tall clump of roadside weeds. "Good morning, Monsieur," he whispered. The *chiffonier*'s sharp brown eyes gave Achille the once-over. "Very good. In that outfit and without your spectacles, you'll pass for a tramp. Are you armed?"

"Of course. But frankly, without my glasses, I could have mistaken you for a large hare."

"If that's the case, I'm glad you're not starving. Anyway, my boss has given you safe passage and no one wants a fight with Le Boudin. But out here, you must always be on the watch for some hopped-up bastard with nothing to lose."

Achille nodded. "I understand, Moïse."

"Good. Now follow close, and don't lag behind. The short cut up the hill to the compound is steep, narrow, and treacherous in the dark." He glanced up. "And we could have done without this fucking rain."

Achille followed the *chiffonier* across the footbridge and up a muddy path lined with scrub. The moon hid behind a cloudscape. Achille could barely make out the obscure rounded form of his guide's rump. In the near distance, a band of foraging cats yowled as they huddled for shelter in the neighboring trash pits. Near the crest of the hill, he heard the bleating of goats in their pen and smelled the sharp stench of animal and human waste. The welcoming, dim yellow glow of candlelight penetrated the darkness.

They mounted the rickety porch of Le Boudin's shanty, where the wary growl of an old yellow dog greeted them. Moïse held his hand out for the blind dog to sniff. "Good morning, Bazaine. I want you to meet a friend."

Bazaine got up from his crouch and sniffed Achille's pant leg. He held out his hand, and the dog licked it. In reply, Achille stroked the animal's muzzle.

"He's got your scent and likes you, Monsieur; a good sign." Moïse opened the makeshift door and entered, followed by Achille.

Le Boudin's massive form emerged from the shadows and walked around a counter stacked high with his most valuable trinkets. A broad grin breached his bushy, chest-length, salt-and-pepper beard. The one-handed ex-legionnaire saluted with his hook. "Welcome, Monsieur Lefebvre. You honor my humble place of business with your presence."

Achille smiled and approached his host. "Good morning, Le Boudin. I'm likewise honored to be here."

Le Boudin's prodigious belly quaked with laughter. "Now that we've kissed each other's arse-holes, we must cleanse our palates with rum." He turned to Moïse. "You may go, but don't stray too far. M. Lefebvre must be back at the gate no later than five. We wouldn't want the cops swarming out here looking for him, now, would we?"

"Sure thing, boss. I'll return in plenty of time."

Le Boudin waited until Moïse had gone, and then gestured to a chair near the counter. "If you please, Inspector." Achille sat while Le Boudin retrieved a bottle of rum and two glasses from behind the counter. Le Boudin pulled the cork with his teeth and was about to pour when he noticed a speck on one of the glasses. He spat on it, and then wiped the spittle on his sleeve before pouring. He noticed Achille's wince.

"Don't worry, Monsieur. This stuff's guaranteed to cure rabies and kill plague germs." Nevertheless, as a matter of courtesy, he handed Achille the un-spat-upon glass.

Achille lifted his drink, said *"À votre santé,"* and gulped the fiery liquid. A coughing fit seized him. Le Boudin came over and slapped his back. After a minute or so, Achille turned to his host with red face and tears in his eyes. "What is this stuff?" he sputtered. "Lamp fluid? Rat poison?"

Le Boudin smiled. "I reckon it might be put to many such useful purposes. Anyway, if the first shot kills, the next one resurrects." With that friendly solicitude, he refilled his guest's glass.

His mouth and gullet numbed, Achille sipped the liquor judiciously. As he did so, his carefully concealed fear dissipated the way a dental patient inhaling nitrous oxide loses his dread of the dentist. Nevertheless, through the rotgut-induced mental fog, he retained a sense of urgency.

"I appreciate your hospitality, but we must get down to business. I'm requesting your assistance in an unusual case."

Le Boudin nodded. "I know, Monsieur. You're investigating the death of the man found hanging from the bridge on the Buttes-Chaumont."

Achille wondered how much Le Boudin already knew about the case. He suspected it was more than what the newspapers had printed. Achille had good reason to trust his host; Le Boudin owed him a favor, and the *chiffonier* king was known as a man who always paid his debts.

Nevertheless, Achille proceeded cautiously, as though he were shadowing a dangerous criminal through a dark, unknown alleyway. "That's right, and I've reached a point where I require some expert surveillance, but for certain reasons, I can't use my own men on this job."

Le Boudin narrowed his eyes, his bearded lips twisted in a shrewd grin. "Would one of those 'certain reasons' be Inspector Rousseau?"

Le Boudin hated Rousseau and he almost certainly knew that Achille was working the case with his former partner. He would play his next card carefully. "As you may know, Rousseau is back with the police, but he's working for another brigade. I've been *ordered* to cooperate with him, but between you and me, my faith in Rousseau and his methods has eroded somewhat."

Le Boudin laughed and shook his head. "'Eroded somewhat'? You talk like a gentleman, M. Lefebvre. Well, that's all right by me. After all, you *are* a gentleman. But I'm not, so I'll speak bluntly. You don't trust the bastard, and for good reason. And you need better spies than those plodders who work for that pig. Why else would you risk meeting me in this place? The answer's simple: I've the best spies in Paris and Rousseau's men haven't the balls to tail you into the Zone."

Achille smiled and nodded his agreement. "That's the gist of it, my friend. Can you help me?"

Le Boudin raked through his beard with his hook as he pondered the request. Then he said, "One more shot of rum before we talk business, eh?"

One more shot and Moïse will have to carry me back to the gate, he thought. But he could not refuse his host's convivial liberality. "Thank you, my friend. Just one more, if you please."

Le Boudin poured the drinks and set them on the counter. "We'll hold this round for a toast to seal our bargain. I once said I owed you a debt of honor that could never be repaid. You saved two of my best men from a frame-up, and you tracked down Virginie Ménard's murderer." For a moment, he stared silently at the dirt floor. "My daughter, Delphine, was in love with Virginie. I can't say I understand that sort of thing, but I care very much for my girl. I assure you, we're both grateful for what you did in that case."

Achille's throat tightened with emotion and he answered spontaneously, without calculation. "I did my duty, Monsieur. You owe me nothing for that."

Le Boudin stared at Achille, and a single tear appeared in the corner of the old legionnaire's eye and slowly trickled down his hairy cheek. "You're an honest man in a crooked world, M. Lefebvre. For that alone, I'll do what I can to help." He cleared his throat before continuing. "Moïse and his brother Nathan are the best I've got for a job like this, but Rousseau's marked them for revenge. One slip-up and they're goners. But before we consider our alternatives, you must tell me who you want shadowed. As for the why of it, you may keep that to yourself."

In response to Le Boudin's reference to his honesty, Achille decided to be as forthcoming as possible. "My chief suspect in the case, a Russian named Viktor Boguslavsky, has gone to ground. He used to hang out with a group of radicals at the Lapin Agile in Montmartre. I believe one or more of that bunch could lead me to the suspect's hiding place, but . . . but Rousseau's handling the surveillance. I want information from a source that's reliable and loyal to me. And I must warn you, I believe there's a conspiracy brewing, which adds to the danger."

"Russians, radicals, and conspiracy, eh? Perhaps you've told me *more* than I wanted to know." Le Boudin stared at Achille as if he were probing for something, like a surgeon picking fragments out of a wound. Detecting nothing suspicious in Achille's frank, steady gaze, he outlined a plan. "I believe I've a solution to your problem. First, I'll put you in touch with two blind beggars. They're master spies, as I'm sure you know, and with my recommendation and for a reasonable compensation, which I'm sure you can arrange, they'll gladly work for you."

Achille's eyebrows lifted in surprise. "The blind beggars? But I thought they worked for Rousseau."

Le Boudin smiled slyly. "They've had a falling-out. Rousseau won't say anything about it; he's trying to lure them back. I'll see to it you get to them first. But there'll be hell to pay if Rousseau gets wind of it."

"I'll risk it to get the blind beggars on my side. Was there something else?"

Le Boudin lowered his voice and frowned, as if he were about to say something profound. "Have you ever used a woman in this line of work? There's nothing like a woman when it comes to prying out secrets or luring an enemy to destruction."

Achille knew about sexual honey traps. He disliked them, but he would not be so squeamish when it came to cracking a tough case. "Have you someone in mind for that job?"

"Yes, I do, Monsieur. Have you considered Delphine?"

The proposition shocked Achille, but he tried hard not to show it. He knew Le Boudin had many women and numerous children and grand-children, but he believed the old rascal was especially fond of Delphine. Yet what Le Boudin proposed was tantamount to selling his daughter. To Achille, such a thing was unthinkable. But he was in no position to turn down whatever help he could get.

"Frankly, your suggestion is surprising," he said cautiously. "I'm sure you understand the danger. She might get herself into a tight spot and I may not be there to pull her out."

Le Boudin grinned and patted Achille's shoulder with his hook. "You don't know my Delphine, do you, Monsieur? When the time comes, more likely you'll be up to your neck in shit, and she'll lift you out. She can come off sweet as sugar, when she needs to, but she's as tough as a legionnaire.

"And here's something that must remain a secret, between you and me. After Virginie's funeral, Delphine said something to me that I'll never forget: 'Papa Le Boudin, M. Lefebvre is the finest man I've ever known. I'd do *anything* for him.' Ah, Monsieur, you should have seen the look in her eye and heard her voice, especially when she said 'anything.' I speak plainly. My Delphine is a whore; she sells herself to both men and women. But she's in love with you, of that I've no doubt."

Achille stared blankly, dumbstruck by the revelation. After a moment of uneasy silence, he stammered, "But . . . but you've just given me more reason not to use her."

Le Boudin's mood changed suddenly. His eyes blazed, and his jovial expression turned menacing. "Listen, M. Lefebvre, you led me to believe that this was important. You're not out here playing some fucking game?"

Achille glared back at Le Boudin and put a sharp edge on his voice. "No, it's not a *fucking* game. If I don't solve this case soon, innocent people might suffer."

Le Boudin leaned forward and gripped Achille's shoulders. "That's right, Monsieur," he said, his aspect softening as quickly as it had turned hard. "You're decent and just; that's why my girl loves you. So be a man and do your job. Use her. You don't have to fuck her. Just see that she's paid fairly, and say 'thank you' when it's done."

Achille stared at Le Boudin, trying to read his face. He soon realized that he had misunderstood the man, and that this misunderstanding might have been the result of his own prejudice. "Very well, my friend. I'll use her, as long as she understands the danger involved—and the nature of our relationship."

Le Boudin leaned back in his chair, smiled, and shook his head. "You're still speaking like a gentleman. What does 'the nature of our relationship' mean?"

"Cordial and professional. Or, if you prefer, businesslike, but friendly."

Le Boudin shrugged. "As you wish, Inspector." He reached over to the counter, grabbed a glass of rum, and handed it to Achille. Then he took one for himself. "Time to toast our bargain. Moïse should return presently. We'll be in touch, and you can use him as our messenger."

They downed their drinks, then Achille staggered to his feet and leaned against the counter for support.

There was a knock on the door followed by the announcement, "I'm at your service, M. Lefebvre. Whenever you're ready."

Le Boudin turned to Achille. "You'd best be off now, Inspector. You'll hear from me soon. And don't worry about Delphine."

Achille took a deep breath, made an effort to clear his head, and tried not to slur his words. "Thank you, Le Boudin. I appreciate your assistance and I'll see to it that you receive a just compensation. And please be assured, in this matter, you've the honor of serving our country."

The old legionnaire glanced down at his hook. "I already served my country, Inspector." Then he looked back up and smiled. "But now I have the pleasure of helping a friend. Good luck, M. Lefebvre."

~∞~

"Papa's home! Papa's home!" The little girl broke free from her mother's hand and streaked toward Achille as soon as he crossed the threshold. Achille smiled and hoisted the child in his arms.

Jeanne's angelic face screwed up into a disgusted *moue*. "Oh, Papa, you look like a tramp and your breath stinks."

"I'm sorry, little one. Papa was out playing tramp with his friends. But now I must clean up and go to work."

Jeanne rested her head on his shoulder and clung to him desperately. "Please don't go. I want you to stay here and play tramp with *me*."

Adele came over in a snit. "Achille, you're filthy and you've been drinking. I just bathed and dressed her. Now, I'll have to do it all over again." She pried the little girl from his arms.

"No, no, I want to play with Papa!" Jeanne whined.

Adele wrestled the child down and grabbed her hand to drag her up the hallway. "Behave, or I'll spank you," she snapped at her squirming daughter. The threat transformed the whining into howls and shrieks that echoed through the apartment and continued with intensity behind a locked nursery door.

Achille sighed and turned up the hallway toward the master bedroom. He'd almost made it to the door when his mother-in-law confronted him.

Mme Berthier loomed before him, a malevolent gnome in black bombazine and white widow's cap, imbued with the overwhelming wardrobe odor of attar of roses and camphor. "Good morning, Achille. Have you been attending a masquerade with your Montmartre friends?"

Achille winced. "Pardon me, Madame. I've been on duty since three this morning. I'm tired and I've had nothing to eat since last evening. Now I must wash, change, and report to headquarters directly."

Madame's eyes narrowed within a spiderweb of wrinkles. She sniffed. "Ah, it's a pity you've had nothing to eat. At least you were fortunate enough to find something to drink."

Achille was in need of many things, the least of which was a conversation with his mother-in-law. Nevertheless, he tried to be civil. "Madame, I'm afraid the drink was in the line of duty. I assure you, I did not enjoy it. Now, if you'll excuse me—"

"I understand, my boy. No need to apologize for your condition. You were on a covert assignment, no doubt in emulation of your idol, the *great* Vidocq." She referred to Eugène François Vidocq, founder of the Sûreté. Among other things, Vidocq had been famous for his disguised forays into the Parisian underworld. But her reference reeked of sarcasm; she had nothing but contempt for the reformed criminal-turned-detective and had made her feelings known to her son-in-law on several occasions.

"Yes, Madame, it's something like that. Now, if you please—"

"I knew it, I knew it," the old woman chirped redundantly. "Only the other day I was discussing the case of the hanged man with my friend Mme Gros. As always, she's developed an interesting theory." Mme Gros was the proprietress of a vegetable stall at the local market; she was famous for her cabbages and conspiracy theories.

Achille decided to play along—up to a point. After all, his mother-in-law could make the homecoming at the end of the day pleasant by squaring things with Adele. "And what, pray tell, is Mme Gros's theory?"

Madame's eyes darted as though there were little spies concealed in the nooks and crannies of her face. Then she approached Achille's chest, tilted her head up, and whispered in the direction of his inclined chin. "Berlin's behind it. The hanged man was a double agent and the Germans found him out."

Achille tried to keep a straight face. "That's an intriguing conjecture. Of course, Madame, you understand I'm not at liberty to comment."

"Absolutely, my boy. And I'm pleased you've been given an assignment worthy of your talents." She paused a moment before adding, "Jeanne's been difficult all morning, and the baby's colicky again. Adele's out of sorts, but I'll set her right before you come home this evening."

Achille smiled appreciatively. "Thank you, Madame. And please be discreet when discussing the case." He lifted a finger to his lips for emphasis.

She smiled conspiratorially. "Mum's the word. You can count on me." With that, she bade him good morning.

Achille watched for a moment as Madame shuffled up the shadowy hallway toward her boudoir. He shook his head sadly. *German spies. If only it were true. I could dump the damned case into the Deuxième Bureau's lap and be done with it.* Then he opened the bedroom door, went straight to the washstand, and dunked his drowsy head in a basin of cold water.

⁓∞⁓

Viktor Boguslavsky moved his black knight—QN-Q2. Chess solitaire provided a diversion; he was grateful for the gift of the board and men. His handler's indulgence—the provision of the game, reading material, cigarettes, comestibles, and adequate sanitation—had eased the chemist's mind, providing him with a sense of security. *This cellar is merely a waypoint*, he thought, *not the end of the line.*

He stroked his beard and took a puff on his Sobranie. As many times as they had played the Queen's Gambit Declined, Kadyshev always fell into

Black's trap on the fourth move. Boguslavsky shook his head and sighed. *You ought to have been more clever, Lev Dmitryevich.*

Viktor recalled the last game they had played together at a rough picnic bench—one had to sit carefully to avoid splinters—on the patio fronting the Lapin Agile. They had lingered beneath the shade of a tall, leafy tree, a warm wind rustling the branches and stirring a row of bushes on the steep, narrow Rue des Saules. They had smoked cigarettes and sipped a decent *vin ordinaire*. A fine day. But that evening, Comrade Rossignol had ordered Kadyshev's execution.

Why make me participate? Each time the question surfaced, he tried to shove it back into the murky depths at the bottom of his consciousness. But it had the bad habit of reemerging, like a bloated corpse inadequately weighted down to keep it concealed beneath the river. The chess game, an association with the hanged man, had been sufficient to raise the unwelcome remains, the evidence of his betrayal, and the source of his guilt.

He tried to justify his actions to himself. *We must use all means necessary to achieve universal justice, a goal that will benefit all humanity.* But how many must suffer and perish for the greater good? Hundreds, thousands, millions? In the end, who would remain to enjoy the brave new world that had required so much sacrifice, so much suffering and blood?

I gave them the formula. Why wasn't that enough? The formula was Boguslavsky's improvement on Nobel's gelignite, the means to the production of a powerful explosive stabilized in a waxy substance, easily shaped and molded like clay. In addition to the formula, he had provided explosives stolen from his employer, and instructions for the manufacture and detonation of a shrapnel-spraying bomb. Comrade Rossignol, the dandified young bicyclist, had given the orders, and Viktor had obeyed to the letter.

Boguslavsky pushed away from the table and stubbed out his cigarette. He glanced at the boarded windows. Still disoriented, he had lost his sense of time and place.

The door lock clicked; the bolt slid. A man known only as the Porter entered. He carried a parcel under his arm. "Greetings, comrade," the man said in a flat monotone.

Boguslavsky returned the greeting. He had grown accustomed to the Porter's laconic demeanor. The man brought food, emptied the slop bucket, and swept the floor. He spoke little, and his answer to any question was either terse, evasive, or a simple "I don't know."

The Porter set the parcel down on the table. "I'm here to shave you, cut your hair, and provide you with a change of clothing."

Boguslavsky's eyes glowed with hopeful anticipation. "Does this mean I'll be leaving soon?"

The Porter opened the parcel and then gathered up the washbasin and pitcher. He removed a razor and whetstone from his jacket pocket. Then he turned toward Boguslavsky. The Porter's little eyes narrowed to slits; his scrubby moustache and pale lips twitched in what seemed like a grin. "I don't know," he replied.

❧

Féraud puffed furiously on his cigar while pacing around his office. Achille sat quietly, patiently allowing his chief to blow off steam. After his third circuit, the chief dumped his cigar in the ashtray, placed his hands on his desk, leaned over, and glared at Achille. "On whose authority did you enter the Zone?"

"My own, Chief. I thought you wanted me to use initiative. Of course, if you'd like to take me off the case and assign someone else—"

"Oh, no, Inspector." The chief smiled sarcastically and shook his head. "You don't get off as easily as that. I *want* you on this case, as you well know. But more importantly, the *prefect* wants you on the case. In fact, he insists upon it, so there it is. As for initiative, I expected you'd use judgment like the experienced man you are, rather than playing cloak-and-dagger like a green recruit. You might have been killed this morning or, worse yet, taken hostage. I would have been up to my neck in shit with the prefect and the newspapers."

"It would have been tough on me, too," Achille observed.

Féraud grimaced. "It would have been tough on you, too, eh? Well, M. Lefebvre, you are to take no other such risks without first clearing it with me. Is that understood?"

Achille frowned, but answered calmly, "I understand, Chief. But you must appreciate the urgency of the situation. Boguslavsky's an explosives expert with a history of radical activity, both here and in Russia. And we've recently learned that his employer reported pilferage to the local police. The missing items could provide the makings for a powerful bomb, and perhaps more than one. It all adds up to a terrorist plot centered right here in Paris. If we find Boguslavsky, we've a good chance of breaking up the conspiracy before they strike. Innocent lives are at stake."

Féraud sat back in his chair. He closed his eyes, took a deep breath, and twiddled with his watch fob. Finally, he looked at Achille and moderated his reply. "I understand, Achille, and I know you've been working hard on this case. Perhaps too hard. You should rely more on Rousseau and his network. Aren't they making progress in locating the fugitive?"

"Not that I'm aware of, Chief. And you may rest assured that I'm cooperating. But in a case like this, I think we should use all our resources, and I have some that aren't on friendly terms with Rousseau. Let me employ them. I've spent years developing my relations with the people on the Butte and in the Zone. In the past, they worked as spies and snitches for Rousseau, for pay and out of fear. With me, the money is, of course, a factor, but we've also formed a bond of mutual respect, akin to friendship."

"I appreciate that, Achille, but aren't you duplicating efforts?"

"No, Chief. That might be the case if I were using our detectives for surveillance, as they and Rousseau's men would be tripping over each other's feet. My plan is to supplement Rousseau's intelligence. I believe that gives us the best chance for success.

"And there's another thing. I fear Rousseau's too bound up in the old 'round up the usual suspects' mentality. That sweeps too broadly in a case like this. If we rousted out all the radicals and their sympathizers in Montmartre, we'd have to arrest more than half the population. We don't need butchery with a meat cleaver; we need precise surgery for such a delicate operation."

Féraud realized that Achille's deprecation of the old methods was an indirect criticism of his tenure as chief. It vexed him at times, but he was big enough not to resent it, as long as Achille got results. "All right, my boy, we'll play it your way. But keep me informed. If you muck this up, we go down together, like galley slaves chained to the same oar."

Achille nodded grimly. "I understand perfectly, Chief. May I go now?"

Féraud started shuffling papers. "Yes, you may." But before Achille opened the door, the chief added, "Get out and have some fun this weekend. Take Adele for a row; the weather should be lovely."

Achille turned around and smiled. "Thanks, Chief. I'm sure she'd like that."

Féraud returned to his paperwork. "Just let me know where you are, in case I need you. And don't go too far from headquarters."

⁓∞⁓

Bright rays flooded in through a skylight, concentrating their intense beam on a young woman posed on a dais. Dressed in freshly laundered white underwear and black cotton stockings, the woman sat on a stool, her arms raised behind her head as if doing her hair while gazing into a mirror. A short, well-dressed man with neatly trimmed black hair and beard focused on the model; his keen, dark eyes peered through a pince-nez, darting between subject and canvas.

Wooden shelves stacked with plaster casts encircled the dais. Paintings and Japanese prints decorated the half-timbered walls. The sharp, bitter-sweet odor of turpentine and linseed oil saturated the studio. The artist worked quickly with short, precise brushstrokes, applying thin washes of oil paint over a chalk under-drawing. Then he stepped back a few paces to judge the result. Satisfied with his progress, he set his brushes and palette down on a table, uncorked a bottle, and poured a glass of cognac.

Dripping with perspiration, her arms, shoulders, and back aching from the difficult pose, the model glanced toward the artist. Relieved to see him taking a break, she asked hopefully, "May I rest now, M. Lautrec?"

Toulouse-Lautrec finished his glass. His critical eye glanced from model to canvas and back. "You may wash and dress, Delphine. I'm done for the day."

"Thank you, Monsieur." Delphine sighed with relief, lowering her arms and taking a moment to stretch and rub her muscles.

Toulouse-Lautrec lit a cigarette and poured another glass, then leaned back in an armchair and continued his observation. His eyes drank in the firm, round contours of her body, rippling beneath her clinging linen chemise and drawers. A student of the morgue and operating theater, Lautrec intellectually processed every fluid detail of her movements and gestures as anatomy in motion, from internal organs, bone structure, veins, arteries, muscles, and tendons outward to her glistening café au lait skin and glossy black hair. However, he also knew her sensually and sexually, and that intimacy added singular context to his artistic vision.

Delphine stepped down from the dais and retired behind a Japanese silk screen decorated with flying cranes gracefully ascending a cloud-stippled sky. Lautrec closed his eyes and, for a moment, lost himself in a reverie.

But a knock at the door interrupted his daydream. "Yes," he answered gruffly, "what is it?"

The concierge opened the door a crack and poked in her head. "There's a man here, a *chiffonier* by the look of him, who says he has a message for Mlle Delphine. Shall I admit him?"

"Does this individual have a name?"

"Yes, M. Lautrec. Moïse, or so he says."

Lautrec recognized the name. "Very well, Madame, you may send him up."

Delphine emerged from behind the screen, fully clothed except for an enormous feathered hat she held at her side. "I wonder what he wants," she mumbled, half to herself.

Moïse crossed the threshold and greeted the artist familiarly. "Hello, M. Lautrec." Then, without awaiting a reply, he turned to Delphine. "Hey, Delphine. How goes it, kid?"

Delphine smiled affectionately, but answered with a hint of annoyance, as if the *chiffonier* were an obstreperous little brother. "I'm well, thank you. Though I notice your manners haven't improved since last we met."

Moïse gave a mocking retort. "My *manners*, eh? They're the same as yours, girlie. Remember, we grew up on the same dung heap. But it seems you're hoity-toity now that you're a star of the café-concerts. You've come up from a snot-nosed kid lifting your skirts and shaking your tail at the Moulin Rouge."

Delphine's eyes flashed; she approached Moïse menacingly. "It's time you learned how to treat a lady, you little plague rat."

Moïse raised his fists and began capering about in comedic imitation of a boxer. He sniffed and wiped his nose with a thumb. "All right, kid, let's see what you've got."

Lautrec stepped between them. "At another time, in another place, this might be amusing. However, please remember that this is my studio and I am a busy man. Now, Moïse, I assume you have a message for Mlle Delphine?"

Moïse immediately stopped his antics, bowed his head, and apologized. "Pardon me, M. Lautrec. I've a message for Delphine from my boss, Le Boudin. It's a private matter, but you might be of assistance." He looked Lautrec squarely in the eye. "You see, it involves Inspector Lefebvre."

"Inspector Lefebvre?" Delphine broke in. She stared at Moïse with a worried frown. "Is he in trouble?"

Moïse nodded in reply. "He's investigating the case of the man found hanging from the bridge on the Buttes-Chaumont. It's a tough nut to crack. He could use your help."

"How can I help?" Delphine asked.

"I can't say. You'll need to speak to Inspector Lefebvre. Will you do that?"

"Of course," she replied without hesitation. "Can you arrange a time and place?"

"You met here in the Ménard case; it was safe then. And no one will notice if you're modeling. The inspector can come disguised." He turned to Lautrec. "Is that all right with you, Monsieur?"

Lautrec cocked an eyebrow and smiled. "I'm always up for a little intrigue. Shall we arrange our rendezvous for tomorrow afternoon?"

Delphine nodded her agreement. "I'm available."

"Very well. I'll contact Inspector Lefebvre and get back to you. Are you working tonight, Delphine?"

"Yes, I'm singing at the Divan Japonais."

"I'll be there, too," Lautrec said.

"Then I'll get a message to you both this evening at the Divan Japonais." Moïse smiled at Delphine sheepishly. "Sorry about the ribbing, kid."

She laughed. "Take care of yourself, Moïse."

"You, too, Delphine. And thanks again, Monsieur. *Au revoir.*"

⌒∞⌒

Around ten o'clock on a mild summer evening, the benches and tables outside the Lapin Agile were running over with chattering customers. The cramped barroom was packed to the walls with men and women discussing art, literature, politics, the happenings of the day, and plans for the evening and early morning, raising a din within a yellowish haze of tobacco smoke and sputtering lamplight. Waiters scurried about amid the convivial welter, bearing trays rattling with glasses and bottles of wine, beer, brandy, and absinthe to fill the needs of the thirsty crowd.

Gilles sat at a small round table near the bar, drinking wine and discussing his craft with two fellow photographers. Armand, a frail, chain-smoking consumptive, coughed into a handkerchief, examined the result, and lit another cigarette. Then he cleared his throat and asked his friend about the status of his experiments in color photography.

Gilles smiled wistfully, shook his head, and took a sip of wine before answering. "I've come to a dead end. I can duplicate the trichromatic process of Ducos du Hauron and Cros, but I can go no further. For example, I photograph a subject through green, orange, and violet filters, and print my negatives on sheets of bichromated gelatin containing carbon pigments of red, blue, and yellow, the complementary colors of my negatives. Thus, I obtain three positives in the form of transparencies, and superimpose them, producing a full-color photograph. An intriguing result, but time-consuming and complex. There will be no progress until someone produces a color-sensitive plate, or film that's as simple to use as black and white. I'm afraid that individual won't be me."

Gabriel, a robust, ruddy-cheeked mismatch to his consumptive companion, chimed in. "Leave color to the painters. I get the effects I want in black and white and sepia."

"But, my friend," Gilles argued, "color is in nature—it's *there*."

Gabriel shook his head vehemently. "The camera is my eye, and the camera's perception renders images in black and white. To paraphrase the English painter Turner, I photograph what my camera sees, not what I know."

Gilles smiled. "What you *know*? But you're editorializing in black and white."

"That's precisely my point," Gabriel replied.

"Asnières," Armand broke in between coughs. "I met that crazy Dutch painter at a *guinguette* in Asnières. He was sketching by the railway bridge, the same scene I was photographing. You know who I mean; the shabby fellow who used to room with his brother on the Rue Lepic."

"Vincent van Gogh," Gilles said. "I wonder what happened to him. Last I heard, he was locked up in an asylum, poor bastard."

Gabriel emptied his glass and gestured to the waiter for another. After a moment, he returned to the subject of their conversation. "I heard he was released to the care of an art-loving doctor in Auvers."

"An art-loving doctor, eh?" Armand said between coughs. "That'll finish him for sure."

Gabriel noticed a blind beggar approaching their table. "Don't look around, fellows, but we're about to be cadged."

"Damn," Armand muttered. "The poor scrounging off the poor. A just society would care properly for such people. I've nothing for him."

Gilles smiled. "Don't worry, my friend. I'm flush this week. I can spare him a coin or two."

A tapping cane announced a raggedly dressed man with long, greasy hair, a scraggly beard, dark glasses, and a sign round his neck: *Blind from Birth*. He rattled a tin cup while pleading, "Charity for a poor blind man?"

Gilles reached into his pocket, took out two ten-centime pieces, and dropped them into the cup.

The blind man lifted his battered hat and smiled, showing a rash-covered bald crown and the brown remains of a few front teeth. "Bless you, my friend," he said, before continuing his circumambulation of the room.

Gabriel watched the man as he made his way toward a table occupied by a small group of anarchists and old Communards. He turned back to his companions. "You better watch your words around these ostensibly *blind* fellows," he said *sotto voce*. "I've heard some of them spy for the police." Then he added with a sly grin, "But our friend Gilles works for the police, so perhaps we ought to be careful what we say around him?"

Gilles finished his drink and laughed. "You've nothing to worry about, my friends. I work for Inspector Lefebvre. He's different."

"Don't be so simple, Gilles," Gabriel muttered. "They're all alike. Lefebvre or Rousseau, what difference does it make? They're lackeys who do their master's bidding."

Gilles frowned and his face reddened. "I'll remind you that M. Lefebvre is my good and trusted friend."

Gabriel did not want to pick a fight with Gilles; he moderated his tone accordingly. "Pardon me, Gilles. It's the drink doing the talking."

Gilles relaxed and smiled reassuringly. He clapped Gabriel's shoulder. "You're too cynical. Achille's a good, honest bourgeois. The bourgeoisie aren't all so bad. As a professional with my own business, I'd say I'm now one of them. Speaking of drink, I'm thirsty. How about another round?"

∽∾

The way up the Rue des Martyrs was precipitous. On a clear evening, with the aid of moonlight and a ladder-like procession of streetlamps, one could gaze upward and make out the inchoate Sacré-Cœur looming above the treetops at the summit of the Butte.

According to legend, the Romans beheaded Saint Denis, apostle to the Gauls, first bishop of Paris, and patron Saint of France, on the site where the new basilica rose. The martyrdom occurred in the third century under the anti-Christian emperor Trajanus Decius, and most would assume that the street and the hill had been named in honor of the headless saint. However, the Romans venerated the summit as a place sacred to Mars, hence the pagan Mons Martis. There was even speculation that before the Romans and Christians, it had been a center of druidic worship. Today, the residents on both Left and Right had their martyrs of 1871. Thus, the name and place had connotations that varied, according to one's perspective.

A legion of ghosts, from different centuries and millennia, affirming disparate beliefs, haunted the hill. However, if any among the crowd pushing through the arched doorways at Number 75 had perceived a wandering spirit or two descending the street with a head tucked under an arm or ectoplasm ventilated with bullet holes, he or she would have reasonably put it down to overindulgence in absinthe and moved on. Amusement was their objective, the names and images on lithographed posters plastered over kiosks and walls their guiding lights.

The Divan Japonais capitalized on the modish trend for the *Japonaiserie* that had influenced artists like Toulouse-Lautrec and Vincent van Gogh. Silk and bamboo furnishings, with red and black lacquered tables and chairs, appealed mainly to the slumming bourgeoisie who mixed with the rowdy working class. The neighborhood proletarians were largely indifferent to fashion and the decorative arts. They came to see and hear one of their own, Delphine Lacroix, the *chiffonier*'s daughter. They knew her from the Moulin Rouge, the Folies Bergère, the *boîtes*, the cabarets, and the streets.

She performed to the accompaniment of a small pit orchestra, on a gaslit platform at the bottom of the basement. Ascending rows of customers, as many as two hundred on a good night, crammed like sardines into the badly ventilated little room. They were boisterous, sometimes belligerent, and filled the air with shouts, laughter, and curses, the pungent odor of sweat and perfume, and the eye-stinging, throat-choking smoke of dozens of cigars, cigarettes, and pipes. Disappoint them and they booed, hissed, stamped, shouted, and hurled objects at the stage; if you pleased them, they could make you a star.

Toulouse-Lautrec sat near the orchestra, sketchbook and charcoal in hand. As the crowd filed in, his eyes darted around the room, scanning the scene for intriguing subjects. A quartet seated near the end of his row caught his eye: two men spruced up like toffs, escorting a pair of young girls wearing the scarlet silk gowns, feather boas, and enormous plumed hats of their profession.

Lautrec recognized the older man and the girls; he had sketched them before in various dance halls, cabarets, and clubs. His brain, eyes, and hand coordinated with machine-like precision rendering their charcoal gray forms on paper. They developed magically, like the latent images emerging from a photographic plate, but they were merely background to the focal point of his composition.

The younger man's elegant detachment intrigued the artist. He was dressed *comme il faut*, but no better than his elder. Still, his middle-aged companion seemed vulgar in comparison; his baggy eyes, well-fed paunch, waxed moustache, and imperial, rouged lips and cheeks displayed a *louche* sensuality. These physical and cosmetic attributes, coupled with his insinuating gestures (a hand on the young whore's knee, an obscenity whispered in her ear), made him appear like the dirty old man in a stage farce, a perfect subject for Lautrec's caricature.

The young man remained aloof. His female companion clung to his arm, made faces, laughed loudly, told dirty jokes, all of which he acknowledged with insouciant minimalism—a nod, a smirk, a subdued snigger. When her hand strayed toward his crotch, he slapped it—hard.

From Lautrec's perspective, the youth treated the whore as though she were a pet monkey. His clear blue eyes remained fixed on an empty stage; his kid-gloved hands rested on a silver-handled cane. The artist emphasized the boy's androgyny, his smooth cheeks, fair curly hair, and delicate features. Nevertheless, Lautrec's sharp eyes and acute intellect detected a singularly arrogant cruelty in his subject's behavior toward his companion and barely concealed contempt for the crowd. He glanced down at the finished sketch. *The old fellow's a scoundrel, but the boy is a sadist.*

The orchestra warmed up their instruments in a flurry of scales, intervals, long tones, and rumbling beats on the kettledrum. For a while, the musical cacophony clashed violently with the audience's nattering din. Presently, their leader appeared and brought them to order by rapping his baton on the music stand. He called upon the oboe to give the musicians a tuning "A." The houselights dimmed. Delphine emerged from the wings and stepped boldly into the footlights' glare. The audience greeted her with whistles and applause.

She posed like a streetwalker under a lamppost, dressed in the shabby costume of the lowliest in her profession. Delphine was an admired exponent of *Chanson réaliste*—her songs told stories about the life she had lived in the Zone and on the streets of Pigalle and Montmartre. Her voice was a throaty mezzo-soprano tainted with cigarettes and absinthe. However, she projected her songs with the power of experience that breathed life into the words, and she had an instinctive sense of rhythm and pitch. The leader and orchestra members praised her natural musicianship. The greatest compliment to her acting was that it never seemed like an act.

When Delphine opened her mouth, the room vibrated with the defiant battle cry of a badly abused but undefeated spirit. The effect was electrifying. The rowdy crowd fell silent. She had once again subdued the beast, like a legendary hero braving the dragon in its lair.

Lautrec sketched Delphine, as he had many times before. But as he worked, he noticed something out of the corner of his eye: the self-important youth sat transfixed, as if mesmerized.

A wry smile crossed the artist's lips. *Try her on for size, you little shit. I wager you'll get more than you bargained for.*

7

DE CAPE ET D'ÉPÉE

At the brink of dawn, the Eiffel Tower's ten thousand blazing gas lamps cast their beams into the purple sky, highlighting the dome of the Institut de France on the Quai de Conti. *Does technology illuminate reason, or is it the other way around?* This thought occurred to Achille as he viewed the two structures from his perspective on the left embankment near the Pont Neuf.

His eyes wandered from the brilliant display to the shadows beneath an arch where a small gathering of clochards slept in a heap. Did this incongruity require investigation? Could scientific and artistic glory peacefully co-exist with such human misery in a just society? *What Then Must We Do?* He had read Tolstoy; he sympathized. As he watched the sleeping clochards, he recalled a particular passage: "However we may try to justify to ourselves our treason against mankind, all our justification falls to pieces before evidence: around us, people are dying from overwork and want; and we destroy the food, clothes, and labor of men merely to amuse ourselves."

How would Chief Féraud have answered Tolstoy's question if his subordinate had put it to him? Perhaps: *This is France, not Tsarist Russia. You're a detective, Achille, an important public servant. Do your job, and leave the rest to the Republic and God.* Simplicity itself.

This morning, his job involved a rendezvous with one of his spies, a man known to him only as Blind from Birth. Achille had arranged their meeting for five, but the spy was already ten minutes late.

Achille wanted a smoke, but he feared the glowing tip of his cigarette might draw unwanted attention. Waiting made him edgy; he kept glancing up and down the embankment from his cover beneath a large chestnut tree. He wore his workingman's outfit to make him less conspicuous but here, near headquarters in central Paris, he carried his badge concealed under his blouse, next to his Chamelot-Delvigne. At last, he was relieved to see a dark figure approaching and hear the telltale tapping of a cane against the embankment wall. *His eyes are better than mine, but he does well to stay in character.*

The man came up to Achille, smiled, and tipped his battered hat. "Good morning, Monsieur."

"You're late," Achille replied testily.

"Pardon me, Monsieur. For reasons that must be obvious, I don't carry a watch. I make do with public clocks, bells, and the signs of nature."

Achille's eyes darted from his spy to the clochards. "Do you think it's all right if we speak here?"

The man turned his head toward the shadowy archway. "You're worried about *them*? You needn't be. Eyes open or shut, they're dead to this world and could not care less about what we have to say to each other. For now, this is as safe a spot as any for us to meet. But we oughtn't hang around here too long."

"Very well. You have something for me?"

"Indeed I have, Monsieur. I spent last night and much of this early morning in Montmartre. I shadowed two known anarchists from the Lapin Agile: friends of Viktor Boguslavsky. Here are their names, addresses, and descriptions." The spy reached into a jacket pocket and handed a piece of paper to Achille. "You should have files on both of them. They're Leon Wroblewski, a Polish exile, and Laurent Moreau, a common seaman between voyages. They both live in a fleabag on the Rue Ravignan, but they didn't return there last night. Instead, I tailed them to a house on the Rue Ronsard—"

"Ronsard, did you say?" Achille immediately remembered the poem code.

The man raised his eyebrows. "Does that address have some significance?"

"It might. Please continue."

"My brother, Blind by Accident, is still on the watch up there—we work in shifts. We'll have more for you tomorrow morning, Monsieur."

Tomorrow was Sunday. Achille had planned to take Adele for a row, but he figured he could make the five A.M. rendezvous and still have most of the day off. "Very well, but please try to be on time. Will there be a problem with Rousseau and his men? I imagine they'll be tailing these individuals, too."

The man raised his hand to his lips to stifle a laugh. "Pardon me, Monsieur, but this is amusing. Rousseau hasn't said anything to his men about the state of our . . . business arrangements. We're in ongoing negotiations of a confidential nature. So his men think we're still working with them."

"That's a dangerous game. What if Rousseau finds out you're working for me?"

"This is the way we blind beggars see it. You and Rousseau are like a pair of thoroughbreds from the same stable. You race against the field, but you also compete with each other. If one of you wins the purse, your owner is pleased, but that does not mean the other goes to the butcher—as long as he runs a good race.

"We are hedging our bets. Whether you or Rousseau cracks the case, it's still a win for the police, and for us. And I don't see why we shouldn't bet on you, at least until we settle our dispute with M. Rousseau."

Achille replied with a twisted grin. "I appreciate your honesty."

"Thank you, Monsieur. It always pays to have fair and honest dealings in my profession."

"I would have thought just the opposite."

The man was silent for a moment. Then he remarked, "Of course, you will pay the agreed-upon price?"

Achille reached into his pocket and retrieved a few gold pieces. "This is for what you've provided so far, plus a little on account. I pay a bonus for good results, but rest assured there is a penalty for failure."

Blind from Birth took the coins and sighed. "Alas, Monsieur, there's always a price to be paid for failure. We'll be in touch. *Au revoir.*"

Achille watched the man walk down the embankment, under the arch, past the clochards, and out of sight. He then turned toward the river and rummaged in his pocket for cigarettes and matchbox. A little tug chugged past, towing a barge in its wake. Light from the lamps on the embankment and bridge reflected in ripples on the dark water. *I'd like to be out in a skiff rowing, with Adele at the tiller.* He watched for a while, and then walked toward the entrance to the bridge and on to headquarters.

∞

Achille met Legros in the evidence room at the Palais de Justice. He examined the ligature Legros had removed from the evidence bag and placed on a lamp-lit table. "Our forgotten clue. Good work, Étienne. Tell me how it was found."

Legros smiled. "A snot-nosed kid came across it while he was playing in the reeds by the lake. He used it as a whip to beat his sister, who'd been tagging along and tried to claim the prize for herself."

Achille laughed. "The little devils!"

"Indeed. Anyway, the girl screamed bloody murder and flailed away at her brother. Their mother ran over, broke up the tussle, grabbed the ligature, and gave them both a good hiding. You can imagine the commotion. The row caught the attention of one of the men Rodin detailed to patrol the crime scene. *Et voilà!*"

"That was a lucky break, combined with good police work. Please convey my thanks to Sergeant Rodin." Achille stretched out the ligature and held it up to the light. "You see how the cord was cut cleanly, and the strength of the knot?"

"Yes. They had a sharp blade ready and made good use of it. And I believe that's a sailor's knot, isn't it?"

Achille nodded and returned the ligature to the bag. "A figure eight, to be precise. I tie them myself. This one's first rate, and under the circumstances, I imagine it was tied expeditiously as well. And that bit of evidence dovetails nicely with some information I received this morning concerning a sailor named Moreau."

"Is he a suspect?"

Achille nodded the affirmative. "He's one of the anarchists who hung out with Boguslavsky at the Lapin Agile. I'm having him shadowed, along with his pal, a Pole named Wroblewski. What's more, I've checked their records and they've both been up to no good in the past." He lowered his voice to a whisper. "I got all this information without the aid of our friend Rousseau. No need to spread that around. Understood?"

"I understand, Achille. Do you have enough on them to ask the *juge* for a warrant?"

Achille thought for a moment. If it had been a routine homicide, the *juge d'instruction* would have already been leading the investigation. "Perhaps, but I want to give them enough rope to hang themselves. And we'll have more for the prosecutor than Kadyshev's murderers. If this is a terrorist conspiracy, as I suspect it is, we want to nab the whole gang right on the point of committing the act. It's risky, but that's how I caught the smugglers on the Marseilles docks.

"Wroblewski and Moreau could lead us to Boguslavsky. According to my theory, it took three to hang Kadyshev. If we can bring in these three all together and put the screws on, I'm sure we can persuade one to rat on the others to save his neck. And let's not forget the knight. I won't be satisfied with three pawns; there's more to this game than that. Anyway, the *juge* and the prosecutor will thank us for making their jobs easier.

"Remember what I said about the coded messages and the dead drop? If we can intercept a message and decrypt it, we'll really have them by the short hairs. I've a rendezvous tomorrow morning with a spy who's tailed them to a house on the Rue Ronsard. Here's the address." Achille took out a pencil and notepad and passed the information to Legros. "I want you to begin a discreet inquiry. Find out everything you can about the place: property owner, residents, concierge, unusual activity, and so forth. Report what you find directly to me."

"I understand. But tomorrow's Sunday. I thought you were taking a day off to go rowing with your wife."

Achille frowned. "Duty first, Étienne. Anyway, my meeting is at five in the morning and won't last long. I'll still have the rest of the day." He made another note and handed it to Legros. "That's the name of a *guinguette* in Croissy. Except for an hour or so on the river, I'll be either there or at home. Pass this along to the chief. If something comes up, you'll know where I am. All right?"

"Very well, Achille. Where to next?"

"I've a meeting in Montmartre. More cloak-and-dagger, I'm afraid."

Legros smiled broadly. "Sounds exciting. Good luck to us both."

Achille grinned back and slapped Legros's shoulder. "You know what our chief says about luck?"

Legros grimaced in bewilderment. "I'm not sure?"

"He quotes the great Napoleon, and it's usually in reference to promotion. When considering one of his young generals for higher command, the Emperor said, 'I know he's brilliant, but is he lucky?' Frankly, I'm dubious when it comes to brilliant detective work, so in this case let's pray that we're both damned lucky."

∞

Blind by Accident crouched behind a *poubelle* in a tight, unpaved passageway between two buildings on the Rue Ravignan. He rubbed his sore hams, having tailed Moreau and Wroblewski down from the summit along the dark, winding streets and stairways.

The first light of dawn touched the heights; the lamplighters had made their rounds, extinguishing countless gas jets; the night-soil collectors had pumped out their quota of cesspools and emptied collection vats from numberless cellars; the *chiffoniers* had finished picking through the trash-filled *poubelles*; the dung collectors had carted off piles of horse manure for fertilizer. Cleansed and refreshed, the Butte was ready for another day.

Through dark glasses, Blind by Accident's eyes scanned the entrance to a doss house on the other side of a small square. *I hope the bastards catch some shuteye, at least until my brother relieves me. I could do with some rest, food, and a bottle of wine.*

To kill time, his mind wandered to idle speculation. According to legend, the Emperor Napoleon had stopped in this place on his way to inspect the semaphore telegraph atop the church of Saint-Pierre. The road, which was then called the Vieux-Chemin, proved too steep for the horse, so the Emperor tied his mount to a pear tree and continued the journey on foot. Displeased with his experience on the old road, the Emperor ordered the construction of a new street that became the Rue Lepic.

Blind by Accident pondered the legend skeptically. He had been up and down the Butte many times, and had blistered feet, an aching back, and sore hams to show for it. Granted, the precipitous Old Way had been a damned tough slog for a horse. Nevertheless, the canny spy had a hard time believing that the great general, who had led his army from horseback across the Alps through the Great St. Bernard Pass, could not coax his mount up the old road to the top of Montmartre. And anyway, didn't the Emperor have other business that was far more pressing than inspecting a signal tower? Blind by Accident sighed and shook his head. *In this world of lies, we must take everything with a grain of salt.*

The spy glanced up from the shadows to the blue sky above. *Where is that brother of mine?* he questioned silently, as if God might provide an answer. Vexed with impatience, he looked down again, and an unwelcome sight greeted his overworked eyes: Moreau exited the doss house and began walking up the Rue Ravignan.

Blind by Accident was now at a singular disadvantage. In the evening and early morning hours, he could operate beneath a cloak of darkness; in daytime, he would dissolve in the stew of humanity. The in-between time, when daylight first penetrated his shadowy shield, was the most dangerous hour. Not many people were about at this time of morning, which made it impossible for him to blend and fade away within a perambulating crowd. If he followed Moreau too closely, there was a risk of detection; if he tailed the suspect too loosely, he could lose him.

He immediately decided that losing Moreau was a much better alternative to being burned. The Blind Beggars could only be effective as long as their subjects did not suspect their dodge. Blind by Accident set out after Moreau nonchalantly, as if his stroll up the hill were the most natural action imaginable. Experience had taught him that the quickest way to betray oneself as a spy was to act like one.

His feet and legs tingled as though pricked by a thousand needles. His heart throbbed, and he gulped air through his mouth as he endured the torment of climbing the Rue de la Mire for the second time that morning. He went slowly, keeping well behind without losing sight of Moreau. But Blind by Accident almost lost his composure when his subject stopped abruptly and glanced up to his left.

The spy did not make the amateur's mistake by darting for cover. Like most pedestrians on the steep little street, he halted as if to catch his breath and rubbed his aching legs, but carefully kept a "blind" eye on his subject. He noticed Moreau focus his attention on a third-story window, the only one that remained unshuttered. *A signal?*

Moreau only paused for a moment, and then proceeded up a stairway to the Rue Lepic. The spy continued his tail uphill, following the street until his subject stopped again outside the entrance to the Café Aux Billards en Bois, at the intersection of the Rue des Saules and Rue Norvins.

Is he going to duck into the café and watch? Blind by Accident wondered. But, after a brief pause, Moreau walked on until he turned the corner. Could Moreau be setting a trap?

The spy made a split-second decision. He knew every inch of the neighborhood. Tired as he was, he dashed through a passageway into an alley, removed his hat and dark glasses, and cautiously peeked around the wall onto the street. He saw Moreau standing by the rear of a building. The subject glanced around furtively, removed a loose brick, and picked up a message. The spy smiled knowingly. *This'll be worth something, for sure.*

⌀

Achille admired the sketched outlines of a new composition, mounted on an easel in Lautrec's studio. The artist leaned back against a wooden column in a corner, observing his guest from the shadows like a cat—wary, but curious.

"It's very striking, M. Lautrec," Achille remarked. "It catches the eye and makes a bold statement. Excellent! I can only wonder at what it will look like when you add color."

The artist's thick, purplish lips curved upward in a shrewd smile and his dark brown eyes glowed with satisfaction. "Thank you, Monsieur. You should have been an art critic instead of a policeman."

Achille stepped back a few paces and kept his eyes fixed on the drawing. *I'd give almost anything to create something like this*, he thought.

"I recognize La Goulue and Valentine le Désossé. Is it a sketch for a new poster advertising the Moulin Rouge?"

Lautrec laughed. "Alas, my secret's been found out by the great Inspector Lefebvre. I trust you'll keep mum?"

Achille turned to face the artist. "My lips are sealed. I'm sure Zidler will be very pleased."

"Oh, I'm sure—he packed them in during the Exposition. But now the tourists are gone, along with their cash. So he feels the need to drum up trade. If he could get away with it, he'd have the girls dance the can-can *sans culottes*. But your prefect's spies are everywhere, guarding public morality. At any rate, the current poster is too dull and uninspiring. He needs something controversial."

The artist left his observation post and walked haltingly toward a liquor cabinet on the other side of the studio. He retrieved a bottle of cognac and two glasses. "You'll join me in a drink while we're waiting for Delphine?"

Achille figured one would be all right, and agreed.

"I don't trust a cop who won't accept a free drink while on duty. That sort of thing smacks of self-righteousness, not to mention bad manners." Lautrec poured and handed a glass to Achille, who joined him at a small rectangular table next to the cabinet.

They sat across from each other, enjoying their drinks in silence, until Achille brought up the subject of surveillance. "You mentioned the prefect's spies. Do you object to them?"

Lautrec put down his glass and lit a cigarette before replying. "Of course I object. It's an invasion of privacy, an affront to liberty and freedom of expression, the most basic of human rights. But I suppose you consider such intrusions necessary to your job?"

Achille sighed. "We've worked together before, Monsieur, and I've come to think of you as a friend. Surveillance and spying are indeed necessary to my job. But, of course, you know the purpose of my visit."

The artist raised his bushy eyebrows and smiled wryly. "I was under the impression you came to admire my work—and perhaps to arrange an assignation with the lovely Mlle Delphine."

Achille frowned, shook his head, and glanced down at his half-empty glass. "I appreciate your humor, Monsieur, but life is no joke."

Lautrec laughed bitterly. "No joke, you say? Life's a jumble of farce and melodrama, the chaotic scribbling of a third-rate penny-a-liner. We mock it to keep from going mad—or at least to display our good taste." Lautrec refilled Achille's glass before his guest could protest. "Drink up, Inspector. I've a theory, you know. Cops, like artists, can find inspiration in a brandy bottle, an opium pipe, or a whore's bed."

Achille frowned and sipped his drink, then wiped his lips. He muttered through his beard, "If anyone else said that, I might take offense."

"Ah, you make an exception for me, Inspector, and I know why," Lautrec answered caustically. "You're a gentleman, but I'm a far grander personage, a scion of the counts of Toulouse. Yet you pity me, in your sentimental bourgeois way, because fate has made me a figure of fun. As a consequence of my deformity, I don't enjoy playing the grand seigneur like my father, or mingling with the upper-class idiots at the Jockey Club. Actually, I do run into those fops on occasion, since we frequent the same brothel on the Rue Chabanais. But unlike them, I make myself useful by contributing to our economy. I live in the shadows, hobbling through the gutters of Bohemia on shriveled legs. Cats yowl at me as I limp by their cozy, trash-laden *poubelles*."

Achille's face reddened, and his hands trembled as though he had received an insult that required satisfaction. But he needed Lautrec's help, and therefore would tolerate the artist's sharp tongue. "This conversation has taken an ugly turn, M. Lautrec. I'll put it down to an excess of brandy."

Lautrec sniggered. "Ugly, you say? Well, I'm *ugly* all right. But you know what's uglier? A man who asks a woman who . . . *admires* him to do a filthy job."

Achille breathed deeply to regain control of himself. "I appreciate your concern for Delphine, Monsieur. Believe me when I say I share your misgivings. However, in this case, I've reason to fear innocent lives are at stake. I'll use any means at my disposal, all means necessary and proper, to protect the honest and peaceful citizens of this city."

Lautrec fixed Achille's eyes with a penetrating gaze. "You say 'all means necessary and proper,' Inspector Lefebvre. So you concede our law draws a line at some point beyond which you will not go?"

Achille answered firmly, "Indeed, M. Lautrec. There are limits—but I'm not there yet."

The artist was about to comment further, but a knock at the door interrupted. "Will you do the honors, Inspector? I fear my legs aren't too serviceable just now."

Achille called out, "One moment, please," then got up and walked to the entrance. He opened the door and saw Delphine half-hidden in shadow on the dimly lit landing. She lifted her face beneath a broad-brimmed hat, smiled faintly in response to his greeting, and then crossed the threshold with a rustle of silk.

The high heels of her leather boots tapped gently on the floorboards; her presence filled the studio with a heady fragrance. Tastefully dressed and studiously graceful in her movements, the *chiffonier*'s daughter had come a long way from the Zone and the streets of Montmartre, so much so that Achille barely recognized her. He offered her a chair at the table and seated her with the attentive courtesy of a waiter at a posh restaurant. Lautrec observed the performance with an amused grin, and his smile only broadened when Achille proffered a cigarette and she accepted, holding his hand seductively to steady the match.

Delphine had never been pretty, not like Renoir's rosy-cheeked models. However, she possessed a marketable *je ne sais quoi* that had earned her a good living in the dance halls, cabarets, artists' studios, and beds. A pair of sparkling emerald eyes complemented her *café au lait* skin, flat nose, full sensual lips, and even, white teeth. Those eyes now fixed on Achille with a probing, questioning gaze. In meeting that look, he felt the sting of Lautrec's admonition: *What could be uglier than a man who asks a woman who admires him to do a filthy job?* He suddenly, inexplicably became tongue-tied.

Delphine recognized shame and guilt in his mute, downcast expression. She had seen it often enough, on the faces of clients when they dropped money on her bed. "Pardon me, Inspector," she said softly. "You've brought me here for a reason. If I can be of service, please don't hesitate to ask."

Achille's mouth was dry, so he finished his cognac to free up his tongue. "Delphine, first I want you to understand the gravity of the situation and the risk." He turned to Lautrec. "Monsieur, you too may be helpful, but I'll understand if you don't want to become involved."

The artist frowned and poured another glass. "The way I see it, I'm already involved. Please continue."

Achille nodded and looked back at Delphine. "I'm investigating a difficult case. You must know that I'm working with Rousseau, a man you despise. What you shouldn't know, although you may have guessed, is that I don't have a great deal of confidence in my former partner."

Lautrec spluttered brandy and coughed into his handkerchief.

Delphine merely smiled. "That's hardly a revelation, Monsieur. Don't worry; you can lay your cards on the table. Do you want me to spy on Rousseau?"

"That's a blunt way of putting it—but it's about the truth. I know Rousseau has clandestine meetings in Montmartre—"

"Like *our* meeting, Inspector?" Lautrec broke in.

"Yes, I suppose so," Achille replied with a hint of irritation. Then, to Delphine: "You know everyone around here; you frequent all the nightspots. If Rousseau's meeting someone on the sly, I'd like to know who that person is. Do you think you can get that information for me?"

Delphine stubbed out her cigarette; her red lips parted in a suggestive smile. "I'm ahead of you, M. Lefebvre. I know two young girls intimately,

Aurore and Apolline. On occasion, we've worked as a threesome for clients who like that sort of thing. Last night they were at the Divan Japonais with two gentlemen—"

Lautrec's head jerked as though he had suddenly awakened from a catnap. "I sketched them! I'll show you." The artist hobbled to a shelf, pulled out a sketchbook, and returned to the table. He flipped the pages until he found what he was looking for. "There, you see?"

Delphine examined the sketch. "That's them, all right. I don't know the pretty boy, but the older fellow is M. Orlovsky."

"Orlovsky?" Achille inquired. "Is he Russian?"

"I suppose so. Anyway, according to the girls, he speaks with an accent and he has money to burn. He keeps them in a flat in Montmartre. They're happy enough with the arrangement, but not long ago they saw him with Rousseau at the Cabaret de L'Enfer. The girls are afraid of Rousseau, and for good reason."

"That's good information. Do you think you could find out more about M. Orlovsky? I'd also like to learn something about the young man."

"You should have seen the way the young fop looked you over, Delphine," Lautrec interrupted with a sly grin. "I'm sure it was love at first sight."

Delphine laughed knowingly. "I caught a glimpse of him last night. If you ask me, his taste is more likely to run to boys."

"Perhaps." Lautrec shook his head. "But I believe I saw something else, and it wasn't very pleasant. You'd better watch yourself with that one."

She shrugged off the warning. "I can take care of myself, M. Lautrec. Besides, if he's bent, I'm sure I'll get all the details from the girls."

Achille placed his hand gently on hers, a gesture that was not lost on Lautrec's keenly observant eyes. "Delphine," he half-whispered, "you must promise not to take any unnecessary risks."

She glanced down at their barely touching hands for an instant, and then gazed at him with a sad smile. "Very well, Monsieur, but I assume you'll leave the *necessary* risks to my discretion?"

Achille lifted his hand suddenly, as though he had carelessly allowed it to stray too close to a flame. "You're a clever woman, Delphine. I trust your judgment in these matters implicitly."

Delphine had clearly read Achille's sudden coolness correctly; she understood. "I'll get onto it straightaway. Apolline's the chattier of the pair, and not too bright. I should be able to get something out of her without much trouble. As for the boy, if he's interested in me I'll play him like a hooked fish. How shall we communicate? I assume you want to avoid direct contact."

"Use Moïse," Achille replied. "If he's unavailable, you can send a message through M. Lautrec—if he's agreeable, that is."

The artist nodded in the affirmative and returned to his bottle.

"Thank you, Monsieur," Achille said. "I appreciate your cooperation. By the way, I'll require your sketch of Orlovsky and the young man for identification purposes. Of course, you'll be compensated and the drawing will be returned at the end of the case."

The artist expressed his indifference with a wave of the hand. "You may keep the sketch for your Rogue's Gallery. As for compensation, how about free drinks for a week at the Moulin Rouge?"

"Thank you again, Monsieur. I know Zidler. I'll arrange it." Achille turned his attention back to Delphine. "Now, Mademoiselle, if you find yourself in a tight spot and I'm not at hand, go directly to my assistant, Inspector Legros, or to Sergeant Rodin."

She smiled at his officious expression of concern. "Don't worry, Inspector. I know what to do." Then she leaned over the table and lowered her voice. "Between you and me, I've lived all my life in a damned tight spot."

⌒∞⌒

Toward midnight, Rousseau sat at Orlovsky's table at the Cabaret de L'Enfer, watching an illusionist turn a staff into a snake. The magician handed the serpent to his scantily clad female assistant, who used it as a prop in her provocative belly dance. She squirmed and wiggled with her serpentine partner to Saint-Saëns *Danse macabre* played by a fiddler cloaked in the shadows behind the low stage.

"A clever trick," Rousseau observed.

"Life's full of illusions," Orlovsky replied. "It's difficult to separate the real from the false, and the deceivers from the deceived." He leered at the dancer. "Take the wriggling girl, for example. From our perspective, in this artificial lighting, she appears to be almost naked. In fact, she's wearing flesh-colored tights, just enough to satisfy the police and keep this place from being raided. But who's fooling whom?"

Rousseau turned away from the show and stared at his drink. "I'm not fooled, Monsieur. Tights or not, you can bet someone's being paid off. Men like me cash in on our opportunities. It's tough making ends meet on a cop's salary."

Orlovsky finished his absinthe and called for another. "Do you notice something different, my friend?"

Rousseau glanced around. "Your girls aren't here, Monsieur. Is that something I'm supposed to notice?"

Orlovsky laughed. "Keenly observant, as always. Do you know why they're absent?"

Rousseau downed his drink and then shook his head. "I couldn't say."

Orlovsky patted the detective's shoulder. "Oh, come, dear fellow, be a sport. Won't you venture a guess?"

Rousseau looked up abruptly and glared. "Pardon me, Monsieur. I'm not in the mood for playing games."

The waiter came with the absinthe. Orlovsky added water and, for a moment, amused himself by watching the cloudy mixture change color. Then, still concentrating on the liqueur, he said, "The little imps are afraid of you. So, you've done me another service without even knowing it. When they're naughty I say, 'Behave, or I'll give you to Rousseau.' Works like a charm. You're their bogeyman. They fear you more than a thrashing."

Rousseau turned back to watch the dancer and snake writhing together suggestively. "You speak of them as though they were your slaves."

Orlovsky took a sip of absinthe, then put down his glass and steepled his hands. "Slaves, you say? I assure you, my little sparrows are as free as air. They may fly away anytime they please. Of course, they would have to take their chances on the streets, with all those un-belled cats. In that regard, they're much like our former serfs.

"You know, my father inherited almost one hundred souls who were bound to the land. However, our martyred emperor freed them, leaving them to fend for themselves. Most still eke out a meager existence as tenant farmers or house servants; some have found work in factories and mills; others wander the roads and crowd together in our cities. Count Tolstoy, our great writer, pities them. Their suffering nettles his conscience. 'What then must we do?' he asks. Not much, I'm afraid. According to Messrs. Darwin and Spencer, the fit will survive and the weak will go under."

Rousseau watched the snake slither between the dancer's legs and up the crack of her buttocks. "Disgusting," he muttered, and returned to his drink.

"Ah, you think me uncharitable?" Orlovsky said. "Or perhaps you dispute the cruel laws of nature, survival of the fittest?"

Rousseau stared at the man with a look that belied his apology. "Pardon, Monsieur, I was referring to the *act*."

Orlovsky caught a glimpse of the dancer, licked some absinthe from his lips, and looked back at Rousseau. "You dislike it, but you won't shut them down. What was it you said about 'opportunities'?"

"That's not my job," he replied.

The music ended abruptly. The audience stopped chattering long enough for a round of applause, and then resumed their conversations. The magician, dancer, and snake exited the stage.

Rousseau eyed Orlovsky wearily. "Can we get down to business, Monsieur?"

"Of course, my friend. Have you made any progress in your search for Boguslavsky?"

"No, Monsieur. We had a tip that led us to a house on the Rue Ronsard, but they must have moved him."

Orlovsky clicked his tongue. "That's too bad. For all we know, he could be out of the country—or this world. Perhaps M. Lefebvre has been more successful?"

Rousseau frowned grimly and shook his head. "The Professor's playing his cards close to the vest. He might be on to them, but he's not sharing information."

Orlovsky smirked. "Is it possible his sources might be better than yours?"

Rousseau resisted a strong impulse to remove the Russian's annoying grin—permanently. "Achille has a way of using people and making them like him for it. It's quite a gift, and he's improved upon it since last I worked with him."

"Yes, that's quite a useful talent for a politician, a pimp—or a detective. Do you know how he pulls it off?"

"Yes, Monsieur, I do. He's made a reputation for honesty, and the poor people of Paris think he really cares about them. That's helped him build a reliable network of snoops and snitches. In my day, we relied mostly on bribery and fear."

"I see. But, of course, he pays for information, doesn't he? And he's not above putting the screws on, if necessary."

Rousseau laughed mordantly. "Achille's no saint, if that's what you mean."

Orlovsky glanced down at his empty glass and sighed. "I shouldn't drink this stuff. It'll be the death of me." After a moment, he looked Rousseau squarely in the eye and continued in a sober, businesslike tone, "Please keep me informed, M. Rousseau. I said once before that I'd like to meet Inspector Lefebvre. That may be sooner rather than later. I'll let you know. *Au revoir*, Inspector."

8

THE EEL UNDER THE ROCK

Achille and Blind from Birth met beneath a chestnut tree on the lower embankment. The familiar group of clochards sheltered under a Left-Bank archway of the nearby Pont Neuf. A steady drizzle had sprinkled the city from late evening to the early morning hours, letting up just before dawn, but raindrops fell from the sodden leaves and plopped on the pavement and the crown of Achille's flat cap.

The spy reported the results of his brother's surveillance from the doss house on the Rue Ravignan to the Café Aux Billards en Bois and back, with emphasis on the dead drop. "*Il y a anguille sous roche*, M. Lefebvre. There certainly was an eel under the rock in this case."

"You and your brother have done well," Achille replied. "Are you certain Rousseau hasn't caught on to our game?"

Blind from Birth grinned reassuringly. "No need to worry on that account, Monsieur. But I must warn you: we're coming to terms with your former partner, and may need to terminate our present arrangement—at least for the time being."

Achille had anticipated the revelation. "Not a problem, my friend. With the information you've provided, my men can stake out the route and take over from here." Achille reached into his pocket and produced several gold pieces. "Here's the remainder of our agreed-upon sum, plus a bonus for good results."

The spy tipped his battered hat, snatched the cash from Achille's extended palm, and flashed a broad smile. "You're an honorable gentleman. That's your reputation, and it's well deserved. My brother and I will gladly work for you anytime, as long as it doesn't create a conflict of interest with M. Rousseau." He noted the hint of a frown on Achille's lips, and added prudently, "In this *particular* case, if we were to become privy to actions contrary to *your* interests, we'd be pleased to tip you off—for a reasonable fee, of course."

Achille smiled. "Of course, my friend." He held out his hand for a hearty shake and concluded his present dealings with the Blind Beggars upon a gentleman's agreement. *I'll keep them on my side*, he thought. *They can be of great help in the future*. He waited until the spy disappeared from view, and then walked up the steps to the bridge.

Halfway across, he stopped for a cigarette. Leaning against the balustrade, he viewed the Conciergerie in the first light of dawn. To most Parisians, the grim fortress had sinister connotations. Parents frightened their wayward children with tales of confinement, torture, and a dreaded early-morning rendezvous with Monsieur de Paris. But to Achille, the detention cells were merely an extension of his office, *a cordon sanitaire* separating the most pernicious elements of society from the general population.

He exhaled tobacco smoke with a sigh. He had enough evidence for a warrant on Moreau and Wroblewski—let the magistrate interrogate them according to law. They could also now search the doss house, the house on the Rue Ronsard, and the one on the Rue de la Mire where the drop had been signaled. There were risks in waiting on the evidence to build a stronger case, but moving prematurely might result in the loss of the person in charge—the king or queen.

Achille shook his head, unsure, and tossed the cigarette into the river; then he checked his watch. He had an early meeting scheduled with Legros, and the rest of the day off for a planned outing with Adele. Gazing up at the cloudy sky, he silently remonstrated with the heavens. *Bonté divine, don't let it rain!*

༄

Achille turned up the lamp, read the note in his hand, and stroked his beard thoughtfully. "So, it seems my friend Rousseau wants a meeting 'at my earliest convenience.' Damned civil of him, don't you agree, Étienne?"

Legros sat facing Achille, on the other side of his office desk. "It must be very important. Will you meet him today?"

Achille set down the note and smiled. "If I were a bachelor like you, I probably would. However, I've promised this Sunday to my family. I'll meet with Rousseau 'at my earliest convenience,' which will be five o'clock tomorrow morning at the Sainte-Chapelle. If it were so damned urgent, he'd be sitting where you are right now. At any rate, I've a good idea why he wants this meeting—M. Rousseau thinks I'm getting ahead of him, and wants me to catch him up. I'll bargain for information from a position of strength."

"I'll convey your reply this morning," Legros said. "Now, I've intelligence about the house on Rue Ronsard. The premises have been let to a M. Rossignol. According to the landlord, he's a well-to-do merchant broker from Lyons. We're checking with the prefecture to see if they've got anything on him."

Achille smirked and shook his head. "Rossignol and Ronsard, eh? He's a cheeky bastard, all right."

"So it seems, Inspector."

"Well, pride before a fall. I want you to check another address, on the Rue de la Mire. It'll be interesting to learn if it's also being leased by M. Songbird."

"I'm on it, Inspector. Now, you wanted me to set up a stakeout in Montmartre?"

"Yes, Étienne. Pick a couple of good men and have them shadow Moreau and Wroblewski night and day. I'm particularly interested in learning the details of how they work their dead drop. The timing of the pickup and delivery is crucial. I've an idea of how to intercept and decode their messages without tipping them off."

"How will you do that?"

"We need to get in touch with Gilles. He has a portable camera disguised as a parcel. It may be possible to photograph the messages at the drop. Anyway, we might have to recruit Gilles for that job. We'll see what he says."

"I'll get a message to him. Anything else?"

Achille shook his head and shuffled through some papers in the opened file. "I think that's all for now. I'm on my way home. Maybe I can catch forty winks before breakfast."

"Good luck, Inspector. And I hope you have fair weather. It pissed down last night."

Achille rubbed the ache around his eye sockets. "If anything, Étienne, this case is warming up, which means our days off from now until it's closed will be few and far between."

cᴏᴏ⋅

Achille pulled the oars with a deft, powerful stroke. Well known among sporting Parisians as a crack rower, the inspector was often the odds-on favorite at impromptu races in the neighborhood of Chatou and Croissy.

The plan had been to rent a skiff at Chatou, row downriver past the bridge, and then return upstream in time for lunch at their favorite *guinguette*, the Maison Fournaise. However, the sky had remained gray and cloudy since sunrise, with intermittent drizzle from the railway station to the dock. Few boaters were out in this weather, but Achille insisted they go, even in the face of the boatman's warnings and Adele's protests.

"I've promised you a row, and that's what you shall have," he said stubbornly. His wife answered with a look at once wounded and wounding.

Adele sat gloomy and silent in the stern as she handled the tiller with one hand and supported her parasol with the other. The weather was not bad as they glided downstream past muddy banks lined with willows and white-walled rustic houses.

But not far beyond the bridge, the sky turned a peculiar tint of green and a flight of noisy sparrows darted from the trees and circled the river ominously. A sulfurous burst of light, like a photographer's powder flash, preceded a low, distant rumbling. Adele's lips silently formed the words "I told you so." The sky answered by spouting like an un-bunged beer barrel.

Achille glanced upward and muttered *"Merde!"* Then he turned to Adele, who glared back at him. "We must be near La Grenouillère. Can you see it?"

"Yes, it's just around the bend."

"Very well. I'm picking up the stroke. Guide me in to the dock."

"Not that horrible place!"

"My dear, we're taking on water. It's La Grenouillère or we go under. Now please help me in, and sing out a warning so we don't crash into the dock."

"All right, M. Lefebvre. But I warned you, the boatman warned you . . . but, oh no, you always know better—"

"You were right, my dear," Achille broke in breathlessly. His chest heaved; his muscular arms and legs worked liked the pistons and driving rods on a locomotive. "I concede defeat. Will you please handle the tiller and keep an eye out for—"

Achille did not finish the sentence. They slammed into a mossy piling with a bone-jarring thud. After quickly assuring himself that the damage was minimal and they were not about to sink, he shipped oars and got up cautiously to balance the boat. Then he grabbed the mooring line, pulled himself up onto the rickety landing, and secured the skiff. Achille reached down for Adele, took her around the waist, and lifted her onto the dock.

You might have helped, he thought while sensibly keeping such criticism to himself. Instead, he grasped her hand and cried, "Come on. Let's run for it."

They dashed to the pavilion that had replaced the notorious floating dance hall, which had burned down the previous year. Inside, they shook themselves off and then sat on a pair of empty seats at the end of a long table. Adele scanned the place critically and made a quick assessment: "It's not as bad as I thought."

Achille smiled wistfully. A decade earlier, in his bachelor days, he had made acquaintance with the Romper, a hall on pontoons named for the rowdiness of the dancing, and the tiny round bathing dock with its lone shade tree, known as *le camembert* because of its resemblance to a cheese. Memories of intoxication, coarse companionship, powdered and perfumed sirens, conquests, brawls, and a quarrel ending in a duel flashed through his mind in an instant. He would share none of these embarrassing reminiscences with his wife.

"It's changed," he said.

Adele leaned toward him with a curious gleam in her eye. "Is it true what they say about the drunken can-can dancing and mixed bathing in the altogether?"

Achille laughed softly. "Bathing costume was the rule, but it was loosely enforced. At any rate, no one would make an effort to stop a few fools from stripping down and jumping in the river. That was part of the attraction, and made for some good jokes about the anatomical attributes—" He cut himself off judiciously. "Well, you understand."

"Indeed I do." She glanced up and around, listening for a moment to the pattering of raindrops against the eaves and windowpanes. "Not much danger of that today, I'm afraid. And not many customers around, either, which demonstrates the common sense of most Parisians on a day like this."

Achille flushed and looked down at his hands. "I'm sorry, my dear," he mumbled. He tried to change the subject. "I met Maupassant here. He was a great rower, back in those days."

She reached over and stroked his hand gently. "Yes, my dear Professor, you've told me about your acquaintance with Maupassant many times. And Renoir, Monet, Pissarro, and others came here to paint when they were still unknown. But that was long ago, before the war."

He placed his hand on hers. "Long ago, when we were very young, before the war," he echoed. "Back then, they all came here, from the highest to the lowest. Even the Emperor and Empress got on a train and came out to have a look. People compared it to Trouville—" He caught himself again.

"*Are* we going to Trouville this summer? You may be frank with me, Achille."

He shook his head and sighed. "I don't know. This case is difficult— very difficult."

Suddenly, Adele let go of his hands, frowned, and hissed, "There's a vulgar little man staring at us. He's with a floozy. She's smoking a cigarette and drinking beer—in public."

Achille glanced over his shoulder. The man smiled and waved. Achille acknowledged the greeting with a nod and turned back swiftly to Adele. "Rats!" he muttered. "It's Fournier."

"Who is Fournier?"

"A blasted reporter."

"Well, the blasted reporter is coming over with his woman."

"Very well. Be polite, but give them no encouragement."

Adele huffed. "You have nothing to worry about on that account."

Fournier approached, a short fellow with a protruding paunch, embellished with a red silk vest and dangling gold watch chains. "Well, Inspector Lefebvre, fancy meeting you here. And in such *charming* company!"

Achille took offense at the implication of infidelity. He rose from his chair and towered over Fournier menacingly.

The reporter calmly ignored Achille's threatening demeanor. "Will you honor us with an introduction, Monsieur?"

Achille glared at the man. "M. Fournier, I have the honor of presenting my *wife*, Mme Lefebvre."

The reporter grinned, lifted his bowler, and bowed. "Your wife? I am indeed honored. Enchanted, Madame Lefebvre. And may I present *my* companion, a young actress of great promise, Mlle Celestine."

Achille made a stiff bow, while Adele eyed the woman with icy contempt. She nodded curtly and said "Mademoiselle."

Celestine was a painted trollop of forty. Despite her apparent maturity, she acted the part of an eighteen-year-old ingénue. Her rouged lips parted in a broad smile, revealing tobacco-stained teeth. "I'm indeed honored, Madame." Turning to Achille, she added, "My dear Inspector Lefebvre, all Paris is buzzing with talk of your latest case. 'The Hanged Man' is on the tip of every tongue."

Achille did not reply to Celestine. He turned from the actress to her companion. Fournier had a bad reputation for bribing police officers to obtain confidential information, and if he did not get what he wanted from the police, he was quite capable of making things up. Associating with such an individual was compromising, but if he and Adele left immediately, the reporter might take it as a slight. His revenge for such a snub could be a fabricated article. Achille had a fine sense of honor—and a temper—and if the story was slanderous, he could be provoked into a duel. An illegal fight between a journalist and an inspector would at the least be scandalous; worse, it could detract from the investigation, even end Achille's career.

Achille addressed Fournier directly in words the reporter would understand. "I'm involved in an investigation, Monsieur, and therefore not at liberty to discuss the case."

The reporter smirked and stroked his waxed moustache. "Ah, yes, your investigation. So many rumors, so few facts. You must be very busy, Monsieur. But at least you have time to spend a pleasant Sunday on the river with your charming wife."

Achille clenched his fists, but Adele sensed trouble and intervened. She rose and made a slight bow. "Monsieur, Mademoiselle, it's been a great pleasure meeting you both, but we were just about to leave. If you will excuse us."

"But, Madame," Fournier protested, "you and your esteemed husband have just arrived. Besides, it's still raining. You might have difficulty obtaining a cab to take you to the railway station."

She smiled sweetly. "Thank you for your solicitude, Monsieur, but I'm sure we'll manage. Come along, my dear." She grabbed Achille's arm and half-dragged him away from the table before the reporter or his companion could get in another word.

All at once, the clouds parted and the rain stopped. On the pathway outside the pavilion, Achille turned to Adele, leaned over, and kissed her cheek. "That was brilliant, my dear," he whispered.

She gazed up at him and laughed. "Did you see the looks on their faces?"

"It was very amusing. But we can't take him too lightly. Remember, the pen's mightier than the sword. And I'm afraid he was right about the cab. We may have a bit of a walk."

She looked up at the brightening sky. "Not necessarily, my love. If the boat still floats, we can row. You were right—it's a beautiful day after all."

◦∞◦

At home, Achille played with Olivier in the nursery. All was going delightfully, until the baby vomited on his father's clean white shirt. After a bath and a change of clothes, the inspector acted the role of horse to his daughter's Napoleon. The child's five-year-old mind transformed the long front hall runner into a snow-laden Alpine pass, or the sands of Egypt (her grandmamma, a colonel's wife, filled the little girl's head with stories about the great Emperor) and her father became Bijou, one of young General Bonaparte's favorite mounts.

"The army will advance! Forward Bijou!" she cried as she kicked her equine papa's aching sides with little bare feet and smacked his sore crupper with the flat of her wooden sword.

Achille began to view his day off as a form of penance for neglecting his family, like performing the Stations of the Cross on bleeding knees. However, the ultimate mortification was yet to come—supper with Mme Berthier.

They dined early in consideration of Achille's early meeting the following morning. Madame opened the conversation with a stern rebuke.

"Achille, it was reckless to go boating in such foul weather. You are fortunate things turned out as well as they did. One expects such foolishness from a college boy, not a man who aspires to become the next Chief of the Sûreté." Then she turned on her daughter. "Adele, you ought to have had the good sense to refuse to enter the boat." Adele blushed, looked down, and remained silent.

"Yes, Madame," Achille replied, with sufficient contrition for both husband and wife. Wishing to avoid any discussion of their encounter with the reporter and his mistress, he immediately changed the subject by commenting on the excellence of Cook's veal chops with sorrel and the accompanying Haut-Brion. Adele followed his lead enthusiastically. These compliments, luckily, elicited a smile from the old woman, who was in charge of going to market and supervised Cook with a sharp eye and a firm hand. Thus, she took credit for the fine meal.

Nevertheless, Achille could not dodge his mother-in-law's rumor-mongering and conspiracy theories, which pervaded the dining-room conversation like a miasma. In response to her speculations concerning the Hanged Man, German spies, and their subversive allies, he replied as he had to Fournier: "The investigation is ongoing, Madame, and I'm not at liberty to discuss it."

Mme Berthier smiled slyly. "Of course, my boy. I understand perfectly."

She understood nothing and, as Achille could foresee but was powerless to prevent, she would continue propagating nonsense among her friends in the marketplace the following morning.

After dinner, Achille read Jeanne one of her favorite stories, *Beauty and the Beast*. As many times as he read the fairy tale, she wanted to hear it again. Afterwards, she looked up at him with a smile so sweet and loving that it almost brought him to tears.

"Papa," she said, "we had so much fun today. Why can't you be with me always?"

Achille's throat tightened. He stroked her long, light brown hair gently and tried to smile. "I would love to be with you always, my darling, but I must go to work. Not just for the good of our family—above all, I have a duty to France."

The little face grew serious. "Are you like the Emperor Napoleon?"

He laughed softly. "No, my dear. More like one of his lieutenants. Although I am a commandant in the reserve."

"Is that like a general?"

"No, little one. It's just below a colonel."

"Like grandpapa?"

"Yes, like your grandpapa Berthier. He was a great soldier—a fine man. So was my father, your grandpapa Lefebvre. He was a lawyer by profession, but he fought in the Crimea. He was wounded and decorated for bravery."

The little mouth quivered. "If there was a war, would you have to fight?"

Achille saw the warning signs in her face and tried to make light of things. "You needn't worry about that. There won't be another war, or at least not for a very long time. By then, you'll be grown up and married with children and I'll be an old grandpa, much too old for fighting." Then he tickled her ribs to make her laugh.

Adele knocked and entered with Mme Berthier. Adele noticed the horseplay and frowned at Achille. "You shouldn't make her excited at bedtime."

He smiled and tousled Jeanne's hair. "We were just playing a game, weren't we, little one?"

"Yes, just a game," the girl echoed.

Adele sat on the edge of the bed, examined her daughter's hair, and began straightening the stray locks. "Look what you've done, Achille. I had it brushed so nicely."

Madame defied convention by defending her son-in-law. "Don't make such a fuss, Adele. After all, he hardly ever gets to see our pretty little cabbage." She smiled and sat next to Adele. Leaning close to Jeanne, she whispered, "Now, say your prayers, darling. Then you may say good night to mama and papa, and give old granny a kiss."

Jeanne behaved beautifully. Adele turned down the bedside lamp, and the three adults passed out into the hall. Out of earshot of the little girl, Mme Berthier observed, "She's a sweet child, Adele; much better than you were at that age. Good evening."

Madame shuffled down the hall to her boudoir, and Achille turned to Adele. "Well, my dear. Are you ready for a smoke and a drink?"

Adele sighed. "I was ready two hours ago." With that pithy comment, they retired arm-in-arm to the drawing room.

They sat together on a small, velvet-upholstered settee, he with his cigar and cognac, she with a cigarette and an *eau de vie de pêche*. For a moment, they savored the quiet pleasure of being together without interference, and they kept their thoughts to themselves.

Achille caught glimpses of Adele with sidelong glances. After seven years of marriage and two children, he could still be surprised by her beauty, and that was especially so in a tranquil evening hour when he could observe her silhouette in golden lamplight. She seemed to be dreaming with her eyes open, and he wondered if she were reflecting on the events of the day.

With all its mishaps and misadventures, it was still beautiful, he thought. How many more such days would they share? No one could tell. *Our grip on life is tenuous, at best*. Achille had seen many coffins lowered into the earth, young men and women, ostensibly healthy, cut down early by disease, accident, crime, or in the line of duty.

Then there were the children, little ones like Olivier and Jeanne. They must run the gauntlet of childhood diseases. Achille had lost three siblings to scarlet fever and diphtheria; he had survived both. He thought of Maître François, the loneliness and decrepitude of old age, the inevitable end, the sickroom smell, a lingering death. *Perhaps it's best to go quickly, unexpectedly*. Achille recalled something he had read about Caesar. When asked how he preferred to die, the great dictator replied "Suddenly."

"You're far away, darling." Adele broke into his thoughts.

He saw her bright green eyes and warm red lips, inhaled her fresh fragrance. Smiling sheepishly, he set his cigar down in an ashtray and placed his empty glass on the coffee table, then turned to her. He reached over and toyed with a pearl earring dangling from a pretty lobe. "How lovely. I remember when I bought these. Wasn't it for your last birthday?"

"Actually, it was two years ago. Is that what you were thinking? My birthday's coming up, you know."

He leaned over and kissed her ear. "No, that's not what I was thinking about, my love," he whispered. "I was thinking about the river. For all my bungling, it still was a fine outing, wasn't it?"

She sighed and rested her head on his chest. "Yes, but I'm worried about that reporter. Do you think he'll write about the incident?"

"Oh, I suppose so, but I expect it'll be something benign." He held her close and stroked her hair. "Anyway, I'm not going to let it bother me, but I'll have to mention the meeting to Féraud."

For an instant, she seemed content to rest quietly in his arms. Then she gazed up at him and said, "There's something about this case that's troubling you more than usual. Would it help if you told me about it? You know I won't tell anyone, especially Mother."

He smiled and brushed her lips with a finger. "Thank you, my dear, but I'm afraid I must give you the formal response: I can't discuss the case. But I will say this: I'm up against something new and pernicious. I'm not quite sure about the nature of the enemy, but I hope to learn more in the coming days. At any rate, I regret we won't have much time together, at least not until this matter is closed." He paused, then continued on to a topic he hoped would be more pleasing to his wife. "We haven't had much of a social life. I've left you cooped up in this apartment with the children and Madame. I hope . . . I'm going to try to see that that changes in the future."

"How will it change?" she asked, a hint of expectancy in her voice.

"We've talked about it, often enough. If I successfully conclude this case, I'll get my promotion, I'm sure of it. Things will change. There will be dinner parties with the prefect and his wife, balls and other social activities among the influential and powerful: magistrates, senators, deputies, generals, magnates, and their spouses. Would you like that?"

Her face clouded over for an instant, as if she were unsure of her answer. Finally, she replied hesitantly, "I . . . I don't know, Achille. I recall how it was for Mother, being the colonel's wife. She trained me for it. I can manage. I suppose I'd become one of those society women who entertains and goes around promoting her husband's career. I know how to play the part; I *believe* I could do it. It's just . . . oh, I don't know." Her eyes suddenly filled with tears and she sobbed on his shoulder.

Her reaction bewildered him. In all their previous discussions about his career, she had seemed enthusiastic. The pain and sadness in her expression hurt him deeply, especially since he believed he was somehow the cause of it.

He lifted her face and wiped her tears with his hands. "I'm sorry, my love. I thought this is what you—what we both—wanted. I can't bear to see you like this. Believe me, I'd chuck the promotion in an instant, if that's what you really wanted."

She shook her head and protested vehemently. "How can you say that? You'd think yourself a failure, and blame me for the rest of our lives." She paused a moment to catch her breath and regain her composure. "I'll be all right, Achille, I promise. It's just . . . the realization that I'm going to live my mother's life all over again. Her life, not *mine*. Do you understand?"

He did not understand, but he had to say something. "It needn't be that way. Women have more freedom nowadays, especially here in Paris. We have a partnership, you and I, and we'll work well together. Think of all the good things our success can bring, for the children and for us. I'm sure you'll enjoy the social whirl once you're into it."

She smiled faintly and nodded. "Yes, I'm certain I shall. For now, I'd like another drink."

Achille reached for the liqueur bottle, but Adele declined.

"I think I'd prefer something stronger—your cognac."

"That's just the ticket," Achille said. "And I'll have another, to brace up for my meeting with M. Rousseau."

Adele laughed. "Are you so concerned about Rousseau? That's not for hours yet." She took her glass from his hand and, for a moment, swirled the amber liquid around before tasting it. "Perhaps you should brace up for a more pressing engagement with me?"

Achille looked her squarely in the eye and twirled his moustache. "Ah, Madame, I don't need brandy to prepare for *that*!"

⁓∞⁓

Aurore filled Orlovsky's glass with champagne. He took a sip and pronounced it "passable." Next, she compulsively tested for freshness one of the cigars she had selected earlier, clipped the tip, and offered it to her patron. He accepted the Maduro-wrapped Havana nonchalantly, leaned forward so she could give him a light, and then relaxed back in his red plush chair, refocusing his attention on a troupe of Japanese acrobats performing on stage.

Aurore and Orlovsky occupied a reserved box at the Folies-Bergère, from which they had an excellent view of the stage, the stalls, and the encircling, mirror-lined promenade. A fog of tobacco smoke pervaded the hall, tinted by the yellowish radiance of hundreds of electric bulbs and gas mantles.

Orlovsky took a few puffs, and then turned from the performance to his companion. "Where is that little chit?" he snapped. "She ought to have come with you. If she doesn't arrive presently, I shall be vexed."

Aurore frowned with remorse. "I'm very sorry, Monsieur. She'll be here soon, I promise," she responded in a mollifying tone. Then, smiling hopefully, she added, "She has a surprise, Monsieur. I'm sure you'll be pleased."

Orlovsky sneered. "A surprise, eh? It had better be good for her sake—and yours."

Aurore trembled at the threat of punishment, her behind having barely recovered from a recent "correction." She glanced nervously in the direction of the entrance to the promenade, and after a minute of desperate searching she sighed with relief. Half-standing, she leaned against the partition and pointed toward the corridor on the other side of the hall.

"You see, Monsieur," she cried, "there they are!" Aurore pulled a handkerchief from her bosom and waved in the same direction to which she had pointed.

Orlovsky grabbed her by the sleeve. "Don't make a scene," he hissed. "And who, pray tell, are *they*?"

Returning to her chair, she replied, "It's Apolline and Delphine Lacroix. Delphine's the surprise. I hope you're pleased?"

Orlovsky scanned the perambulating throng and caught sight of the *poule* walking arm-in-arm with a dark, elegantly dressed young woman. He smiled and nodded in their direction.

"It's all right, then, Monsieur?" Aurore asked timidly.

"Yes, yes, it's all right. But you ought to have told me. At any rate, I am surprised to see Mlle Delphine walking the promenade. I thought she was above that sort of thing."

"Oh, she's no longer a card-carrying regular," confided Aurore. "But she's still on very good terms with the management. And she's not 'walking the promenade,' so to speak. She's here at our invitation, to meet you."

Orlovsky grinned broadly. "I see. A moment ago, you and Apolline were in danger of a good hiding. Now, you might be in line for a nice present or two, provided, of course, that the evening progresses to my satisfaction."

"Oh, thank you, Monsieur," the girl gushed, with a mixture of relief for having escaped a whipping and greed for the anticipated reward.

Delphine and Apolline arrived at the entrance to the box and, bubbling over with excitement, Apolline made the introductions. "M. Orlovsky, permit me to introduce my dear friend, Mlle Delphine Lacroix."

Orlovsky rose to his feet and made a courteous bow. "I'm honored, Mademoiselle. I have admired your singing on many occasions. Will you allow me the great pleasure of entertaining you in my box?"

Delphine smiled seductively. "You are too kind, Monsieur. It will be my pleasure to join you."

She entered, followed by Apolline. Orlovsky gestured to a nearby waiter for more chairs and another bottle of champagne, and this time he specified a better vintage. Once seated and served, Orlovsky engaged Delphine in small talk flatteringly centered upon her career. Aurore and Apolline amused themselves by watching the acts, though they remained attentive to the needs of their master and his guest. Eventually, the conversation turned to Delphine's most recent performance. After thanking Orlovsky for his praise, Delphine referred to the young gentleman in their company who seemed so engrossed in the performance.

Orlovsky raised an eyebrow and smiled shrewdly. "Ah, you mean young M. de Gournay."

"Oh, is that his name?" Delphine replied casually, taking a cigarette from her purse.

"Permit me, Mademoiselle." Orlovsky struck a match and lit her cigarette, then blew out the match and dropped it in an ashtray. "Gournay is a young gentleman from Normandy, a man of good family forced by circumstances to go into trade. Nevertheless, he has made a great success in business and I am one of his best clients." He paused a moment to read Delphine's face. He detected interest in her sparkling eyes and sensually parted lips. "If you'd care to make his acquaintance, I'd be pleased to introduce you."

Delphine took a puff of her cigarette and exhaled a plume of smoke in the direction of the ceiling. Then she looked directly at Orlovsky. "If you please, Monsieur. He seems like an *amusing* young man."

Apolline suppressed laughter at Delphine's comment by covering her face with a fan and coughing loudly, which drew a reproving glare from her patron. Directing his attention back to Delphine, he continued, "Very well, Mademoiselle. I shall speak to him." Then he lowered his voice, leered provocatively, and brushed his fingers against her kid-gloved hand. "Now, my dear, if you are not otherwise engaged, perhaps you'll condescend to spend the rest of the evening with me and my charming little companions?"

Aurore and Apolline held their breaths, anxiously awaiting Delphine's response. They knew exactly what Orlovsky wanted—and expected. Their coveted reward was at stake.

Delphine teased him coyly. "That is an intriguing proposal, Monsieur. What should I say in reply?"

Orlovsky's brain burned with lascivious images of the three young women in bed. He leaned over the table, took her hand in his, and kissed her fingers. Then he looked up with entreating eyes. "Say yes, dear Mademoiselle. Say yes!"

9

THE FRENCH DEFENSE

On his way to the Sainte-Chapelle, Achille diverted himself with a chess metaphor. He imagined Rousseau playing white, opening with the prosaic yet sound P-K4. One could anticipate a respectable but unimaginative response from black, mirroring the opponent's opening move. However, Achille preferred the tricky French Defense—P-K3.

The choice of first move always gave white the initiative, but black had a retort: "We'll dance to my tune, not yours." The reasoning was simple: white may have studied the traditional king's pawn openings—Giuoco Piano, Ruy Lopez—to exhaustion, but he had better know the defenses as well.

A weak player might view black's P-K3 as a blunder, an invitation to charge aggressively like a bull, only to run headlong into a hidden sword. On the other hand, the move could confuse a more experienced player, and that confusion might lead to tentativeness in which white loses the initiative, alters his plans, and winds up playing black's game.

Achille smiled at the analogy, the cat-and-mouse tactics he had adopted with his former partner. Upon arrival at the chapel, he flashed his badge at the guard and entered the dark nave, then spotted Rousseau lurking within the arcade. The detective sought cover habitually, whether he needed to or not.

Achille picked up his pace, footsteps echoing throughout the high-vaulted sacred enclosure. He stopped at the corner of an arch and peered into the shadows. "Good morning, Rousseau. You're early."

"Good morning, Professor." The greeting emerged from the penumbra. "Yes, I'm early and I'm in a hurry. I've a busy day ahead. Things are heating up in our case."

Achille responded to the obvious with a smirk. "Hot as Hades, I'd say, and I appreciate the reference to *our* case. What have you got for me, *partner?*"

Rousseau ignored the sarcasm. "We're closing in on Boguslavsky. We believe he was moved from a safe house in Montmartre to La Villette."

"La Villette's a big place. Have you anything more definite?"

Rousseau frowned with displeasure—he had apparently anticipated surprise, or at least a more enthusiastic response. "We're working on it," he grunted.

"Good," Achille replied. "Please keep me apprised of the situation."

Rousseau's granitic features cracked. "Keep you apprised of the situation?" he parroted mockingly. "You're a cool one, Professor."

Achille smiled. "I'll take that as a compliment. Any leads on the cat burglar?"

"We brought in the usual suspects for questioning. We've turned up nothing, so far. But these fellows don't like outsiders poaching on their preserve. Sooner or later, someone will come forward and inform."

"Let's hope sooner rather than later. At any rate, if we trap the rats, we'll likely bag the cat too. Now, I have a question. What do you know about M. Orlovsky?"

Rousseau was taken aback and remained silent for a moment, eyes smoldering like hot coals. The snoop did not like being snooped. "I should ask you the same question," he answered bluntly.

"Let's not play games, my friend. You've been meeting with the man regularly, and I doubt these are social tête-à-têtes. I can imagine how he fits into *our* case."

"Don't *imagine*. He's my Okhrana contact," Rousseau admitted. "He's on our side. That's all you need to know."

His suspicions confirmed, Achille thought of Delphine. He had launched her on a dangerous venture, like a sacrificial pawn. But he had no time for sentimental weakness. "Fair enough," he said. "Now, what can you tell me about Rossignol?"

"Rossignol? I don't know what you're talking about."

Was Rousseau lying? Covering up? Or just ignorant? Achille had no way of knowing, but he threw a bone to see how Rousseau chewed on it. "You mentioned a safe house in Montmartre. We located a place on the Rue Ronsard, and I assume it's the same. The lease is in the name of M. Rossignol."

Rousseau did not answer directly. "So you know about Moreau and Wroblewski?"

"Yes, I do. And you know nothing of Rossignol?"

Rousseau shook his head in the negative and remained silent. Then he said, "I suppose you're looking for this Rossignol?"

"Of course." Achille paused before adding, "Can you tell me something about one of Orlovsky's friends? A young fop who frequents the dance halls and cabarets."

Rousseau did not hesitate to answer, though he raised a questioning eyebrow. "You mean de Gournay? I know nothing about him, except that he hangs out with Orlovsky. The Russian gentleman has his own way of life. I don't interfere, as long as he remains our ally."

"I see. But there is no formal alliance between France and Russia. What if he turned against us?"

Rousseau's face darkened. He stepped forward and clenched a fist, as though about to strike out. "I think you can answer that yourself," he growled.

Achille remained calm, gazing directly into Rousseau's burning eyes. "I'm sorry, my friend, I know you're a patriot. I trust you'll act accordingly."

Rousseau backed off, but he replied with dignity, "You needn't remind me of my duty."

"I'd never presume to," Achille said. Then he tossed another bone. "I'll contact you immediately if I learn more about M. Rossignol." Of course, he said nothing about the code, the Blind Beggars, or Delphine's espionage. As for the shady M. de Gournay, he would take Rousseau at his word. Achille had other means of acquiring facts about the gentleman. Everything considered, he had learned something about Rousseau's intentions, and revealed little in return.

Rousseau seemed satisfied. "All right, Inspector." Then he solemnly proclaimed, "We'd better pull together, Achille. After all, we're rowing the same boat."

The offer of closer cooperation, coupled with the boating metaphor, caught Achille off guard. Subtlety was hardly Rousseau's long suit. "Before, we were working opposite sides of the same street," Achille replied. "Now, we'll crew the same boat. It's all one to me, as long as we do our job and dispose of the case successfully."

"Very well, Professor. You'll hear from me soon. Until then."

Achille nodded. "*Au revoir*, Rousseau."

The porter gave Boguslavsky's shoulder a rude shake. "Wake up, comrade. You must leave at once."

The snoring man's eyes blinked open to the blinding glare of a lantern. He raised his right hand over his face for shade. "What . . . what the devil's going on?"

"Keep your voice down! The police have this place surrounded. We have an escape route planned, but you must make haste. Get dressed and I'll give you instructions."

Boguslavsky rolled off his palette and grabbed his trousers, shoes, and socks. In response to the porter's incessant urging, he growled, "Shut up, will you? I'm moving as fast as I can."

As soon as Boguslavsky was dressed, the porter guided him to a corner space hidden behind a row of shelves. He set the lantern down, grasped an iron ring, and lifted a trap door. A stench like rotten meat and excrement filled their nostrils.

"What is this?" Boguslavsky growled. "Do you expect me to crawl through a fucking sewer?"

"Be quiet, you fool!" the porter hissed. "This is the only way out. Get down there and I'll point the way. Now listen carefully: You'll crawl on your belly for about twenty meters until you come to a canal. A boat's waiting. The boatman will take you to a prearranged spot, where you'll transfer to a closed coach that'll take you to a railway station. Rossignol will meet you there with a passport, tickets, and cash. Any questions?"

Boguslavsky scowled. "No." He lowered himself into the narrow space, grunting as he stretched out face-down in the muck. "Aren't you coming?" he asked.

"Don't worry about me. Start crawling. It's not far." The porter held the lantern and watched until Boguslavsky disappeared from view. Then he lowered the trap door, leaving the chemist to creep through the slime in total darkness.

⌘

Delphine and Apolline sat at a lace-draped tea table, enjoying their morning chocolate, pears, and brioche. A Moroccan maid served their breakfast near an unshuttered window, with cut velvet curtains partially drawn to admit light and a mild summer breeze. The two young women lounged, partially dressed in petticoats and chemises.

Aurore called to them from the adjoining sitting room. "Are you lazy-bones going to get up and join me?"

Apolline stretched her arms and yawned loudly. "You run along, dear, and take Aisha with you. Delphine will stay here with me and have a nice gossip." Then she bit into a juicy pear and wiped the dribble from her chin with a serviette.

"Do as you please," Aurore replied. "Come, Aisha, we haven't all day."

The Moroccan girl, who looked no more than thirteen, said, "Yes, Mademoiselle." She curtsied politely to Apolline and Delphine and then passed out of the room through a *portiere*.

Apolline grinned as she leaned over the table and whispered, "Aurore likes getting up early and going to market with Aisha. Frankly, I think she's sweet on her. Can you imagine?"

Delphine shrugged and took a cigarette from her silver case. "Would you like one, dear?" she offered. "It's a Turkish blend I have made up special. The tobacconist calls it 'Delphine' and it's becoming popular with the fashionable ladies."

"Oh, thank you, darling," Apolline replied, as Delphine gave her a light. They smoked quietly and picked at their breakfast until they heard the front door close. Apolline smiled conspiratorially. "At last, we can speak freely. What do you think of our little love nest?"

Delphine glanced around at the lavishly furnished bedroom: blue silk-patterned wallpaper adorned with landscapes in gilt frames; raspberry velvet-upholstered settee and chairs; Persian carpets; Japanese silk screens with floating blossoms and soaring cranes; and fragrant, fresh-cut flowers in Chinese vases. There was even a whimsical mechanical parrot in a gilded cage. Finally, her eyes rested on the large Empire-period bed, unmade, and a strategically placed screen.

"Monsieur has fine taste, and he seems generous enough," she stated matter-of-factly. "You girls are lucky."

Apolline nodded her agreement. "This place is a palace compared to where we came from. As for Monsieur, he has his quirks, but no one's perfect. Better him than some old tightwad."

"Is that all he does with you two, watch from behind that screen?"

Apolline laughed and stubbed out her cigarette. "Yes, he likes to hide and peek, watching us romp in bed. With you, he got a bonus. He's very pleased today, I'm sure. Thank goodness."

Delphine frowned. "Last night, I saw evidence of his *displeasure* on Aurore's behind."

"Oh, that." Apolline shrugged. "Last week, Monsieur was playing cards with his crony, de Gournay. Aurore and Aisha served them, and that clumsy fool Aurore spilled half a bottle of champagne over the card table. Monsieur was furious. He made her lift her skirts and lie face down on the settee. I held her wrists while de Gournay grabbed her by the ankles. Monsieur whipped Aurore's bare ass with his riding crop and little Aisha had to count the strokes. The poor girl cried more than Aurore."

"The brute. A pimp beat me when I was fourteen and I swore I'd kill the next man who abused me."

"Fine gentlemen or thugs, so many men are beasts. But if you ask me, Aurore provokes him. I fancy it's just a game for them. They're both bent that way, I'm afraid."

Delphine smirked. *"À chacun son goût."* Then she finished the chocolate, puffed her cigarette, and set it down in an ashtray.

"At any rate, he's never hurt me physically, though he's made threats on occasion. And I've managed to obtain some nice trinkets for my services, and put some cash away, too."

"I'm glad to hear it. We girls should save for a rainy day. By the way, what do you think of M. de Gournay?"

Apolline shook her head and frowned. "He's a queer one. I can't make him out. For example, when M. Orlovsky whipped Aurore, you should have seen the fiendish look on his face. Like Satan himself; frightening. But de Gournay? Nothing—blank as a wiped slate. He might as well have been staring at the wallpaper."

"Well, we see all kinds of things in our profession—and hear them, too. By the way, what is the relationship between Orlovsky and de Gournay? Are they in business together?"

"Now you've touched on an interesting subject." Her eyes darted furtively around the room, as if looking for spies lurking in every corner and crevice. Though they were alone, she lowered her voice. "They're in business, all right, and they're on to something big. If it comes off as planned, they stand to make millions. I guess they let things slip around me because they think I'm too stupid to understand. But I'm not so dumb. I'll let you in on a secret, if you promise on your sacred honor not to tell anyone."

Delphine surreptitiously crossed her fingers behind her back and promised.

"All right. It seems Germany has stopped lending money to Russia. So a syndicate of the largest French banks has entered into an agreement with the Russians for a huge loan on very favorable terms. France will be Russia's largest creditor."

"How big is 'huge'?"

"Orlovsky said a billion francs."

"But what has this loan to do with Orlovsky and de Gournay?"

Apolline grinned slyly. "Ah, here's where it gets really interesting. Orlovsky acts as agent for a large Russian arms manufacturer. De Gournay works for a comparable French firm. When they float the loan, the Russian government will give an immense subsidy to Orlovsky's company and the price of its shares will skyrocket. What's more, Orlovsky and de Gournay share a secret from which both companies will benefit. So the price in the French company's shares will rise as well."

"Do you know the secret?"

Apolline shook her head. "I think it has something to do with a new explosive for the military. Anyway, anyone with shares in the French and Russian companies at today's prices stands to make a fortune when the loan goes through and the public gets wind of it. Frankly, I was hoping they'd let me invest a little, but I'm afraid to ask.

"And here's another thing that frightens me: I've seen Orlovsky with Rousseau. They meet at the Cabaret de L'Enfer. Everyone in Montmartre knows that Rousseau took payoffs from the pimps and cabaret owners. Maybe he's on Orlovsky's payroll. I don't know, and I don't want to get involved. Rousseau's scarier than Orlovsky and de Gournay put together."

Delphine nodded her agreement and smiled sympathetically. "You'd better play dumb and stay out of it." After a moment, she questioned, "Do you think Aurore knows anything? And what about Aisha? Have they discussed this matter with you?"

"I don't think they know anything. At least, they haven't talked to me about it. You're the only one I've told, so far. I don't trust the other girls." She reached across the table and took Delphine's hand. "I wanted to tell someone to get it off my chest. You're different from the others. It's sort of like talking to a priest."

Delphine stared into her friend's trusting eyes, and knew that when she passed the information to Achille, she would have to emphasize the need to protect Apolline and the other girls. "I'm glad you told me. But you realize we can't profit from this information. That would be wrong, not to mention *extremely* dangerous."

Apolline frowned soberly. "I promise I won't speak another word about it, except to you."

Delphine leaned forward and kissed her friend's lips. "I must finish dressing and go now, my dear."

"Oh, so soon?" Apolline pouted with disappointment, like a child who missed her favorite playmate. "I wish we had more time together. Anyway, do you still plan to meet M. de Gournay?"

Delphine got up and patted Apolline's hair affectionately. "Yes, the young gentleman intrigues me. I enjoy a challenge."

Apolline sighed. "Well, you be careful around that man. He gives me the creeps."

Delphine laughed nonchalantly, as if to show her disdain for a mere fop. "Now, where did I leave my dress?" she asked, scanning the room in search of her outfit.

Apolline went to her dresser, sat down in front of the mirror, and began arranging her hair. "It's in the wardrobe, my dear, along with your corset. Your shoes and stockings are under the bed." For a moment, she watched Delphine's reflected image in the mirror as she rounded up her clothes. Then Apolline smiled at her reflection and continued her toilette.

❧

I've seen that face before. But where? When?

Achille stared at Lautrec's sketch of de Gournay. Light streamed through a window opening onto the quay, highlighting the drawing on his desk. He stubbed out a cigarette in an ashtray, lit another, and then closed his eyes and leaned back in his chair.

Who is he? What's his game? I need to contact Delphine.

Opening his eyes, he leaned forward and penciled a note on a chart he had been working on since his meeting with Rousseau had concluded. The sounds of chugging tugboats and steam whistles filtered in from the river, but he hardly noticed, concentrating instead on the chart and the case.

The case could involve the interests of four major powers: France, Russia, Germany, and Great Britain. Two competing factions on the radical left were also relevant to his investigation: Anarchists and Marxists. Kadyshev, the Hanged Man, had been a Marxist. Boguslavsky, Moreau, and Wroblewski were Anarchists. He situated Nazimov and Nazimova in between with a question mark. He indicated Rossignol with a question mark and an exclamation point.

How did all these interests interact? On the French side, he sketched in the hierarchy down to inspector level. He did the same on the Russian side, from Tsar down to the Okhrana operatives. He bracketed Rousseau and drew a line between the inspector, the Russian Secret Police, and Orlovsky. However, he also drew a dotted line between France and Russia. He had no way of knowing for sure, but it was reasonable to assume that cooperation between the two nations, at least in regard to this matter, went up to the highest level. Such covert cooperation between France and Russia could draw the attention of German and British intelligence. Furthermore, all four governments spied on the activities of the radicals.

What do they all want? By "all," he meant the gamut from kings and queens down to pawns. He could not dwell upon overly broad generalities like power, wealth, and prestige. He needed to bring it down to the level of the matter at hand. He reconsidered his conclusions based on Boguslavsky's expertise in high explosives. *Maybe there is more to it than making anarchist bombs. Perhaps he's developed something revolutionary, something powerful.* That was tangible and concrete, something of military value providing a plausible motive for espionage, betrayal, theft, and murder.

Achille put down his pencil, removed his pince-nez, and rubbed his eyes. His thoughts turned to the elusive knight. *Who is the bastard? What is he? Whom does he serve? Is he in it for himself?*

After a moment, he penciled in Rossignol beneath Orlovsky. He added de Gournay, traced a dotted line connecting the two, put them in brackets, took a ruler and drew another dotted line to the "Rossignol" entry among the radicals. He wrote "Infiltrator," "Double Agent," and "Agent Provocateur," and placed question marks next to all three. He added notations as reminders: "Delphine," who was to spy on de Gournay, and "Legros," who was to provide more information about Rossignol.

Achille wanted to talk to Legros, who was currently at the stakeout in Montmartre. Among other things, he was to arrange with Gilles to begin photographing the coded messages. He glared at the brass telephone resting uselessly on his desk. *What good is the blasted thing without more lines, exchanges, and call boxes?* He would have to rely on the telegraph and messengers. He was in the process of scribbling a note to Legros when a knock on the door interrupted him.

"Enter," he muttered, and quickly stuffed his chart in a desk drawer.

The chief greeted him cheerily. "Good morning, Achille. Hard at work on the case, I see."

Achille returned the greeting and offered Féraud a chair. He noticed a folded newspaper in the chief's hand.

Féraud requested a routine update on the case, which Achille provided without too much detail or speculation. He made a point of not referencing his chart. The chief seemed quite satisfied, but he beamed while incessantly tapping the newspaper with his forefinger. Achille thought this behavior peculiar and annoying. Eventually, when he could endure no more, he looked directly at the paper and blandly inquired if there was anything interesting in the morning news.

The chief grinned from ear to ear. He lifted the paper and began smacking it against his palm as if he were about to swat a naughty puppy. "As if you didn't know, my boy!"

Achille shook his head in bewilderment. "I'm afraid I don't know what you're talking about, Chief. Will you please be direct?"

The chief shook his head bemusedly. "Oh, all right, Achille, though I think such coyness more becoming to a maiden at her first ball." He opened the early morning edition of *Les Amis de la Vérité* and turned to a featured article. "Shall I read aloud what M. Fournier has to say about 'France's greatest detective'?"

Damn the man! Achille thought, assuming that the reference to France's greatest detective was a product of the journalist's sarcasm. Anticipating a dressing-down, Achille sputtered, "I can explain, Chief. The man's a rascal. Adele and I—"

The chief broke in with a laugh. "A rascal, you say? That's very droll. A journalist praises you to the skies in a prestigious newspaper, and you call him a dirty name. I wonder what you would say about your enemies."

Achille was perplexed in the extreme. Flushed with embarrassment, he asked, "Pardon me, Chief. May I see the article?"

"With pleasure, my boy. I should think you'd want to clip it, get it framed, and hang it on your office wall. Such acclaim from the press is the next best thing to the Legion of Honor."

Achille took the paper and skimmed the article. There was no mention of the incident at La Grenouillère. Rather, this was a puff piece dedicated to the Sûreté, with Achille singled out as the investigative brigade's rising star. Fournier did not spare the adulatory adjectives: Inspector Lefebvre was "intrepid," "resourceful," "indefatigable," and "brilliant." Achille responded to the flattery with mixed feelings—on one hand, there was the gratification that most would experience upon seeing oneself lionized in print; on the other, he could not avoid skepticism and suspicion as to the journalist's motives. He returned the newspaper without comment.

Féraud stared at Achille for a few moments before asking, with a hint of exasperation, "Well, aren't you going to say anything?"

Achille replied modestly, "It's very complimentary to the brigade."

The chief shook his head and grinned. "Butter wouldn't melt in his mouth."

Achille frowned. "What do you want me to say?"

The chief laughed at his protégé's seemingly affected display of nonchalance. "Do you keep a bottle of cognac in your office? No, of course you do not. Well, I do. If I were in your shoes, I'd pour a couple of glasses, salute our success, and perhaps pour another and one more after that. Then I'd dance a jig around the office."

Achille remained stoically focused on the problem at hand. "That's understandable, Chief. However, I prefer to reserve my celebration for the day we crack this case. May I ask a few straightforward questions?"

"Of course, Inspector. And I shall try to give you straightforward answers."

"Is it true nothing gets published in *Les Amis de la Vérité* without M. Junot's approval?" Junot was the paper's influential publisher and managing editor.

"Most certainly," Féraud replied. "And M. Junot's very particular about what he allows into print."

"I see. And is it also true that the Junots dine regularly with the prefect and his wife?"

Féraud's eyes narrowed; his joviality waned. "That's true; they move within the same social circle, though I'm not sure I understand what you're driving at."

Féraud would not welcome an inference of collusion between the Prefect of Police and the publisher, especially since the article honored his service. Achille realized he had pushed his chief as far as he could on the subject, and so smiled innocently. "I was just thinking how pleased the prefect will be when he reads the paper."

Féraud eyed Achille coolly for an instant before regaining his conviviality. "Oh, I'm certain of it. As for dining with the prefect, his wife, and the Junots, I wager you and Adele will soon have that honor."

A biblical allusion flashed through Achille's mind: *What does it profit a man to dine with the prefect and M. Junot?*

A knock on the door intervened. After apologizing for the interruption, the messenger handed a telegram to Achille. The messenger left, and Achille shared the contents of the message with his chief.

"It's from Rousseau. They've located Boguslavsky in La Villette. Rousseau's men have the place surrounded. I'm going there at once. Legros and Gilles will join me."

"Splendid! It looks like we'll wrap up this case in record time. Then you and Adele can run off to Trouville. I envy you."

"I hope so, Chief," Achille replied laconically.

Féraud left the office. Achille took his revolver out of its holster and checked the cylinder. Then he grabbed his hat and jacket from the coat rack. On his way out, he muttered to himself, "It's all too pat."

The stench of closely confined animals, excrement, offal, and blood saturated the humid, noontime air. Chuffing locomotives rumbled over an iron network, hauling long trains of cars laden with livestock, lowing, bleating, grunting, and squealing their way to the slaughterhouse pens. Other engines chugged in the opposite direction, pulling ice cars packed with fresh meat for the Paris markets.

The police cordoned off a small section of storehouses situated between the great abattoir and a narrow canal flowing into the La Villette basin. Achille joined Rousseau, Legros, and Gilles across the street from a boarded-up, one-story frame building.

Rousseau lifted his bowler and mopped his forehead with the back of his hand. "It smells sweet on a hot summer day, doesn't it, Professor?"

Achille, eyes focused on the canal, thought wistfully of the sea at Trouville and nodded. "It stinks, but I've smelled worse." After a moment, he asked, "How long have you been here?"

"A little more than three hours, and it's too damned quiet. There's one door and boarded windows all around. No one's gone in or out since we showed up," Rousseau replied. He turned to Achille with a grim frown. "They may resist. Are you armed?"

Achille patted the Chamelot-Delvigne, holstered beneath his jacket. "Yes, of course."

"Can you still use it?" Rousseau asked with a sly grin.

"I practice regularly. Do you have a warrant?"

Rousseau reached into his pocket and pulled out the paper. "Here it is, signed and sealed by the *juge*. It's all legal and proper."

"Good. When do we go in?"

Rousseau returned the warrant to his pocket and took out his watch. "Let's synchronize on five minutes from now."

Achille checked his watch and then signaled to the detectives and gendarmes stationed on the barricade's perimeter. At the appointed time, he and Rousseau advanced steadily toward the entrance, escorted by two officers with drawn revolvers and another pair carrying a battering ram. Tactically deployed sharpshooters, armed with Lebel rifles, concentrated on the boarded windows and rooftop.

They walked up a few steps to a low porch. Rousseau stepped forward and pounded on the door. "Open, in the name of the law!" His booming voice echoed around the block. No answer. He pounded again until the hinges almost gave way. "Open or we'll break it down!" Still no response.

"Shall we break in, Inspector?" asked one of the gendarmes with the battering ram.

"Oh, fuck it," Rousseau muttered. He backed up a pace, and kicked out with a massive, hobnail-booted foot. The lock shattered, the hinges broke away from the frame, and the door fell forward, landing on the plank floor with a thud and a plume of dust.

Achille and Rousseau drew their revolvers, pulled back to either side of the doorway, and cautiously peered into the dark interior. Their eyes darted about, scanning for hidden ambushers.

"You see the counter? There's a window behind it," Achille half-whispered.

Rousseau nodded and gestured to the gendarmes. "Rip out the boards on the south-side windows and look in," he ordered. "And be careful."

They waited until the gendarmes gave a signal indicating all was clear, then the inspectors entered warily, covered by the policemen. The storeroom was empty and the air stale, as if long abandoned. Achille pointed toward a short flight of steps leading to a basement door.

Rousseau nodded and gestured to a gendarme. "Get one of the riflemen." When the sharpshooter arrived, Rousseau turned to Achille. "They've had their chance to surrender. Why risk going through the door? I say pull the boards out from the cellar windows, and let the sharpshooter have at them if they don't give up peacefully. We'll guard the door in case they try to break out."

Achille agreed. They waited a few minutes until a gendarme reported back.

"It looks clear, Inspector. We can't see or hear anything, but there are rows of shelves. They could be lying in wait."

Rousseau waved one of his detectives over. "Go to the basement window and lob in a smoke grenade. That'll stir the cockroaches." Then he looked to Achille. "You see, Professor, I come prepared."

They remained in place, silently guarding the door, waiting for the smoke to have its effect. Finally, Rousseau muttered, "I'll be damned. If anyone were alive down there, we'd have heard them coughing their lungs out."

"We've waited long enough," Achille agreed. "Let's knock down the door, air the place out, and go in."

The men broke through the basement door and smashed all the windows from the outside. Several minutes later, with handkerchiefs covering noses and mouths, they entered. There were signs of recent habitation—a palette, food scraps, a slop bucket, and cigarette butts.

Rousseau fumed to no one in particular, "God damn it. The bastards have buggered out."

Achille figured an informer had tipped off Rousseau, but the information had leaked before the police arrived. That was a problem, but they had more immediate concerns.

He gave an order to his detectives. "They must have had an escape route. Look for a trap door." Then Achille called to Legros. "Start gathering evidence, Étienne. I'll bet those cigarette butts are Sobranies."

"Over here, Inspector," a detective cried.

Achille went to a dark corner hidden behind some shelves. Rousseau followed. When they arrived, the detective had already lifted the trap door.

"That was their way out," Achille stated matter-of-factly.

Rousseau nodded. "Are you going down to have a look, Professor?"

Achille turned and gave his former partner a sad but resigned smile. "Since it's your stakeout, I thought you might have the honor."

Rousseau shook his head. "Not me, my friend. I'm too big. Might get stuck in the muck."

Achille had always led from the front; he never asked his men to do anything he would not do himself. He removed his hat and jacket and handed them to the detective. "That's what I expected," he muttered.

"You'll be fine, Professor," Rousseau said encouragingly. "After all, you had plenty of experience with crawl spaces in the Palmieri case."

"Thanks for reminding me." He rolled up his sleeves and removed his pince-nez. Then he continued, "I believe they went to the canal. It's no more than twenty meters from here. Please take a detail of men over there and check for an outlet. I'll head in that direction and we'll meet, unless I run into an obstruction and have to turn back."

Rousseau gestured to a couple of his men. "You, come with me."

Achille lowered himself into the hole and then stretched forward, prone. A red-eyed rodent greeted him, nose twitching. Achille froze as the rat studied his face for a moment, then scampered off.

He began crawling forward, his powerful rowing arms and legs working to his advantage. *Thank goodness I've a change of clothes at head-quarters*, he thought. The ground was muddy, the air rank as a cesspit, and the space cramped and claustrophobic. But several meters on, he noticed a pale light ahead, partially blocked by an obscure heap, as if someone had stuffed a pile of old clothes into the crawl space. He halted and listened to an incessant buzzing. *Flies. Hundreds of them, by the sound.*

He crept on. The sound grew louder, the shape more distinct. Flies attacked Achille's eyes and nose, buzzed in his ears, flew into his hair and beard, crawled over his mouth. A sharp stench filled his nostrils. A familiar shape loomed ahead: the heels and soles of a pair of shoes.

"Rousseau! Rousseau!" he cried. "Are you there?"

"We're out here by the canal," Rousseau answered. "There's a drainage hole, but I can't see you. Something's blocking the way."

"It's a body. Can a man crawl into the hole and pull it out? I can help by pushing on the feet."

"I think so."

"Well, be quick about it. It stinks like hell and I'm into a swarm of bloody flies."

Achille swatted at the flies until he heard grunting. The body began sliding slowly through the mud and he pushed forward against the feet. The body was stuck halfway through the drainage outlet when Achille heard retching—the man hauling the body was puking his guts out.

Achille gave the officer a minute to compose himself before asking, "Are you all right?"

The man coughed to clear his throat. "Pardon me, Inspector Lefebvre. I'm fine now, but we can't get the body out. He's too big."

"*Merde!* Listen. Get a strong rope. We'll need to tie it around his ankles and drag him back and up through the trap door."

"Are you staying in there, Achille?" Rousseau asked.

"Hell, no! Someone else can finish this. I'm going back to give instructions to Legros. Then I'm going to clean up and return to headquarters. I'll meet you at the Morgue."

"All right," Rousseau replied. "I think it's Boguslavsky. He must have gotten stuck on his way out and they garroted him, poor bastard."

Achille spat out a fly. "We'll confirm that at the Morgue. Now, I'm getting the hell out of here."

The space was too narrow to turn around, so Achille worked his way backwards to the trap door. Upon reaching the opening, he got a hand up from a gendarme. As soon as he got his feet on the floor, Achille shook his head, shooed away the remaining flies, and wiped some of the muck from his hands, shirt, and trousers. The gendarme could not help gaping at his disheveled superior. Achille gave him a dirty look, followed by an order.

"Make yourself useful. Go fetch Inspector Legros."

Legros came directly. "Gilles is taking photographs, and we're gathering up the evidence. Someone lived down here for a few days."

Achille nodded. "It was probably Boguslavsky. I found what appears to be his corpse in the crawl space. Assuming it's him, they must have moved him here from the Rue Ronsard. I doubt he's been dead more than a few hours."

"What next, Inspector?"

"The body's stuck. You'll have to haul him back through the trapdoor." He noticed Legros's pained expression and smiled. "You needn't do it yourself, Étienne. There are plenty of idle hands hanging around who could use some exercise."

Legros almost sighed with relief. "Are you returning to headquarters?"

"Yes. I need a wash and a change of clothes. I'll meet you and Gilles at the Morgue. Speaking of Gilles, did you ask him about the concealed camera?"

"He'll be pleased to help."

"Good. We'll talk about it later." Achille glanced about to make sure no one was listening. He lowered his voice and added, "There's a leak in Rousseau's organization. I'm not blaming him, but we need to be careful about sharing information, at least for the time being. That most particularly applies to the code, the dead drop, Delphine, and Rossignol."

"I understand, Inspector. By the way, we confirmed that Rossignol leased both houses in Montmartre, but the transactions were handled by a notary."

"So neither landlord dealt directly with Rossignol?"

"That's correct; they can't describe him. And the notary's left Paris. We're tracking him down, but no luck so far."

"Damn," Achille muttered. "What about Moreau and Wroblewski? Any report on their whereabouts the last twenty-four hours?"

"I was just about to check with the detectives on that."

Achille frowned. "We could bring them in for questioning anytime, but if we can connect them to this murder, we can really sweat them. Though if we arrest them now, we could lose Rossignol and the higher-ups, as well."

Rousseau entered with one of his men and a coil of stout rope. "Still here, Professor?" he called. "Don't worry. We'll take care of the stiff."

Achille walked over to Rousseau. "Thanks, Inspector. Before I leave, there's something important we need to discuss."

Rousseau nodded. Then he ordered his detective to form a detail to retrieve the body. Turning back to Achille, he said, "Come on, Inspector, let's go outside for a smoke. It'll get the stink out of your nostrils."

Achille picked up his hat and jacket. They went out front and around the corner, stopping beneath an acacia tree that spread its cooling shade over the canal embankment. He gratefully accepted one of Rousseau's cigars. After a couple of puffs, he said, "We have a problem. Someone leaked. Do you know who?"

Rousseau frowned and shook his head. "No, but you can be sure I'll find out."

"I understand. But until you've plugged the leak, we'll need to be extremely careful about sharing information."

"Agreed. I'll keep you informed about the situation. By the way, have you been keeping an eye on Moreau and Wroblewski?"

"We have, but I need an update from my men."

Rousseau smirked. "I see. Well, they're small fry. I suppose you'd use them for bait. Leave them wriggling on the line to hook a bigger fish."

Achille smiled knowingly, but did not comment further.

A warm breeze rustled the branches of the trees lining the canal. Achille and Rousseau stood silently together, each deep in his own thoughts. How far could they trust each other? Who had betrayed them? Finally, Achille tossed his half-smoked cigar in the canal.

"Thanks for the smoke," he said. "Until later, at the Morgue." Then he left Rousseau, crossed the street, and walked on in the direction of a waiting carriage.

⚭

The corpse rested on a blood-stained wooden dissection table. A stream of light from two mirror-reflected gas mantles highlighted purplish abrasions on a chalk-white throat. Dr. Cortot leaned over and scrutinized the bruises while palpating the neck. After a moment, he lifted his eyeglasses onto his forehead, stood erect, and pronounced, "Death by strangulation. A homicide. The killer was skilled in the use of a garrote, something like the knotted scarves employed by the Thugs."

Achille had already identified Boguslavsky based upon the description and photograph in his records. Everything matched, except for the recently shaved beard and short haircut.

"Thank you, Doctor," he replied perfunctorily.

"Shall we put him on display?" the pathologist inquired.

"No, Doctor, that won't be necessary. But please preserve the body, at least for the time being." He turned to Gilles. "Take the postmortem photographs and have the prints on my desk as soon as possible."

"I can have them to you by tomorrow morning."

"Thanks, Gilles." Achille looked to Legros. "We're finished here. Let's return to headquarters."

Rousseau had remained at the Morgue long enough to confirm the identification, though he did not stay to hear the doctor officially pronounce it a homicide. Rousseau's immediate concern was the leak in his organization.

Back in his office, Achille took out his chart, set it on the desk, and briefed Legros on his developing theory of the case. "I'm taking you into my confidence. I believe this case goes beyond the agenda of a small anarchist cell, and involves the interests and intrigues of great nations, including our own."

"What has France got to do with it?" Legros broke in, shocked by the implication that his mentor's theory might impugn the honor of their country.

Achille remained calm and smiled reassuringly. "Please, Étienne, be patient. I'm not necessarily implying any wrongdoing on the part of our government. May I continue?"

"I'm sorry, Inspector. Please do."

"Based on the evidence we've gathered thus far, it appears that Boguslavsky participated in Kadyshev's murder, and Moreau and Wroblewski were his accomplices. Moreover, I believe Moreau and Wroblewski killed Boguslavsky. However, I don't think they acted on their own initiative. Rather, they are pawns in a game played by masters. Rossignol is the most likely candidate for their immediate superior. But who is Rossignol?"

Legros stared at the chart. "You suspect de Gournay? And de Gournay works for the Okhrana?"

Achille nodded. "I believe so, and Delphine should be making contact with him soon. Now let's think about motive. What can you deduce from the circumstances of Boguslavky's murder?"

Legros thought for a moment. "The anarchists planned the escape route. It was Boguslavky's bad luck to be stuck in the drainage hole. They couldn't get him out, and they couldn't leave him for the police. So they shut his mouth—permanently."

"Very good. Now, what is it that made Boguslavsky both valuable and expendable?"

Legros paused before venturing, "His bomb-making expertise?"

Achille shook his head. "His expertise died with him. What survived? Could it be something of value to both the anarchists and the Russian government?"

Legros's eyes widened as if Achille had unmasked a monster. "The plans for a new weapon—or the formula for an explosive?"

"Exactly, Étienne. That would be something all the great powers want to gain a military advantage over their rivals. For example, France has developed smokeless powder for our Lebel rifles, and new high explosives for the artillery. Germany, Great Britain, and Russia are all seeking improvements along those lines. The sad truth of it is, Europe is preparing for the next war."

"But how do the anarchists benefit? What interest do they have in a high-explosives formula, besides bomb-making?"

"From an altruistic standpoint, they might keep the secret from the great powers, build a terror weapon, and use it themselves as a means to end all war, like Jules Verne's Captain Nemo or Robur the Conqueror. On the other hand, more realistically, they could bargain with it and sell to the highest bidder. That's a way of raising cash to finance their revolutionary activities."

"But what about Kadyshev?" Legros asked. "Do you think he was killed to stop him from betraying the secret?"

"That's plausible. He and Boguslavsky were friends and they were both chemists, but they had different political ideologies. Regardless, I think this is where Rossignol enters the stage. I believe he works for Orlovsky and has at least two identities—Rossignol and de Gournay. His assignment might be twofold: secure the formula for the Russians, and eliminate the anarchist cell. To accomplish this, he's infiltrated the group and acts as an agent provocateur. The Hanged Man may have been part of his plan, to obtain the formula and set up the anarchists for a charge of conspiracy to commit murder. The deed also foments conflict between the Marxists and the anarchists." He paused a moment before asking, "How do you think our government might fit into this scenario?"

Legros began thinking aloud. "France and Russia have been improving diplomatic relations. Rousseau's branch cooperates covertly with the Okhrana. Both governments have an interest in suppressing radicalism. And—" He broke off and stared blankly at Achille.

"Yes, Étienne," he urged. "Please, continue."

"Russia and France could share the formula, giving us an edge over the other powers—most particularly, our mutual adversary, Germany."

"There it is! We may be witnessing the beginnings of an alliance. Now, if we can get some good intelligence from Delphine and intercept the coded messages, that might be enough to complete the puzzle. But I'm going to try to mine another source as well. I think Mme Nazimova is keeping a secret. Remember, her late husband was close to Kadyshev and Boguslavsky. I'm going to question her in relation to Boguslavsky's murder. She might reveal something of interest to us."

Legros pondered for a moment, considering all the implications. Finally, he asked, "With all due respect, Inspector, where does this end? We've gone well beyond a homicide investigation, and we've gathered some good evidence in the process. Can't we stop and turn the whole thing over to Inspector Rousseau? Let the political police take it from here."

A few days earlier, Achille might have agreed. Now, he would persist to the finish.

"The chief gave us an assignment and it's our duty to see it through," he said. "Though I am now on the point of going to Féraud and placing all my cards on the table, and he will decide our course of action going forward. Frankly, this is uncharted territory. If you have any objections or serious concerns about proceeding, please state them now."

"I'm with you, Achille," Legros answered without hesitation. "But do you think—do you honestly believe—our government might be acting dishonorably in this matter?"

Achille smiled sadly. "Étienne, as always, I follow the evidence wherever it might lead. As for our government, I suppose they are acting the way governments have acted since the dawn of civilization. Whether or not such actions are 'honorable' is a question for a moral philosopher, not a police officer. To quote Lord Tennyson: 'Ours not to reason why . . .'"

Legros nodded without comment. Then he asked, "Are we going to arrest Moreau and Wroblewski? I'm afraid our detectives lost the tail last evening, but those two still need to account for their whereabouts."

Achille shook his head. "We'll let the worms wriggle on the hook for a while longer. Keep shadowing them. We can bring them in anytime we want. Now, we need to intercept a message. You can work with our stakeout to set that up. I'm going to pay a call on Mme Nazimova."

"Very well. I'll be in Montmartre if you need me."

"Thank you, Étienne. You've done a fine job." After he said the words, Achille realized how much he sounded like the chief in one of his patronizing moods. But he could not think of anything else to say.

⌦

The doorbell rang as Achille entered Mme Nazimova's shop. He glanced around, expecting Marie to pop out from one of her cubbyholes. There was no greeting, and he noticed that the shelves were empty. After a moment, he heard the tapping of a cane and saw the back room *portiere* stirring. Nazimova emerged, looking frailer than when he had last seen her, only a few days before. She approached haltingly and her head inclined forward as she tried to focus on him with bleary eyes.

Achille advanced and announced himself. "Good afternoon, Mme Nazimova. I trust you are well?"

She stopped, rested her hands on the cane handle, and breathed heavily. Her eyes lacked expression; her voice was a hoarse rasp. "Is that you, Inspector Lefebvre? Pardon me. My eyes are very weak."

Achille found her appearance distressing and immediately regretted disturbing her. On the other hand, he believed he had a duty to question her. "I'm very sorry, Madame. May I help you to a chair?"

"Thank you, Monsieur. As you can see, Marie is no longer here to assist me."

Achille took Nazimova's arm and helped her to the back parlor, where she slowly and painfully eased onto a settee. He adjusted a bolster behind her back and asked if she was comfortable.

"Comfortable, Monsieur?" she replied. "For me, comfort is a memory. But you are thoughtful to ask." She took a moment to catch her breath before explaining her situation. "I'm closing the shop. I should have done it last week. I felt better then. At any rate, I've made all the arrangements. I sold most of the stock to a bookseller. The rest goes to charity. A notary is coming this afternoon to wind up business. I thought it was he when you entered. Marie's gone home to her village in Normandy. I'm alone, and I'm dying."

Her reference to death almost unnerved him. Could he, in good conscience, continue with his questioning? "Do you want me to go for a doctor?"

Her lips twitched in the semblance of a smile. "I've consulted a doctor, Monsieur. It would be a waste of time and money to call for him now. I presume you are here on official business?"

"Yes, Madame, regrettably, I am. Viktor Boguslavsky is dead. We found his body early this morning. He was murdered. Considering our previous discussions, I wondered if there was more you wanted to tell me."

"You believe I've been hiding something from you?"

His desire for the truth overruled his sense of pity. "Yes, Madame, I do."

"And now that I'm dying, you think I might wish to unburden myself. Are you to be my confessor?"

He stared directly into her cloudy eyes. "I'm obliged to ask, Madame. Two men have been murdered, and I want to know who did it and why. I come in the name of the law."

"But I believe you already know the answers to your questions. Why trouble me further?"

What made her assume he had solved the case? Her statement impelled him to pursue the matter. "I have suspects and a theory, Madame. The information you provide might confirm or refute what I believe to be true."

"Very well, Monsieur. You may ask your questions, and I will do my best to answer."

"In consideration of your condition, I'll come to the point: I have reason to believe your late husband, Kadyshev, and Boguslavsky shared a secret, something of considerable value to the Russian government, and others as well. Moreover, I believe you've withheld this information from me for personal reasons. I urge you to come forward now. If you cooperate, I can offer you protection."

Nazimova laughed feebly. "In my present circumstances, your offer is meaningless. Anyone who took my life would be doing me a favor. But since you insist, I'll answer you candidly and completely.

"Shortly after the Tsar's assassination, during our Swiss sojourn, my husband and his two friends had an idealistically foolish notion. They wanted to create a weapon so powerfully destructive that the mere threat of its use would end war forever. They designed an airship with propellers powered by an electric motor. The ship would carry bombs armed with a high explosive several times more potent than dynamite.

"They discussed their plans with a Swiss engineer who convinced them that the airship was impractical. The explosive was another matter. My late husband and Kadyshev were fine chemists, but Viktor was a genius. They tested his formula and it worked frighteningly well. Clever as they were, they weren't cunning enough to evade the Tsar's spies. The Okhrana discovered their plans, and pursued us to Paris, where they kept us all under close surveillance.

"My husband told me the three vowed never to divulge the secret formula to any of the great powers, most particularly the Tsarist tyranny from which we had fled. Later, Kadyshev confirmed what I'd already learned. Alas, humans are weak and corruptible. My husband took the secret to his grave, but Kadyshev agreed to sell it to Orlovsky, the head of the Okhrana in Paris.

"I only know this because Kadyshev confided in me. You were correct, I did withhold information, though for personal reasons. We were lovers. Lev still cared enough to come to me shortly before he died. He wanted to take me to Buenos Aires for my health, or so he said. That's where he planned to go with Orlovsky's money. I refused. I would not spend my last days with a traitor.

"Viktor must have gotten wind of the betrayal. Perhaps that was part of Orlovsky's scheme. Double-dealing is the Okhrana's stock-in-trade. Regardless, I believe Viktor and his comrades killed Lev; and from their perspective, it wasn't murder, but justice. Now, Viktor is dead. I've told you all I know of the matter, but like you, I too can make deductions. I can venture a guess as to the identities of Viktor's killers."

Achille looked into the dying woman's eyes with a mixed feeling of respect, guilt, and an overwhelming need to know the truth. "Please tell me what you believe, Madame."

"I believe as I suspect you do, Inspector Lefebvre: The Russian Secret Police murdered Viktor. That is to say, they got Viktor's comrades to do the dirty work. They must have planted an agent among the anarchists. Once they had what they wanted—the formula, of course—Viktor became expendable." She held his eyes with a steady, penetrating gaze.

For a moment, Achille was speechless. Then he asked a final question. "You referred to the formula. Did your husband keep copies?"

"Yes, Monsieur, he did. But I burned them the day he died."

Achille wanted to leave her in peace, but he could not help expressing concern for her condition. "Madame, I thank you for your candor. You said you were expecting a notary, but I don't feel right leaving you alone like this. Permit me to fetch a doctor. Or, if you'd prefer, I could go for the notary. Please, let me be of service."

Nazimova shook her head. "No, thank you, Inspector. Actually, I'm feeling better. They say confession's good for the soul. Perhaps it helps the body as well. You needn't reproach yourself. Your devotion to duty is commendable, even though some might think it misplaced."

He bid her good afternoon, but as soon as he returned to headquarters, he notified the local police to keep an eye on her.

⚭

After Achille left, Nazimova walked to the mantelpiece and, with great effort, removed a loose brick from the hearth. She retrieved a locked iron box from within and opened it with a key on her chatelaine. She removed a copy of Boguslavsky's formula and stared at it for a moment, before striking a match and setting the paper alight. She dropped the blackened notes into the fireplace and watched the flames transform her memento of Boguslavsky's misguided genius into ashes.

Tears streamed down her wrinkled face. This world that she had longed to change for the better was as bad as the one into which she had been born. "An exercise in futility," she murmured.

Gripping her cane with one hand and clinging to the banister with the other, she slowly mounted a flight of stairs to her bedroom. There, she took her last few painful steps to the bed. A brown medicine bottle rested on a bedside table, containing a mixture of morphine and chloral hydrate. She pulled the cork stopper and drank the contents. Then, with her hands clutching the empty bottle, she reclined on the counterpane with her head resting on a bolster. She closed her eyes and took one deep breath, followed by a long sigh. Her hand opened and the bottle rolled over the bedstead and clattered onto the floor.

Two hours later, the notary arrived. He discovered the body and reported Nazimova's death to the police.

∽∞∾

Delphine answered an anticipated knock at her front door. A smiling lackey greeted her with a bow and a spray of yellow acacia blossoms. "Good evening, Mlle Delphine." He proffered the small bouquet. "For you, Mademoiselle, with Monsieur's compliments."

She accepted the flowers and sniffed their fragrance, thinking it would have been more gracious if de Gournay had presented them himself. "Where is Monsieur?" she asked with a hint of annoyance.

"He waits below in the carriage. If you please, Mademoiselle."

Delphine followed the lackey down three flights of stairs, stopping once to check her appearance in a large wall mirror on the first landing. They passed through the foyer and exited to the street where a closed coach, drawn by two handsome grays, was parked by the curb beneath a blazing gas lamp. The horses snorted placidly as the servant helped

Delphine into the carriage. The door closed behind her before she caught a glimpse of the individual seated in the interior.

As the carriage pulled away from the curb, Delphine's first impression of her companion was scent—an earthy, masculine, fern, and floral fragrance, *Fougère Royale*, interfused with tobacco smoke. A throaty but distinctly feminine voice greeted her.

"Good evening, Mlle Delphine. I trust you like the flowers?"

Closed blinds cloaked the passengers in shadow, but Delphine's eyes gradually adjusted to the darkness. She stared in the direction of the voice and of the heady odor emanating from the seat next to her. Her ears detected a rustle of silk as her companion shifted about. Delphine made out the inchoate form of an elegantly dressed woman wearing a veiled hat.

"Monsieur?" she inquired dubiously.

A pair of delicate white hands lifted the veil, revealing the painted and powdered features of the young gentleman at the Divan Japonais. "Permit me to introduce myself. I am Marie Madeleine de Gournay. However, I would be very pleased if you called me Mado."

Delphine frowned, incredulous. "Is this a jest? If so, I believe it's in poor taste and unbecoming a gentleman."

De Gournay smiled apologetically. "Forgive me, Mademoiselle. I assure you, this is who I am. I'm an actor who plays many parts, and this evening I greet you in the role I hoped you'd find most agreeable. With all due respect, it's well known that you prefer women to men."

Delphine controlled her temper, remembering that she too was an actor, playing her role under the direction of Inspector Lefebvre. She put on her sweetest smile. "Pardon me . . . Mado. You took me by surprise. I'm not in the least offended; I appreciate the gesture. And thank you for the lovely flowers."

De Gournay smiled. "I'm relieved that you're pleased with my gift, Mademoiselle."

"Please, call me Delphine."

"Thank you, Delphine. Did you know yellow acacias have a special meaning?"

She lifted the spray and inhaled the fragrance before answering. "I did not. What do they mean, Mado?"

De Gournay leaned over, brushed away a curl from Delphine's ear, and whispered "Secret love."

Her eyes still focused on the bouquet, she said, "Ah, how enchanting." Then she gave a sidelong glance. "Where are we going?"

"First, to the Hanneton for drinks and some chat. Then, to the Moulin Rouge for dancing and a show. Afterwards, I'd like to offer you a late supper at my apartment."

"That sounds lovely," she replied.

De Gournay smiled, took Delphine's free hand, and caressed her kid-gloved fingers.

⁂

Upon Delphine and de Gournay's arrival at the Hanneton, the tough, half-blind proprietress, Mme Armande, stepped out from behind her cashier's cage and greeted the couple with a familiar embrace. "It's been too long, Delphine. And who is your charming companion?"

Delphine smiled and made an introduction. "Mme Armande, may I present my new friend, Mlle de Gournay?"

The beefy proprietress smiled broadly and kissed de Gournay's lips. "My humble establishment is honored by a lady's presence. We'll have to mind our manners, won't we, Delphine?"

Delphine winked at the proprietress and then turned to her companion. "Don't worry, Mado. The girls can get rowdy at times, but Madame knows how to keep them in line."

Madame laughed and flexed her muscles. "Oh, that I do, indeed." Her one good eye leering at de Gournay, she added, "Just let me know if anyone gets fresh with you, dearie. I'll tan her hide and pitch her out the door."

De Gournay smiled demurely and nodded in reply to Madame's gallant offer. They passed on into the intimate room decorated in the familiar style of the *brasserie à femmes*: red curtains and carpets, a few strategically placed marble-topped tables, and a baize banquette backed by wall mirrors that made the place seem larger than it was. A gas chandelier and wall sconces filled the room with a warm golden glow.

This place was different from others of its ilk in that both clientele and servers were women. As Delphine and de Gournay made their way toward a small corner table, a handful of females eyed them with curiosity, envy, and desire. Delphine was a local celebrity and her companion was handsome and dressed to perfection—they would be the subject of gossip and speculation for some time to come.

One pair of critical male eyes examined the couple from the vantage point of his reserved corner table. Toulouse-Lautrec was an honored regular, Madame's friend and one of the few members of his gender welcome in the otherwise female establishment. *She sees me and ignores me,* he thought. *Why?*

Turning his attention from Delphine to her companion, Lautrec's sharp eyes scrutinized de Gournay as the subject of a sketch. Before long, his memory conjured the image of the young man at the Divan Japonais. *No wonder Delphine's avoiding me,* Lautrec thought. Smiling wryly, he put charcoal to paper. *Is she a woman posing as a man, or a man masquerading as a woman? Intriguing. More grist for M. Lefebvre's investigative mill.*

De Gournay opened a beaded handbag, removed a gold cigarette case, and offered Delphine a smoke. They were smoking and chatting when a curious young server approached them without being beckoned.

"Good evening, Delphine," the attractive young girl said, impudently ignoring de Gournay. "We've missed you, but perhaps you've no time for old friends?"

Delphine set down her cigarette in an ashtray and picked a strand of tobacco from her teeth. "Good evening, Clo. I regret I've been busy with my career. But I see nothing's changed—you're cheeky as ever. Didn't Madame teach you not to come until you're called?"

Clo pouted. "Oh, my, aren't we hoity-toity. I suppose I must call you 'Mademoiselle.' All right, *Mlle* Delphine. Now, won't you be polite in return and introduce your *friend*?"

Delphine frowned disapprovingly, but made a curt introduction. "Mado, this is Clo. Clo, this is Mlle de Gournay."

Clo made a mock curtsy. Then she winked at de Gournay and smirked. "So, what'll it be, dearie? I assume you're playing Monsieur for the evening?"

Delphine glared at Clo. If she had not been "on duty," she would have grabbed the girl's reddish-blond topknot, dragged her outside, and slapped her insolent face. Madame would have approved. But under the circumstances, Delphine remained silent and calm.

De Gournay smiled, savoring the bitchy ambience. "Two beers, Mademoiselle, if you please," de Gournay ordered with excessive politeness.

The girl melted. "Oh, you're nice, darling. I mean, Mademoiselle," she simpered. "Do you prefer short or tall?"

De Gournay turned to Delphine. "Which do you prefer?"

"I like mine tall and strong," she replied.

"Two tall beers, please," de Gournay rejoined.

"Coming right up, love," Clo chirped. As she turned, she brushed her hip against de Gournay's arm, a provocative action not lost on the vigilant Madame. On the way to the bar, the girl heeded the warning implicit in Mme Armande's icy stare.

Their next visitor was a small dog that stood on its hind legs, placed its forepaws on de Gournay's thigh, and wagged its tail in greeting. De Gournay petted the dog's head and scratched behind its ear.

Delphine smiled. "It's Madame's dog. He's friendly. Nevertheless, I must warn you. He has the bad habit of sneaking under tables and peeing on the customer's skirts."

De Gournay pushed away the dog. "Goodness, I hope not. I'm wearing the latest Worth creation."

Delphine laughed and patted de Gournay's hand reassuringly. She admired the emerald green silk dress. "It's very beautiful, Mado. Much too fine to be pissed upon."

De Gournay held her hand. "Would you care to have a dress like this?"

Delphine sighed. "It would be lovely, but I couldn't wear it."

"Why not?"

"If I put on that elegant gown, I might forget where I came from."

Puzzled by her answer, de Gournay's brow wrinkled. "Don't you want to forget?"

She shook her head. "I mustn't. If I did, my songs would be false and meaningless. The audience would jeer me off the stage."

"But you've improved yourself. You live well, and your audience doesn't seem to mind."

"Oh, they don't mind that I've bettered myself. In fact, they admire me for my success. And they know that, deep down, I'm still one of them. Of course, they tease me on occasion, as we just got from Clo. I shouldn't mind, really. It reminds me who I am."

"'This above all: to thine own self be true,' eh?"

"Pardon?"

Before de Gournay could reveal the source of the quote, Clo came with two large glasses of beer balanced on a tray. She served them courteously, without comment, and then went about her business.

"Her attitude changed awfully fast," observed de Gournay.

Delphine took a draft and then wiped foam from her lips with a serviette. "Remember what Madame said about the girls getting too fresh. She's quite capable of carrying out her threat, as Clo knows only too well."

De Gournay stared at Delphine. For an instant, her eyes blazed with a cruel passion, which she masked with a benign smile.

Lautrec finished his sketch. *I'll set this one aside for Inspector Lefebvre,* he thought, closing the book and packing away his charcoals. Placing his hands on the tabletop, he rose slowly and painfully. Lifting his "button-hook" cane from the back of the chair, he gestured to Madame to indicate he was leaving, and made for the door. He was off to one of his other haunts, the Moulin Rouge.

⁓

Toulouse-Lautrec sat at his favorite table, on the dance floor perimeter below the mezzanine, not far from the bar. From this location, he had an excellent view of the hall, a perfect vantage point for sketching. He drank, sketched, and assimilated the atmosphere into his art.

Delphine and de Gournay entered while the quadrille was underway. The elegant couple passed by the bar, their images reflected in a row of sparkling mirrors. They ignored the alluring scrutiny of many amorous eyes, until they found a recently vacated table not far from Lautrec. De Gournay ordered champagne and they huddled together on the banquette, watching the dance, holding hands. They made small talk, occasionally shouting in each other's ears to compete with the orchestra. Lautrec captured their facial expressions and gestures in charcoal.

The dance ended to cheers and applause and the orchestra took a break. Lautrec kept his eyes on Delphine and de Gournay. *Thus far, she plays her part well*, he thought. *However, the next act will be more difficult.* He finished his cognac and signaled the waiter for another.

Zidler approached with a bottle, poured Lautrec a drink, and set the cognac on the table. The portly, dark mustachioed owner-manager looked very prosperous in his white tie and black tailcoat. "Good evening, M. Lautrec."

"Good evening, Zidler. A good crowd tonight. You must be pleased."

Zidler rubbed his hands together and winked. "Not bad, Monsieur. Not bad at all. But not like it was during the Exposition."

Lautrec shrugged. "Well, every day can't be the first day of spring."

Zidler stroked his moustache. "Very true, Monsieur." He glanced in the direction of Delphine and de Gournay and noted, "Our Delphine has found a chic new friend."

"Yes, so it seems," Lautrec muttered and drained his glass.

"I'd like to have her back at the Moulin, Monsieur," Zidler said to Lautrec, "but I'm afraid there would be too much competition with Jane Avril."

Lautrec refilled his glass. "I suppose so."

Zidler peered down at the sketchbook. "Hard at work as always, I see. Excellent!" He paused a moment, then inquired, "How's the poster coming along?"

Lautrec sighed. Without looking up, he said, "I shall have something for you presently."

"Splendid!" Zidler replied. He noticed the orchestra beginning to warm up and glanced at his watch. "I look forward to the new poster, and it's always a pleasure to see you. *Au revoir.*" With that, he walked away in the direction of his office.

A few minutes later, the orchestra was tuned and the conductor tapped his baton on his stand. They struck up a polka and an eager crowd, including de Gournay and Delphine, streamed onto the dance floor. Lautrec flipped a page in his book and began a new drawing, his eyes following the couple around the dance floor, his deft hand working in perfect harmony with his penetrating eye. He captured fluid motion, posture, gesture, and expression with a striking economy of line. Were his observations cool, detached, and clinical? Did he approach the subject objectively, the way he recorded Dr. Péan's operations?

Perhaps, on this singular occasion, more emotion than usual crept into his composition. A cloud of jealousy hovered over his consciousness, as noxious as the tobacco haze permeating the dance hall. He recognized the danger. He would not permit such a base passion to interfere with his art.

One dance followed another, then another, until the couple left the floor, panting with fatigue. *A fine pictorial record for the inspector,* Lautrec thought to himself. *Much better than a concealed camera.* He watched de Gournay settle the bill, take Delphine by the arm, and escort her to the exit. Lautrec set down his charcoal and sketchpad, and took a long draft of cognac. *Now, Delphine, you must give your best performance, until the curtain descends on the final scene.*

10

DISCOVERED ATTACK

Achille and Legros pondered the ashes in Nazimova's fireplace, the empty iron box on the floor, and the displaced brick in the mantelpiece. "She lied to me, Étienne. She didn't burn Boguslavsky's formula when her husband died. What else might she have hidden in the box?"

Earlier that morning, the medical examiner had certified the cause of death an accident—an overdose of medication. According to the Morgue pathologist, Nazimova had suffered from a rare bone cancer.

"Excruciatingly painful," he had observed, following the autopsy. In such cases, he always determined death by accident rather than suicide, giving the deceased the benefit of the doubt.

Achille removed his watch from his vest pocket. "Let's have lunch. We're finished here, at least for the time being."

He and Legros left the bookstore and walked up the boulevard to their favorite café. Achille perceived what a fine, mild day it was, so different from his mental landscape. The circumstances of Nazimova's death troubled him deeply, in a way he did not want to admit to himself.

They sat at a small round table on the sidewalk fronting the café, in the shade of a tall linden tree. The proprietor welcomed them, as the inspectors were regulars. They ordered coffee and croissants, and remained silent until the proprietor left them and entered the café.

Achille began the conversation with a chess analogy. "A discovered attack with check is one of the most powerful and dangerous moves in chess. Imagine this position: Rossignol, the knight, occupies a square next to our queen. He moves and checks our king, uncovering an attack from his queen against ours on the diagonal. We have no choice but to move our king out of check, thus losing our queen and the game. How do we prevent the knight from making such a move?"

Legros replied without hesitation. "We must avoid placing ourselves in that compromising position. Otherwise, our only hope is that our opponent blunders, that he does not see our weakness and take advantage of his opportunity."

Achille smiled. "Precisely, Étienne. We've advanced into the middle game of this investigation. We must anticipate our adversary's moves and forestall any of his actions that might harm us. However, if it looks like he's about to blunder, we won't interfere. As the great Napoleon said, 'Never interrupt your enemy when he is making a mistake.' At any rate, we need more information. I expect a report from Delphine today."

"Have you received a message?"

"Yes, I'm meeting her at Lautrec's studio this afternoon."

The proprietor interrupted with their order. Achille and Legros exchanged a few pleasantries with their friend until he left them to attend to another table.

Legros took a sip of coffee and a bite of croissant before continuing. "Things are quiet at the stakeout. No new messages. Do you think they suspect we're watching them?"

Achille frowned and shook his head. "I have no reason to believe so, but they would be cautious nevertheless. Why would they risk sending a message when there's no urgent need for it? However, my gut tells me they're going to move soon. When they do, we'd better be prepared to act fast. Have you been working with Gilles?"

"Yes, he's studied the area at the stakeout, and he's trained two of our men to use his camera. I've picked up on it myself."

"Good. There's one more thing—a hunch. It stretches our resources, but I want to detail a couple of good men to watch Nazimova's shop, at least for the next few days."

Legros grimaced. "What are you thinking, Inspector?"

Achille fidgeted nervously with his pince-nez before answering with a question. "Nazimova had a shop assistant, Marie—Marie Léglise, the type who could blend into the woodwork. You'd hardly know she was there, but on occasion, I detected something about her in a look, a gesture, a tone of voice. There seemed to be a hidden strength and conviction that she kept well concealed. Overall, she might be the sort of person who makes a good spy.

"Nazimova told me that Marie had returned to her home in Normandy. Nazimova was closing the shop, providing a reasonable explanation for Marie's sudden disappearance. But what if she didn't leave Paris? She might be here, waiting for an opportunity to enter the shop to search for the papers that Nazimova burned."

"You're thinking about the cat burglar who took Kadyshev's papers, aren't you?"

Achille nodded the affirmative, finished his coffee, and lit a cigarette.

"But wouldn't she know that Nazimova destroyed the papers?" Legros pressed.

"Why would she know? I trust we have no leak in our brigade. The Russians could have planted Marie to keep an eye on Nazimova, or they might have recruited her for the job. They knew, or at least must have suspected, that Nazimova had a copy of Boguslavsky's formula. However, they don't know that we're on to their game. Anyway, they wouldn't want to leave any evidence behind for us to discover."

"Very well." Legros could not argue with Achille's logic. "I'll work with the schedule and assign a couple of men."

A flight of sparrows darted among the lindens and a soft breeze ruffled leaves and stirred branches, projecting moving shadows onto the pavement. The café patrons drank, ate, smoked, and chatted, pausing at times to observe the passersby. After a few minutes of quiet enjoyment, Legros ventured a personal question. "You liked Nazimova, didn't you?"

Achille looked down at his folded hands. "Yes, Étienne, I did." He raised his eyes to Legros. "We discussed art, literature, poetry, and philosophy. At times, her shop became my refuge from our workaday world." He stubbed out his cigarette and rested his elbows on the table. "She was an idealist. She wanted to change the world for the better by peaceful means. Frankly, I think she was a dreamer, a utopian. What she wanted affronts reason and experience. Nevertheless, I understood her longing.

"We dwell too much on revenge for the lost provinces, Alsace-Lorraine. What's more, the wounds of 1871 have never healed completely. Nation against nation, class against class, race against race. Who will fight the next war, my friend? Will it be our generation, or our children, or our grandchildren?"

Achille sighed and shook his head. "I'm sorry, Étienne. Such thoughts distract from the job at hand, but I can't help thinking. After all, we're civilized; we have a will and a well-developed sense of right and wrong. If we follow orders without question, we're nothing but automata doing our master's bidding."

The turn in the conversation disturbed Legros, but he put it down to Nazimova's death. He reminded the inspector of a recent comment.

"I understand your feelings, Achille, but you did say 'Ours not to reason why. . . .'"

Achille smiled sadly. "Thank you for reminding me. At any rate, I'm glad I got that off my chest." He reached into his pocket and checked his watch. "We're in danger of becoming idlers, Inspector. Time to settle our bill and return to headquarters. Our day has barely begun."

∞

Delphine met Achille at Lautrec's studio. She sat with the artist and inspector at the same table they had occupied at their last meeting. Delphine began her narrative with a detailed description of the lackey, which Achille recorded in his notebook, and then de Gournay's appearance, which drew an immediate response from the inspector.

"Is de Gournay a man or a woman?"

Delphine shook her head. "I'm sorry, Inspector. I can't say for sure."

Achille's bewildered look amused Lautrec. The artist would have grabbed his sketchpad and charcoals to capture the inspector's expression, had the materials been nearby.

Achille sputtered, "But Delphine, surely you saw . . . I mean you must have felt . . ." His face reddened and he stopped speaking, averting his eyes. Lautrec could not contain his laughter, which brought angry stares from both his guests.

"I understand your hesitancy, Inspector," Delphine said. "You're a gentleman, and wish to spare me embarrassment. Frankly, the evening did not end as I expected. We kissed, held hands, and talked. That's all." She opened her purse and removed a slip of paper. "We spent the evening at a house on the Rue de la Mire. Here's the address."

Achille immediately recognized it. It was the house the anarchists used to signal a mail drop. He put the paper in his pocket and pursued his original line of inquiry. "Did you notice anything that might indicate gender? Beard stubble, or perhaps a protrusion of some sort?"

189

The reference to a "protrusion" was too much for Lautrec. He coughed into a handkerchief to stifle his laughter, excused himself, and retreated to his liquor cabinet.

Delphine glared at the artist, and then turned her attention back to Achille. "I'm afraid I couldn't tell one way or another. At any rate, if he's a man, he gave a great performance. For the most part, I was convinced he was not."

Lautrec returned with a bottle, three glasses, and his sketchbook. "Will you join me?"

Delphine accepted a glass, but Achille refused. After Lautrec poured for himself and Delphine, the artist opened the sketchbook and handed it to Achille.

"I sketched de Gournay at the Hanneton and the Moulin Rouge. I thought you might be interested."

"Thank you, Monsieur. Indeed, I am." Achille scrutinized the sketches. The face seemed familiar, but he could not place it. "Did de Gournay give you a Christian name?" he asked Delphine.

"The only name he gave was Marie Madeleine, Mado for short," she replied.

Marie. He stared at the sketches, applying his skill in Bertillon's identification method. Could de Gournay and Marie Léglise be the same person? *There is a resemblance in the key features*, he thought, *but it might just be coincidence.*

Eventually, he looked up and declared, "This individual is a master of disguise and deception, a chameleon-like person who changes roles and identities with ease. A dangerous adversary, without doubt. Now, Delphine, please recall your conversation, and don't spare the details."

She began with a reference to the information she had received from Apolline, concerning Orlovsky and de Gournay's lucrative joint venture. The intelligence related to the Russian arms deal, bank loans, and market speculation with French cooperation confirmed Achille's suspicions.

"Did de Gournay elaborate further on their scheme?" Achille asked.

"No, Inspector," she replied, "but he did indicate he would be leaving Paris soon, perhaps within the next couple of days. He didn't say where, though I believe it will be out of the country."

"What gave you that impression?"

"He talked about faraway places, long days and nights at sea. And he asked if I'd enjoy a journey to some exotic destination."

"I understand. Please continue."

"He asked me to accompany him. He even offered me a thousand francs, which I refused."

Her information supported Achille's hunch that de Gournay was about to make a critical move. "How did he react to your refusal?"

"Oh, he was quite a gentleman . . . or lady, as the case may be. He said if I changed my mind, I should notify him no later than this evening."

Achille took a moment to consider the situation. *The game is evolving, developing with every move. I must keep ahead, anticipate and preempt. But I don't want to expose Delphine. She has done enough.*

"Thank you, Delphine," he replied at last. "Your efforts have been invaluable. From now on, I want you to avoid de Gournay. Since you've already rejected his offer, you needn't have any further communication with him. However, if he's importunate, you may give him a polite refusal, something simple and direct. Say you have too many commitments in Paris to leave on such short notice. It's quite plausible. He shouldn't expect you to jeopardize your career for a thousand francs and his charming company.

"Should anything develop with de Gournay, or if you feel threatened, notify me immediately through the usual channels. Likewise, if you hear further from Orlovsky or your friends Apolline and Aurore, please get in touch with me at your first opportunity. But regardless of the circumstances, try to maintain a secure line of communication."

"Very cloak-and-dagger, isn't it, Inspector?" Lautrec interjected.

"Yes, Monsieur, it is," Achille stated matter-of-factly. "Based on Delphine's information, I believe the next forty-eight hours are crucial, and I ask you to be similarly circumspect. Please keep your eyes and ears open, and report anything suspicious."

Lautrec downed a glass and poured another. "You may count on me, Inspector. As always, I'm at your service."

Delphine made a wry face, indicating her doubt as to the habitually inebriated artist's usefulness in a tight spot. "I'm performing tonight at the Divan Japonais," she said to Achille. "Orlovsky, de Gournay, and the girls might be there."

"I'll be in the front row," Lautrec broke in with tipsy enthusiasm. "I wouldn't miss it for the world."

Delphine glanced at the painter with a sigh, then turned back to Achille and continued. "If they approach me after the performance, I'll play it by ear. Of course, if I learn anything of interest, I'll pass it on to you."

Achille smiled. "Thanks, Delphine." He checked his watch. He wanted to get to the stakeout near the Café Aux Billards en Bois as soon as possible, as he suspected a new mission was due to be put through soon. "I must be off," he said. "Is there anything else before I go?"

Delphine said no, but Lautrec chimed in with a question.

"Are we in any danger?"

Achille frowned, but answered honestly. "The question is rather broad, Monsieur. To narrow it down, I believe, at present, you are in no more danger than usual. However, I must caution you both to be on your guard in the presence of both Orlovsky and de Gournay."

Lautrec grinned. "Oh, good. Anything to relieve the boredom of our quotidian existence." He poured another drink.

⌑

Wroblewski and Moreau sheltered from the noonday sun beneath a broad chestnut tree planted in the center of the square near the doss house. Wroblewski smoked a foul-smelling cigarette made from discarded butts. Between puffs, he nervously picked at a few stray threads dangling from the edges of his frayed shirt cuffs. "What's taking so long?" he muttered. "We ought to have had our marching orders by now."

Moreau smiled at his excitable friend. "Calm yourself, comrade. Rossignol knows what he's doing. We'll have our instructions soon enough."

Wroblewski exhaled a cloud of gray smoke. "I hope you're right," he replied without conviction. "Anyway, I'd best be off. It's my turn to check the mail."

Moreau patted his friend's shoulder. "Good luck, comrade. Maybe today's the day."

Wroblewski shrugged and dropped his cigarette on the pavement, then trudged off in the direction of the Rue de la Mire.

A detective, watching from his hiding place in an alley on the other side of the square, checked his watch, opened a notebook, and recorded the time.

When Wroblewski arrived at the signaling house, he glanced up at the third-story window and immediately noticed that it was unshuttered. In response to the eagerly anticipated signal, he turned, walked rapidly away, and practically bounded up the precipitous stairway to the Rue Lepic. A detective concealed in a narrow air space between two houses across the street noted the time, the signal, and Wroblewski's reaction.

Wroblewski continued to the Café Aux Billards en Bois, at the intersection of the Rue des Saules and Rue Norvins.

Achille, Gilles, and another detective waited in the secreted alleyway observation post staked out by Blind by Accident. Two hours earlier, Gilles had photographed an unidentified suspect, the porter from the La Villette storehouse, depositing a message behind the loose brick in the wall around the corner from the café. The detective stationed on the Rue de la Mire had already spotted the message carrier and written a *portrait parlé*. As soon as the "postman" was safely out of view, Gilles had gone to the hiding place and taken two exposures of the concealed note.

The photographer had two plates left and used them to photograph Wroblewski retrieving the message. As soon as the subject was out of sight, Achille turned to his detective. "Remain here until you're relieved." Then to Gilles, he said, "We must return to your studio immediately. How long will it take to develop and print the negatives?"

"About an hour."

The knight's making his move, Achille thought. "All right, then. I need to decrypt the message and get descriptions of the new suspect to Legros. Then I need to arrange a meeting with Rousseau. We have no time to lose."

⁕

Achille paced up and down the floor outside Gilles's darkroom, chain-smoking and muttering to himself. As always, he deplored the scarcity of telephones. In a matter of utmost urgency, he would rely upon the ubiquitous *petit-bleu*, a closed telegram sent by pneumatic tube and delivered by messenger. He took cold comfort in knowing that his adversaries were subject to the same limitations.

Gilles emerged from his photographer's lair, prints in hand. "Good news, Achille! They all came out beautifully. The light was perfect, and my new camera performed like a charm."

Achille muttered "Thanks" and dashed to a nearby table with the prints. He sat, laid out the photographs before him, and concentrated on the encryption. At last, a broad smile crossed his lips. "You fucked up!" he cried.

Gilles winced as if he had been struck. He ran to the table and stared at the photographs. "What are you saying, Achille? They're perfect, absolutely perfect."

Achille glanced up at Gilles. "I'm sorry, my friend, I wasn't referring to your work. I was speaking of the clever M. Rossignol. As I'd hoped, he failed to change the key to his poem encryption. I've got the bastard by the short hairs."

"Oh, thank you very much," Gilles replied with a mixture of consternation and relief.

Taking the Ronsard poem, some paper, and a pencil from his pockets, Achille went to work on the decryption. Operating quickly but accurately, he soon had the message decoded. Then he dashed off two messages marked "Urgent Police Business": one to Legros, the other to Rousseau. As soon as he was finished, he got up from the table and stuffed all the material in his pockets.

"I'm off to the telegraph office and then to headquarters. If anyone comes looking for me, especially Étienne, please tell him to meet me there directly."

"I'll do that, Achille."

Achille smiled and took his friend by the hand. "I can't tell you how much I appreciate your work on this case. When it's over, I'll take you out on the town and thank you properly."

"I'll look forward to that, my friend. But don't you have a holiday planned? I assume Adele takes precedence."

Achille shook his head. "Ah, yes, Trouville. Thank you for reminding me. Our 'bachelor' spree will have to wait until I return."

Gilles laughed and clapped his friend's shoulder. "I understand. Now off with you, Inspector. And good luck!"

∾

Mme Berthier and Cook returned from the market, their baskets brimming with fresh produce. In addition to a variety of vegetables, Madame's basket carried the latest edition of *Les Amis de la Vérité*, a gift from Madame's friend, the noted cabbage vendor and gossip, Mme Gros.

Madame and Cook met the nanny and Jeanne in the first-floor foyer. The nanny, Suzanne, pushed a perambulator bearing Olivier, who was sound asleep. "Good afternoon, Mme Berthier," Suzanne said as she halted her excursion party.

"Good afternoon, Suzanne," Madame replied. "Taking the little ones out for some air?"

"Yes, Madame, we're going to the Tuileries Gardens."

Madame inspected the dormant infant in the pram. "Very well, but mind Olivier carefully. He's been a bit fragile lately. He must take after the Lefebvres." With a rustle of old-fashioned crinoline and a creaking of stays, she bent over gingerly and patted Jeanne's head. "Not like my pretty little cabbage. She's a true Berthier, strong as a cavalry horse."

Jeanne beamed with pride. "Yes, Grandmamma, and when I grow up, I'm going to be a colonel, just like Grandpapa."

Madame shook her head. "I'm afraid you'll have to settle for being a colonel's wife."

Jeanne pouted and stared at her shoes. "Oh," she muttered. But a moment later, she looked up again with an excited grin. "You're invited to an English tea!"

"An *English* tea, eh? How elegant. And what is the time and place of this social event?"

"It takes place in the nursery this afternoon, as soon as we come back from the park. You will be the guest of honor."

"If that's the case, I'll surely come. Who else, may I ask, will be present?"

"Suzanne and my dollies," Jeanne replied matter-of-factly.

"Oh, no one else? What about your mama?"

The little girl frowned and shook her head. "No! Mama is *not* invited."

Madame imagined the snub was the result of a minor scolding that had not yet worn off. She smiled and patted Jeanne's cheek gently. "Well, perhaps you'll change your mind and add Mama to your guest list."

"Perhaps," she replied without enthusiasm.

Madame kissed Jeanne's forehead and whispered, "*A bientôt*, my angel." Then Suzanne passed out the front entrance with her charges, while Madame and Cook proceeded upstairs.

Adele greeted her mother and Cook at the door. "How was the market, Mama?"

Madame removed the newspaper and handed her basket to Cook. The servant excused herself and moved on to the kitchen.

"Not bad," Madame replied. "Prices were reasonable, though, as always, I had to bargain them down. The quality is good, especially Mme Gros's cabbages." With the mention of Mme Gros, her eyes twinkled. She rolled her newspaper around in her hands. "Have you read the latest edition of *Les Amis de la Vérité?*"

Speechless, Adele eyed the newspaper. *My God! Did Fournier write about our meeting at La Grenouillère?*

Madame smiled mischievously. "You seem at a loss for words. Let us go to the drawing room. There's a matter I wish to discuss with you—in private."

Adele followed her mother silently with downcast eyes, like a naughty child on her way to a familiar place of punishment. When they arrived in the drawing room, Madame eased herself into a comfortable armchair.

"It's early, but I'd like a sherry. Why don't you pour two glasses?"

Perplexed by her mother's conviviality, Adele retrieved the bottle and glasses from a nearby cabinet. She served Madame, took a glass for herself, and sat on the settee across from her mother.

Adele braced herself with sherry before breaking her silence. "Is there something of particular interest in the newspaper?" she inquired hesitantly.

"You needn't be so modest, my dear." Mme Berthier noticed her daughter's blank stare. Her face wrinkled; her eyes narrowed skeptically. "Is it possible you don't know? Why, all Paris is abuzz with it."

Adele's apprehension and bewilderment evolved into exasperation. "Abuzz with what, Mother? Please be kind enough to inform me."

Madame snorted dubiously and took a sip of sherry. Then she opened the paper to Fournier's article and handed it over to Adele. "Read it for yourself."

Adele read the puffery with a bemusement even greater than that of her husband. When she finished, she set down the newspaper on the coffee table. After taking a minute to gather her thoughts, she stammered, "I had no idea M. Fournier was . . . that he admired Achille so greatly."

Madame smiled shrewdly. "Oh, you didn't, my dear? Well, his great admiration for your husband is obvious, but more important is M. Junot's esteem. Junot is a man of consequence, with influence at the highest level of government, and with M. Junot backing him, there's no limit to what Achille might achieve.

"I'll admit to having misjudged your husband. I thought he was nothing but a common policeman, chasing criminals through the gutters of Paris. His ambition seemed confined to the office of the chief of detectives. Well, I was wrong and I apologize. Achille has risen considerably in my eyes. Why, only this morning, Mme Gros said he could be our next Prefect of Police. Do you realize what that means? The prefect is a position of great honor, the equivalent of a general or a cabinet minister. Men in such positions reap great rewards; fortunes are made overnight. Achille could assume a title based on his ancient lineage. You might become a baroness with apartments on the Rue du Faubourg Saint-Honoré."

"Please, Mother, think of what you're saying," Adele broke in with alarm. "It's true, Achille's well-regarded. He's solved difficult cases and been promoted for his accomplishments. But he's still a young man. You mustn't leap to conclusions based upon one newspaper article and Mme Gros's predictions."

"Young, is he?" Madame sniffed. "The great Napoleon was a general at twenty-four and ruler of France at thirty. Of course, I will not liken Achille to the incomparable Emperor. Nevertheless, you should be proud being the wife of such a promising individual. Your father was a brave man, a brilliant officer. He ought to have been a general, but he had powerful enemies. They ruined his career and forced him to retire. You must not let that happen to Achille. As his wife, you have a duty to him and to our family. You must support and encourage him, and do your utmost to help him succeed. Do you understand?"

"For heaven's sake, Mother." Adele trembled and her eyes filled with tears. "Remember Scripture: 'Pride goes before destruction and a haughty spirit before a fall.'"

Madame laughed bitterly. "Oh, my dear, when did you become so religious? You and your freethinking husband rarely attend mass—not a good example for your children, I'm afraid. Admit it: You don't turn to the Bible from piety, Adele. It's fear, pure and simple. You married a man with a destiny and you're afraid to live with the consequences. Well, I took the colonel, for better or worse, and I would have ridden to heaven or hell with him, as long as I could remain by his side." Madame reached for the sherry and poured another glass.

Adele composed herself. Following her mother's example, she refilled her glass and took a draft before responding. "I'll admit I'm frightened," she said, "but it's not what you think. I won't hold Achille back. I'm afraid that as we gain wealth and social status, we'll lose sight of something precious, something closely bound up in our love for one another. For want of a better word, I'd call it innocence."

The old woman sighed. "Adele, you're a married woman with two children. You're hardly *innocent*. What's more, I think you're too sentimental to be my daughter. At any rate, innocence has nothing to do with it. You can be happy or miserable in a shack or a palace. All things considered, it's better to live in the palace." She leaned over and took her daughter's hand. "Your life will change. You'll meet new people and enter a higher social sphere. Achille spends too much time with his rowing companions and bohemian friends. They're all a bunch of loafers, drunkards, dope fiends, and degenerates, not to mention their floozies—"

"Please, Mother," Adele interrupted. "You exaggerate. Gilles is a good friend, and M. Lautrec is a great artist and a gentleman."

Madame smiled. "All right, my dear, we won't speak of it anymore. Now, tell me why you're not invited to Jeanne's tea party."

Adele raised her eyebrows in surprise. "Did she tell you that?"

"She certainly did." Madame mimicked her granddaughter to perfection: "'No! Mama is *not* invited.'"

The imitation was so ludicrous, it got a laugh out of Adele. "I scolded her this morning," she explained. "You know how she's always leaving her toys on the runner. Suzanne and I pick up after her, but it does no good. She just takes them out again and leaves them. Then, when Achille comes home, tired and near-sighted as he is, he trips on the toys and swears awfully."

Madame doubled over in a giggling fit. "Oh, I *know*," she said between bursts of laughter. "I've heard him often enough—his favorite curse word, though I won't repeat it." Presently, she calmed down and remarked, "Don't worry, my dear. I'm sure your name will be put back on the invited list." She turned her attention to the bottle. "You know, this sherry is excellent. Shall we have another?"

Adele smiled. "Just one more wouldn't hurt," she said, as she filled two more glasses to the brim.

⚭

Achille and Legros stood side by side, each leaning against the walkway balustrade on the Pont Neuf, gazing in the direction of the Eiffel Tower while discussing the case. Passersby walked up and down from Left Bank to Right, ignoring the detectives who were, on this clear, pleasant day, anonymous, hidden in plain sight.

Achille spoke over the chugging and churning of a tugboat passing beneath the arch. "As soon as we're finished, go to Records and look for the letter carrier. From the photograph and description, I believe he may be Guy Renard, alias the Porter, wanted for burglary in Liège. He's an expert second-story man. He used to work in the hotels; that's where he got the moniker."

"Do you think he's our cat burglar?"

"Could be. If you find a match in Records, wire our Belgian contact for more information. In the meantime, keep shadowing him, and maintain the stakeout on Nazimova's shop."

"What about the message?"

"The decoded message read, 'Rossignol team. Meeting at Ronsard re: Guest, four A.M. tomorrow.'" Achille took out a pack of cigarettes and offered one to his companion. He lit up and took a drag on his smoke before answering. "The 'team' is the knight and his pawns, Moreau and Wroblewski. The unidentified suspect, possibly Renard, may not be part of the inner circle. The place is the house on the Rue Ronsard. The purpose of the meeting and the identity of the 'Guest' are unknown. I'm hoping Rousseau will shed some light on the subject."

"You're meeting him here?"

Achille consulted his watch. "Yes, in twenty minutes. Afterwards, I'll make our case to the chief."

Legros turned to Achille. "And what will that be, Inspector?"

Achille smiled and shook his head. Without looking back at Legros, he answered, "I won't know until I speak to our big friend."

"Why not arrest the whole gang at the Rue Ronsard tomorrow morning? They're all suspects in the murders of Kadyshev and Boguslavsky, and we've built a good case against them."

"Assuming the meeting isn't a ruse or diversion, I'd say that's the best way to proceed. But Rousseau might think otherwise, not to mention the chief. And we still don't know what Orlovsky and Rossignol are up to. Rousseau might be on to something, or at least have a clue. And he's been investigating the leak at La Villette. I believe Rossignol tipped off the anarchists, but I want Rousseau's opinion. Regardless, something significant is happening within the next twenty-four hours, and we must prepare for all contingencies."

Legros sighed. "I've had enough cloak-and-dagger to last a lifetime. Give me a good old criminal investigation any day."

Achille nodded and tossed his cigarette into the river. "A beautiful day, isn't it, Étienne? Suzanne's taking the little ones to the Tuileries Gardens. They ought to be there by now. I'd like to be with them."

"It must be nice, having children."

"It's a great responsibility—and a headache at times—but I wouldn't give it up for the world. Anyway, you'd better get over to Records. When you're done, meet me back at headquarters. The next couple of days will be pure hell. Don't expect to go home or get much sleep."

"Thank God I'm a bachelor. Have you notified Adele?"

"I already sent a message." He turned toward Legros and smiled wryly. "I'm sure she'll be pleased. Now, get a move on, Inspector. I'll stay here and enjoy the view until my friend Rousseau arrives."

At the appointed time, Achille saw Rousseau approaching from the Right Bank. A well-dressed man exhibiting the distinctive military bearing of an officer in civilian attire accompanied the detective. Surprised by the appearance of someone unconnected to the case, Achille adjusted his pince-nez and then recognized Commandant Bazeries of the Deuxième Bureau.

Rousseau displayed his best manners as he made a brief introduction. "Inspector Lefebvre, I believe you know Commandant Bazeries?"

Achille smiled and shook the officer's hand. "Indeed I do. I'm pleased to see you Commandant, though frankly I'm puzzled. Has our case come to your bureau's attention?"

Bazeries was on the point of explaining when Rousseau broke in. "Gentlemen, I'm hungry," he said. "I suggest we discuss this matter over lunch."

Achille frowned and protested, "We hardly have time for a leisurely luncheon."

Rousseau shook his head and laughed. "I'm a big man with big appetites, as you well know, Inspector. Unlike you, I can't survive on coffee and cigarettes. We're going to be as busy as the devil the next day or two, so we might as well eat while we can. Now, I want a beer and a croque monsieur, so let's be off."

As they crossed to the Left Bank and proceeded up the boulevard, Achille speculated as to Bazeries's involvement. *It must have something to do with the code*, he thought. He had gone to great lengths to guard the secret. Was there a leak in his organization? Regardless, he found the officer's presence reassuring, evidence of Rousseau's good intentions. After all, Bazeries was a man of spotless reputation.

They arrived at the café and the proprietor seated them at Achille's favorite sidewalk table. Achille took Rousseau's advice and ordered a sandwich and a beer. Bazeries made do with coffee and a brioche.

"I won't keep you in suspense, Inspector, though what I'm about to tell you must remain strictly confidential," Rousseau said as soon as the proprietor was out of earshot. "I have a mole working in the Paris Okhrana. This individual reports directly to me—and me only. My agent has been providing me with information on de Gournay and early this morning identified him as the source of the leak at La Villette. I'd suspected de Gournay for some time, but Boguslavsky's death confirmed it. Now Orlovsky's in the shit because we've caught his best agent double-dealing. According to the mole, Orlovsky planted de Gournay among the anarchists to spy on them and provoke them to illegal acts, but not to feather his own nest at the expense of Russia and France."

"Pardon me, Inspector," Achille interrupted. "Did you say de Gournay *provoked* them to illegality?"

"You *have* heard the term agent provocateur, haven't you?" Rousseau replied.

"I was just wondering what our government would think of a foreign agent instigating crimes on French soil."

Rousseau smiled knowingly. "If by 'crimes on French soil' you mean dangerous subversives killing others of their ilk at the instigation of a friendly government, our superiors would *think* 'Thank you very much.' Of course, they would deny all knowledge of the affair and demand that we bring the killers to justice. May I continue?"

Rousseau had confirmed another of Achille's suspicions. "Please do," he said calmly.

"Now that de Gournay's gone rogue, M. Orlovsky will have to square things with his masters in Saint Petersburg. So far, he's playing it cool, acting as though nothing's gone wrong within his organization. His predicament could be to our advantage—he'll cooperate, and be indebted to us if we can pull his chestnuts out of the fire. That's where the commandant comes into the picture."

Bazeries paused a moment to brush a fly away from his beard. His eyes followed the insect until one of Rousseau's hands lashed out and dispatched the intruder.

"Our bureau has also had de Gournay under surveillance for several weeks, M. Lefebvre," Bazeries began. "When he first came to our attention, we thought he was a woman going by the name of Marie de Gournay. Regardless of gender, de Gournay has formed a liaison with a military attaché at the German Embassy. They have exchanged certain communications in code, which is how the matter came to me."

"Excuse me, Commandant. Is it a poem code, similar to the one used in the Marseilles smuggling case?" Achille asked.

Rousseau, who had been leering at a pair of pretty girls walking up the boulevard, stopped and stared at Achille. Bazeries raised his eyebrows. "Yes, Inspector," he answered. "Is that an educated guess, or did you know?"

Achille replied with another question. "Do they use a poem by Ronsard about a nightingale?"

"That's correct, Inspector. So you did know."

"I suspected de Gournay, but I knew nothing about the German."

"Wait a minute," Rousseau broke in. "You never said anything to me about a code."

"How could I tell you, my friend," Achille replied, "when your organization had a leak?"

Rousseau's face reddened. "It's not *my* organization," he fumed. "It's the fucking Russians."

His comment caught the attention of a couple at a nearby table.

"Please keep it down, Inspector," Achille said sotto voce.

Rousseau grunted and stared at his hands. "I'm hungry, that's all. Where's my bloody sandwich?"

As if on cue, the proprietor arrived with the order. As soon as the man left, Achille continued with a question for the commandant. "Has de Gournay passed on any secret information to the Germans?"

"Not to our knowledge. He's negotiating with them. We believe he's trying to sell a high-explosives formula that's relevant to your case. The Germans want it, but so far they haven't met de Gournay's demands."

"How much does he want?" Achille inquired.

"Two million francs. The Germans have offered him one."

"Did you know that one of my informers has been spying on de Gournay?"

The commandant nodded in the affirmative. "De Gournay's lackey works for us. He's provided a full report of their evening together."

"I see. Did you also know that de Gournay told my informer that he was leaving France soon and that he asked her to accompany him?"

"Yes, M. Lefebvre. We have that information."

Achille thought of Delphine. Would de Gournay risk going to the Divan Japonais so close to a critical meeting with his cell? Achille doubted it. Under the circumstances, he did not think Orlovsky would appear in public with his turncoat agent. Moreover, how could he arrest de Gournay at the Divan Japonais without creating a scandal that might compromise Delphine and the *Sûreté*? Much better, he thought, to capture or otherwise eliminate de Gournay away from his spymaster and out of the public eye.

He addressed his next question to Rousseau. "Does the code word 'Guest' mean anything to you?"

Rousseau was busy wolfing down his croque monsieur. He coughed loudly and continued hacking into his serviette.

The commandant slapped the inspector's back. "Are you all right?" he asked.

The crimson-faced detective nodded in the affirmative and held up his hand to signal: *One moment, please*. Rousseau took a long swig of beer to clear his throat. Then he turned to Achille. "How did you learn about 'Guest'?"

"We recently intercepted a message from de Gournay to his cell. They're meeting tomorrow morning at four to discuss 'Guest.'"

Rousseau lowered his voice. "'Guest' is a code name for the Russian foreign minister. He arrives in Paris tomorrow evening for a secret meeting with his French counterpart."

Now it was the commandant's turn to be surprised. "I knew nothing of this. My bureau should have been informed."

"With all due respect, Commandant," Rousseau replied, "this matter is in my brigade's jurisdiction."

Bazeries was about to make a sharp retort when Achille intervened. "Gentlemen, please. Let's not squabble over jurisdiction. From now on, we must coordinate closely and efficiently. Agreed?"

Bazeries and Rousseau concurred. Achille continued with reference to the cat burglar.

"One of the individuals we're investigating may be a common criminal, a burglar named Guy Renard."

"The Porter?" Rousseau interjected. "I thought he was safely locked up in a Belgian prison."

"Perhaps not," Achille replied. "We have photographs and a description that matches. Inspector Legros is wiring our Belgian contact for more information. At any rate, I have reason to believe there will be a burglary within the next twenty-four hours at Nazimova's bookstore."

"Why do you think that?" the commandant inquired.

"I believe Mme Nazimova kept some papers that belonged to her late husband, and it's likely the high-explosives formula was among the documents. Nazimova burned the papers just before she died, but de Gournay wouldn't know that. Perhaps she hid something more than copies of Boguslavsky's notes. Regardless, the papers would be something de

Gournay would not want us to find. And here's another twist. It's possible de Gournay worked as Nazimova's shop assistant under the name Marie Léglise, to spy on Nazimova and gain access to the documents.

"My detectives will arrest anyone who enters the shop. If it's Renard, I believe we can persuade him to rat on the others to save his neck. He's a professional thief, not a committed ideologue like the other members of de Gournay's cell. And I don't believe he was in on the murders, though we can still charge him as an accessory and co-conspirator if he doesn't cooperate."

"Will you take him to the Conciergerie and turn him over to the *juge* for interrogation?" Rousseau asked.

Achille frowned and shook his head. "No time for that, I'm afraid. I suggest you detail one of your men at the stakeout. We can turn the prisoner over to you, let your brigade handle the interrogation."

Rousseau grinned. "Don't worry, Achille. If we get him, we'll make him talk."

"Oh, I'm sure."

Rousseau shrugged and returned to his croque monsieur.

"Now," Achille continued, "we must take extra precautions to protect the Russian minister. Even if we make our arrests before he arrives, we can't take any chances. They may have planned for that contingency. What's his itinerary?"

Rousseau put down the remains of his sandwich and wiped his mouth with the back of his hand. "He arrives at Saint-Lazare station tomorrow evening, on an eight o'clock express from Le Havre. The meeting will be held in a suite at the Hotel Terminus."

Achille thought for a moment. "I'm afraid the express will have to make an unscheduled stop. The minister could detrain at Asnières and proceed to the hotel by coach, where we would escort him through the tradesmen's entrance and up to his suite. Orlovsky should be present to reassure the minister that it's a routine precaution. Can you arrange it?"

"I can," Rousseau replied.

"I have another question. If you were de Gournay, planning an assassination along the minister's travel route, what would be the most likely place for an ambush?"

Rousseau drummed his fingers on the table, and looked away as if in deep thought. After a moment, he answered with conviction, "The pedestrian overpass between the station and hotel would be a good spot. It's an enclosed space, about twenty meters from end to end, and narrow. A bomb would be devastating. Of course, the assassin would have to be fanatically devoted to his cause, since his chances of escape would be slim. But he'd certainly get publicity and set off a panic, which is what these terrorists want. Moreau and Wroblewski are mad enough to do the deed, but I'd say Moreau's the steadier of the two for a job like that."

"Thank you, Inspector. That's my thinking, too." Achille paused, then moved on to the next item on the agenda. "One problem is the timing of the arrests. Do we try to take them piecemeal to forestall further action on their part? Picking them up now would save us a lot of time and trouble, but what happens if we lose one or two of them?"

"I believe it may be best to wait for their four A.M. meeting, when all the rotten eggs are in one basket, so to speak. We'll set up a cordon on the Rue Ronsard, then enter the house and wait for them. We'll arm ourselves in case they put up a fight. What's more, the place might be a bomb factory, so we should alert the Fire Brigade and keep an explosives expert on hand. In the meantime, we'll maintain our surveillance on all the suspects. Are we in agreement?"

Bazeries frowned and said, "I'm a cryptographer, not a policeman or a spymaster. There's not much more I can do personally, but I'll inform the appropriate parties in my organization. I agree, Inspector."

Rousseau grunted and nodded in the affirmative.

"Two thoughts occurred to me that are worth considering," Achille said. "If de Gournay comes to trial, the facts of the case would raise an awful stink. Moreover, if the Germans will not pay full price for the explosives formula, I wonder what they would pay for the assassination of a Russian foreign minister traveling incognito on French soil, especially if we were to be blamed for lax security. That might nip our prospective alliance in the bud, don't you think?"

After a moment, Bazeries said gravely, "It might precipitate a war."

Rousseau drained the last drop of beer. He put down his glass and grinned at Achille. "It's a festival of shit, isn't it, Professor?"

"Are you speaking of life in general, or our particular situation?" Achille replied.

⧉

Achille had invited Bazeries and Rousseau to join him for his meeting with Féraud. Now, they sat in his office, watching as the chief paced around, his hands clasped behind his back, his teeth grinding away at an unlit cigar. After a few tense minutes, the chief stopped near his desk, took the chewed-up cigar out of his mouth, and stared at the small group of officers assembled before him, which now included Inspector Legros.

"Gentlemen, our duty is clear in this matter. The honor of France is at stake. I agree to Inspector Lefebvre's plan. The Russian minister will detrain at Asnières and I will greet him, along with a group of picked men and M. Orlovsky. If necessary, I'll defend our distinguished guest with my life."

Achille thought his chief's declaration overly dramatic, though it was not far from the truth. If the anarchists assassinated the Russian minister on Féraud's watch, he would be in the same position as General Ducrot at the Battle of Sedan: *Nous sommes dans un pot de chambre, et nous y serons emmerdés.*

The chief looked directly at Achille. "Inspector Lefebvre, I leave the matter of the arrests to you and Inspector Rousseau. My preference would be to bring them in now, but I understand that's impossible."

"That's correct, Chief," Achille replied. "We could arrest Moreau and Wroblewski immediately, but we're not sure about Renard. Unfortunately,

209

after he delivered his message our detectives lost track of him. Moreover, I'm afraid as of this morning, de Gournay's given us the slip. Fortunately, the Deuxième Bureau has him under close surveillance."

The chief scowled and turned to Bazeries. "Do your agents know de Gournay's present whereabouts, Commandant?"

Bazeries hesitated before answering, "I can't be certain, Chief Féraud. I haven't seen the latest report."

The chief pointed to the telephone on his desk. "Can you use this thing to communicate with your office?"

"I believe so," the commandant replied, somewhat dubiously, and went to the telephone. Bazeries began fidgeting with a pencil on the chief's desktop.

Rousseau rolled his eyes and tapped his foot in synchronization with the commandant's pencil. After a while, he began whistling a popular cabaret tune. The chief's icy glare stifled the impromptu performance. Rousseau looked down and twiddled his thumbs.

"Hello . . . hello. Am I connected with the Deuxième Bureau? Good. This is Commandant Bazeries. Ba-zeh-ree! Yes. Could you please connect me to Captain Duret? Yes, I'll wait." A few moments passed. "Good afternoon, Captain. Bazeries here. This matter is urgent. Do you have the de Gournay file at hand? Goor-nay! Yes, yes, of course I'll wait." A minute passed. "I'm here. Do you have the most recent report from our agent?" Bazeries sighed and glanced at the ceiling. Another minute passed. "Of course I'm still here. If I weren't here, I wouldn't be shouting into this damned contraption!" Bazeries frowned. "Yes, yes. Is that all? I see. Very well, Captain. Thank you. Good afternoon." Bazeries put down the receiver.

"Gentlemen, we've had no contact with our agent since yesterday," he announced to the assembled group with a downcast look. "He should have reported this morning, and he's punctual. Moreover, the house on the Rue de la Mire is empty. We've lost de Gournay."

"*Sacristi!*" the chief sputtered. "He's a slippery devil, and too clever by half. Achille, you'd better pray this bastard walks into your early-morning trap. In the meantime, don't lose sight of Moreau and Wroblewski and do your best to catch Renard."

Then the chief turned to Rousseau. "Inspector, I want to meet with Orlovsky to make arrangements for the minister's arrival. We must notify the railway management and hotel immediately. As soon as our preparations are made, I'll report to the prefect." Finally, he thanked Bazeries. "Commandant, as always I appreciate your assistance. I leave the business with the Germans to you and your bureau. I've enough on my plate for now."

The officers dispersed without further comment, each among them thinking that this case was indeed a "festival of shit." Whether or not that sad state of affairs applied to life in general was a problem best left to the philosophers.

11

ENDGAME

P lease permit me to escort you to your apartment." Lautrec made this gentlemanly offer to Delphine following her performance at the Divan Japonais. His gesture was more than mere politeness; it reflected his genuine concern for her safety.

"That's very kind of you, Monsieur, but I've been walking these streets for years and I know how to take care of myself." Her reply was not bravado; Delphine carried a razor in her purse and she was quite capable of using it to fend off an attack. Moreover, she knew how Lautrec struggled up the steep winding streets and stairways of the Butte. She did not want to add to his misery without reason.

A light rain fell on the Rue des Martyrs. The crowd had scattered and moved on to their beds, *boîtes*, brothels, or whatever other amusement was obtainable at that late hour. De Gournay, Orlovsky, and the girls were not among the audience that evening, much to Delphine's relief. She hoped never to see de Gournay again, though not because she feared him. Rather, she felt an unwanted attraction to Inspector Lefebvre's adversary.

Delphine turned in the direction of the Rue des Abbesses and Lautrec bid her good evening. He descended the dark street in the direction of the still-lively boulevard, his tapping cane echoing on the pavement, while she trudged upward on strong legs, walking as rapidly as her high-heeled leather boots would permit on the rain-slicked pavement.

She turned the corner and walked on through silent squares, past shuttered houses, shops, and alleys alive with whining cats. When she reached the narrow, unlit passage with its precipitous stairway climbing to the Rue Lepic, she paused. Sensing something ominous in the shadows, she glanced around and then reached into her purse. She drew out the razor and felt for her other weapon, a hatpin that she could resort to as a backup in a tight corner. Having checked her weapons, she raised her skirts halfway to her knees and started up the slippery stairs.

As she reached the summit and turned onto the street, she took comfort from the gas lamps and the glimmering yellow lights in a few unshuttered windows. Her apartment was only two blocks ahead. She recalled how her best friend and lover, Virginie Ménard, had walked this way in the early morning hours, the final moments of her brief, tragic life.

As she neared the gated entrance to her flat, she heard a low, familiar voice calling her from a murky passageway. Her grip tightened on the razor, her thumb poised to flick it open with a well-practiced action. She approached cautiously until she made out the obscure form of a woman hidden in shadows.

"Is that you, Mado?" she asked.

"Yes, Delphine. Please come closer; there's something I must say to you."

Delphine shook her head. "I'm sorry. If you want to speak to me, step forward and show yourself."

The figure revealed itself in lamplight. Delphine recognized de Gournay's form and features through the slanting raindrops. "I've met you halfway. Won't you do me the same courtesy?"

Delphine took one step and halted. "Whatever you have to say, please say it now. It's late, and I'm wet and tired."

"I told you I was leaving Paris and I asked you to come with me. I offered you money and I regret it. I believe I insulted you. I wanted to apologize."

"Put your mind at ease, Mado. I'm not insulted. Your offer was simply too generous. I've sold my body for much less than that."

De Gournay smiled sadly. "Your body, perhaps, but never your heart."

Delphine had loved one woman and one man. The former was dead, the latter unattainable. She felt something for de Gournay, but she knew it was not love. "You're too romantic. Goodbye, Mado."

"Just one moment," de Gournay cried, "that's all. I wanted to tell you that our evening was the happiest of my life. You understand what it's like to be . . . different. I've never understood, never really knew who or what I was until I met you. Now, I must leave Paris, perhaps never to return. But I'd like to know your true feelings. Please say you don't despise me. Give me a little hope. Can you at least do that much for me?"

At that moment, Delphine understood her feelings for de Gournay—compassion for an outcast. But despite her empathy, she could never betray Achille.

"I don't hate you, Mado, but I could never love you. I don't wish you harm, but I never want to see you again."

De Gournay reached out to her with one hand, as if he were a drowning man grasping for a lifeline. Delphine turned from him and walked toward the bell-pull. Faced with the finality of her declaration and the futility of his position, de Gournay retreated into the darkness and disappeared.

The concierge answered the bell and opened the gate. Delphine passed into the courtyard and entered the front door. Across the street, Moïse huddled under a blanket behind an overflowing *poubelle* in a cramped, arched passage. Le Boudin had ordered the *chiffonier* to keep a close watch on Delphine. *She's safe for tonight.*

For an instant, Moïse considered tailing the strange woman. *Inspector Lefebvre might make it worth my while.* But he had his orders. He stretched out his hand and felt the heavy drops. *The devil with it,* he decided. *No need to traipse all over the Butte in filthy weather.*

He settled back in his damp hidey-hole, fixing his eyes on Delphine's room until the shutters closed and the lamp went out.

∽

Clouds covered the moon. The streetlamps below left the rooftops cloaked in shadow. His feet encased in plimsolls, Renard crept noiselessly over slippery roof tiles. The cat burglar wore gloves and tight-fitting black clothing. A knit cap covered his head and a mixture of grease and soot darkened his face. He crawled up to the cornice, where he rested for a moment. Then he took a deep breath, braced himself, and leapt across the narrow space between buildings, landing with a dull thud on the roof over Nazimova's shop.

Two detectives observed Renard's progress from their surveillance post, an unlit fifth-story window in a building across the boulevard. One of the detectives nodded to his companion before opening and closing the shutter on his lantern, a signal to their counterparts on the street. The police waiting below spotted the signal and walked across the street to the shop entrance.

Unaware of the looming police presence, Renard crouched on the roof and scampered to the skylight. There he removed tools of his trade from a canvas bag securely fastened to his leather belt: a glasscutter, a lump of putty, and a clean rag. After drying the selected pane, he applied putty to prevent glass fragments from falling noisily onto the landing below. Then he began cutting near the skylight latch.

He worked swiftly. After a moment, he removed the cut glass, lifted the skylight, and propped it open. He eased himself through the opening, hung by his hands from the sill, and then dropped to the landing.

Renard clutched a small bull's-eye lantern dangling from a hook on his belt. He struck a match on his thumbnail to light the wick, then raised the lamp and scanned his surroundings. The cone of white light revealed the door to Nazimova's bedroom and the narrow stairway leading down to the small room in the back of the shop. The burglar walked downstairs and entered the back room, where he spied the mantelpiece and went straight for the loose brick in the hearth.

"Stop, in the name of the law!" a detective shouted.

Renard glanced over his shoulder into the glare of two unshuttered lanterns. The burglar flung his lantern at the police and bolted for the stairway. The detectives cursed and ran after him.

Renard mounted the landing and leaped for the skylight sill. Pulling up with powerful arms, he was almost halfway through the skylight when a warning shot hit the wall just below the burglar's dangling feet.

"Stop, or the next shot won't miss!" the detective cried.

Renard lowered himself and leaned back against the wall with his hands up. Trembling, he glared at the approaching detectives. The cramped space reeked with the sharp stench of sweat and gunpowder.

His smoking revolver at the ready, the detective climbed the stairs with his partner close behind. Upon reaching the landing, he pointed his gun at Renard's belly. "Pull another stunt like that and you'll wish you were dead. Face the wall and lower your hands behind your back."

The burglar complied without a word. The second detective stepped forward and bound Renard's hands tightly before patting him down for weapons, while his partner kept their quarry covered with his pistol. When the detective was satisfied that his quarry was defenseless, he grabbed Renard by the shoulder, spun him around, and slammed a fist into his gut. Renard doubled over in pain, retching, and puked on the carpet.

"That'll teach you not to fuck with us," the first detective growled.

"It was a fair cop," his partner added. "An old pro like you should have known better. Now you're going to have a nice chat with Inspector Rousseau, so you'd better behave yourself."

Renard's eyes widened. "Rousseau?"

The detectives laughed. The first detective holstered his revolver and said, "You should see your face, Renard—like a comedian who just got his rear whacked with a slapstick. You'd better be nice and sing like a bird for Rousseau, or the clochards will have your guts for fish bait. Now let's get a move on. We mustn't keep the inspector waiting."

⌀

At four A.M., Moreau and Wroblewski arrived at the house on the Rue Ronsard. Moreau turned the latchkey and they entered the front hallway. The blinding white light of several police lanterns greeted them.

"Laurent Moreau and Leon Wroblewski," Achille said, "I arrest you in the name of the law."

The pair replied by turning to run, but landed in the arms of two beefy officers. A struggle ensued, ending when a gendarme whipped out his truncheon and cracked the back of Wroblewski's skull. Stunned, the fugitive dropped to his knees like a poleaxed ox. Seeing his companion fall at his side and realizing the hopelessness of the situation, Moreau gave up the fight and surrendered.

The officers bound the prisoners and dragged them to Achille and Legros.

"Where's Rossignol?" Achille demanded.

Wroblewski, his eyes glazed over, shook his head and mumbled incoherently. Moreau scowled and spat in the inspector's face. Achille calmly wiped the spittle with a handkerchief; his partner was not so unflappable.

"Filthy swine!" Legros struck Moreau's face with the back of his hand, knocking the prisoner down. Legros's signet ring split Moreau's lip and cracked a tooth. "Stay on your knees and lick the floor!"

Achille put his hand on his partner's shoulder. "That's enough, Étienne." He ordered the gendarmes to stand the prisoner up.

The officers grabbed Moreau's bound arms and lifted him to his feet. One of the gendarmes yanked the prisoner's hair and held his head in Achille's direction.

"It's over, Moreau," Achille said calmly. "You're facing the guillotine or transportation. Cooperate, and we'll recommend leniency. I'll ask one more time. Where is Rossignol?"

Moreau scowled. "Go to hell."

"Take them to the Conciergerie," Achille ordered.

The officers carried the groaning, semi-conscious Wroblewski feet-first out the door. Moreau followed. As soon as he was in the street, Moreau cried, "You may cut off our heads, but the voice of the people will be heard. Long live anarchy!" Several dogs barked in reply.

"Gag him before he wakes the whole neighborhood," Achille directed. Then he turned to his partner and shook his head. "De Gournay's given us the slip. All we have are the pawns. I wonder what Rousseau's doing with Renard."

"Getting valuable information, I hope," Legros replied. "I'm sure the Porter will talk to save his neck. Among other things, our Belgian friends said he's a gutless canary. However, I doubt the *juge* will get anything out of Moreau or Wroblewski."

Achille nodded his agreement. "They aren't cowards, if that's what you mean. They want to be martyrs for the cause, but scoundrels have duped and betrayed them and their ideals. Who will profit from their sacrifice? De Gournay? Orlovsky? Others of their ilk? Anyway, the poor fools we arrested this morning wouldn't believe us if we told them. I'm afraid there's no chance of justice in this case unless we catch Rossignol."

Legros tried to lift his partner's spirit with a sanguine observation. "Sergeant Rodin's men are searching the house on the Rue de la Mire. Maybe de Gournay's hiding there?"

"That would be too lucky, my friend," Achille said with a sigh. "At any rate, they should be reporting soon. In the meantime, let's go to the cellar and see what the chemist has found."

The police had entered the house and begun searching a few hours earlier. An expert from the Central Explosives Laboratory accompanied them. They were particularly concerned about the potential hazard from a cache of nitroglycerin.

Achille and Legros went down to the cellar, where they found the chemist and another detective examining a stockpile of explosives and weapons by the light of kerosene lamps. The chemist crouched by a box in a corner, sifting through its contents until he heard the inspectors approach. He turned his head and smiled up at Achille.

"I've some good news, Inspector. There's no nitro down here. We've found dynamite, gelignite, blasting caps and fuses, and an interesting timing device. But once it's all been inventoried, it will be safe to transport."

"I see," Achille replied. "So there's no evidence they were making an explosive from a formula?"

The chemist got up and walked over to Achille and Legros. "No, Inspector, they have neither the equipment nor the chemicals required for manufacturing explosives. They either purchased or stole everything. Everything, that is, except for the timer, which is quite ingenious."

"May I see it?"

The chemist led Achille and Legros to a workbench in the middle of the basement. "As you can see, it's a cheap alarm clock connected to a detonator. It could be placed in a parcel or briefcase, left somewhere, and timed to explode after the bomber had made his escape."

Achille lifted the device and examined it carefully. "Yes, it's devilishly clever, all right." He set down the mechanism and added, "I appreciate your efforts, Professor. Your assistance in this case has been invaluable."

The chemist smiled and shook Achille's extended hand. "I'm glad to be of service, Inspector." He paused before asking, "Do you anticipate more cases of this nature?"

"Yes, I'm afraid so. It's the way of our world, after all."

The chemist frowned and shook his head. "Ah, yes. *Our* world." He looked Achille in the eye. "What then must we do?"

∽

Chief Féraud folded his hands, leaned forward over his desk, and stared at his lead investigators, clearly impatient. "Well, gentlemen, three out of four isn't bad. And we have all their explosives and weapons, haven't we?"

Achille, Legros, and Rousseau sat facing the chief. A tense moment of silence passed among them before Achille replied, "I'm sorry, Chief. We can't claim victory with de Gournay on the loose. As for the explosives and weapons, we have no idea what he took with him as he went to ground. We need more information, but one of our prisoners is in the hospital with a concussion and the other's withstood the magistrate's grilling for hours."

"I'd make him talk," Rousseau broke in.

"I'm afraid that's impossible, Inspector, as M. Lefebvre has placed them in the magistrate's custody." The chief glared at Achille, his meaning clear: Féraud would have handled the matter differently.

Rousseau noticed the chief's displeasure and grinned. "My canary's been singing his little heart out. I'm confident he's told us everything he knows. The plan was to bomb the Café Terminus this evening. Our prisoners would get their final marching orders this morning at four. De Gournay must have gotten wise to our planned raids, but too late to tip off his confederates."

"Did Renard say anything about the papers he was sent to steal?" Achille asked.

"No, it was just another job to him, like the Kadyshev burglary. De Gournay paid the burglar and told him where to go and what to look for. Renard also took care of Boguslavsky in the La Villette storehouse for a while, brought him food and so forth. He swears he had nothing to do with the killings. He says that was de Gournay's, Moreau's, and Wroblewski's work, and he'll testify against them."

"Do you believe him?" Achille pressed.

Rousseau turned to Achille with a sarcastic smile. "Really, Achille, do you think the little rat would lie to *me*?"

Achille addressed his next comment to the chief. "I believe the café bombing was planned as a diversion. De Gournay's target is the Russian foreign minister."

"Are you still convinced of that?" Féraud asked.

"I can't be certain without further evidence, but I believe the assassination plot is most probable."

The chief seemed confused. "Please explain, Achille."

"The minister, traveling incognito, was scheduled to arrive at Saint-Lazare station on the Le Havre express at eight o'clock tonight. We must presume that de Gournay has no knowledge of our plan to have the minister detrain at Asnières. The Café Terminus is just around the corner from the station. A bombing shortly before the train's arrival would create panic that would soon spread through the hotel and the station. De Gournay could kill the minister as he stepped onto the platform and escape during the confusion."

"That makes sense," Rousseau said, "but with Moreau and Wroblewski in custody, who would throw the bomb at the café?"

A timid knock on the door interrupted the discussion. The chief growled, "Enter."

A nervous clerk opened the door a crack and poked his head in. "I apologize for the interruption, M. Féraud, but there's a gentleman here to see you. He says it's most urgent."

"I gave strict instructions not to be disturbed. Who is he?"

"Uh . . . it's Commandant Bazeries."

"Bazeries? Of course we'll see him."

The commandant entered the office and took a chair next to Achille. He did not keep the group in suspense. "I have good news, gentlemen. Captain Duret has made contact with the Lackey."

The chief seemed bewildered. "Which lackey is that, Commandant?"

"I apologize. 'The Lackey' is a code name for our agent, de Gournay's servant."

"I sometimes get confused with all this cloak-and-dagger. Please continue."

Bazeries nodded and smiled politely. "With your permission, Chief Féraud. As you may recall, the Lackey failed to report on schedule, which had Duret worried. We now have an explanation for this sudden change in our agent's behavior. The man's terrified. De Gournay, who is ordinarily very cool in his actions, has suddenly seemed desperate and erratic. They left the house on the Rue de la Mire late last night and checked into a hotel on the Rue de Parme as the Viscount de Saint-Valery and manservant."

"The Rue de Parme? That's not far from the railway station," the chief remarked.

"That's correct, Monsieur," Bazeries replied. "Unfortunately, de Gournay's not there at present. We've lost track of him again."

"Pardon me, Commandant," Achille said, "but you said your agent is terrified. Is there something specific that's worrying him?"

"De Gournay left a package and five hundred francs compensation with his servant, with instructions to leave the parcel under a table at the Café Terminus at eight o'clock this evening."

"My God, it's a bomb!" Achille exclaimed. He turned to Bazeries. "Before you joined us, we were discussing de Gournay's plot to bomb the café. Inspector Rousseau questioned who would throw the bomb with Moreau and Wroblewski in custody. With the information you've provided, I'm now certain of the answer. I believe de Gournay means for the Lackey to plant it unknowingly.

"This morning, an explosives expert from the Central Laboratory helped us search the house on the Rue Ronsard. In the course of the investigation, he discovered a new type of infernal machine, which we subsequently took as evidence. The device has an ingenious mechanism employing a common alarm clock and an electric detonator. A dry-cell battery provides the electricity. Boguslavsky tinkered with that sort of thing."

"What the deuce is a dry-cell battery?" the chief inquired.

"It's a recent invention," Achille replied. "It's much more compact than a wet-cell battery, portable, and adaptable. Electric ignition makes a lit fuse unnecessary. The bomber can set the clockwork mechanism to give him time to escape. At any rate, I believe de Gournay planned the café as a diversion, rather than the primary target.

"In my opinion, he intends to assassinate the 'Guest.' Initially, I thought they would attempt the deed by lobbing a bomb into the overpass connecting the station with the hotel. Now, I think it's more likely to occur on the platform. I believe that would give de Gournay a better chance for escape. Moreover, I believe his motivation is money rather than ideology, but I still don't know who's paying him, other than the Russians whom he has betrayed." He turned to Bazeries. "Does the Deuxième Bureau suspect the Germans?"

Bazeries answered firmly, "We do not, Inspector. The Germans would pay for the high-explosives formula, but they would not be so rash as to instigate an assassination that would provoke an international crisis."

"Are you certain they wouldn't try it, if the anarchists were blamed?" Achille asked.

Bazeries shook his head and remained firm. "In our opinion, they would not risk it."

"I agree," Féraud said. "Besides, I'm a police officer. Matters of foreign affairs are outside my sphere of operations, thank God. From my perspective, our job is to prevent the assassination and the bombing and, if possible, capture or kill de Gournay. We already have a plan for the former, we now need one for the latter, and time is short."

"I have an idea, Chief, but it requires precise coordination among our police brigades, as well as the assistance of the Deuxième Bureau and the explosives expert, Professor Martin."

"Very well, Achille," the chief replied. "I leave it in your capable hands. I'm off to report to the prefect, and then I must meet with M. Orlovsky and discuss our plan for meeting the minister's train at Asnières."

⌘

At seven o'clock, the Lackey stepped into a *pissoir* on the Rue d'Amsterdam. Captain Duret was waiting at the urinal. They exchanged parcels, identically wrapped in brown paper and bound with string, and then the captain walked out without a word. A minute later, the Lackey exited with a tremendous sigh of relief and proceeded down the busy thoroughfare in the direction of the railway station and Hotel Terminus.

Captain Duret walked in the opposite direction, toward a closed coach parked near the Hotel Britannia. The driver opened the door and the captain stepped up into the dark interior, where Professor Martin waited patiently. The door closed and the driver climbed to his box, snapped the reins, and clicked at his horses. They pulled away from the curb and soon broke into a quick trot.

The captain handed the parcel over gingerly. "Do you think we have enough time?"

The professor received the package and cradled it in his lap. With a faint smile, he replied, "I sincerely hope so. At any rate, I've studied the mechanism. If we can't make it to the arsenal, I'll try to disarm the bomb in the coach. I trust you've paid your insurance premiums?"

∞

Achille stood near the gate separating the concourse from the train shed, scanning the immense iron-and-glass structure. Several plainclothes officers patrolled the area, awaiting a signal from Achille.

Arriving and departing trains belched smoke and hissed steam, saturating the atmosphere with a thick grayish haze. The sky above the sooty glass panes was pitch dark, moonless and starless, but the concrete platforms stretching out beyond the shed into the busy rail yard were ablaze with rows of electric lamps. Passengers bustled in and out; porters stacked and hauled baggage; guards blew their whistles and slammed carriage doors shut; chuffing engines shuttled back and forth; wheels rumbled and brakes squealed.

Legros approached from the crowded concourse and tapped Achille's shoulder. "Good news, Inspector. The Lackey made the switch on schedule."

Achille checked his watch. The captain and chemist had barely one hour to take the bomb to a safe location and disarm or explode it. "Let's wish them well, Étienne. We'll need a bit of good luck, too."

"You haven't spotted him yet?" Legros asked.

"Not yet. Though with the exception of Rousseau, who's met him, we're all working from descriptions. De Gournay's a chameleon. Who knows what color he'll display this evening?"

Legros smiled. "I doubt he'll play the female. Skirts, high-heeled shoes, and a corset would be quite a nuisance if he had to make a run for it."

Rousseau joined them. "Tsk-tsk, Inspectors. Talking about women's unmentionables, eh? I'm shocked."

Achille scrutinized his colleague, who wore a railway guard's cap and uniform and hid his face behind a false beard and glasses. "Nice disguise, my friend. Have you been taking lessons from the elusive Rossignol?"

"It's no joke, Lefebvre," Rousseau snorted. "I've the best chance of identifying him, but without a disguise he'd recognize me on the spot."

"I'm sorry, old man," Achille said, and smirked, "but you do look elegant in that outfit. Perhaps the railway will take you on when you retire from the force."

Rousseau shook his head with a frown. "Enough clowning, Achille. I know it helps when we're all on edge, but he could show up at any minute, armed and desperate. Have your men closed off all his escape routes?"

"He'll be blocked if he tries to go through the station or to cross over to the hotel. His only way out is through the rail yard."

"What good would that do him?" Rousseau asked.

"I haven't a clue," Achille replied. "Maybe he could climb the Pont de l'Europe?"

"How the hell would he do that?" Rousseau growled.

"Damned if I know."

"Then we'll be up against a trapped rat; there's nothing worse. God help us if he grabs a hostage." Rousseau looked up the platform. "Where is the bastard? The Le Havre train's on schedule; it must be nearing the Batignolles tunnel." His eyes darted around the milling throng. After a moment, he grabbed Achille's arm and whispered in his ear, "Keep quiet, and look over there."

Rousseau nudged Achille in the direction of a man entering the platform with a Gladstone bag in his left hand. He was a young man wearing a nondescript brown suit and a slouch hat with the brim pulled down low over his forehead.

"Do you see him?" Rousseau hissed. "That's Rossignol."

Achille tapped Legros's arm and then signaled his men with a hand to his bowler's brim. A squad of plainclothes detectives and gendarmes began closing in on the subject. As soon as the man stopped, the police halted and waited for another signal from Achille.

"He's mine, Lefebvre," Rousseau snapped and began moving toward de Gournay.

Achille grabbed the inspector's coat sleeve. "Don't be a fool. Let's take him as we planned."

Rousseau shook him off. "It's my affair!"

The blast of the signalman's horn echoed through the train shed, the express train arriving on time. "Damn him," Achille muttered. He turned to Legros. "Follow me."

The express chugged into the platform bay, enveloped in a cloud of steam. The crowd stirred as the train screeched to a halt. Rousseau approached the suspect rapidly; he was more than two meters ahead of Achille and Legros. A great arm extended; a strong hand gripped the suspect's shoulder.

"You're under arrest, de Gournay!" Rousseau bellowed.

In an instant, de Gournay spun around, whipped out a British Bulldog, and aimed. Rousseau swatted at the pistol, knocking it out of de Gournay's hand and deflecting the shot, but not before the Bulldog barked. A .44

caliber ball slammed into Rousseau's shoulder. Rousseau staggered from the impact and lost his grip on the prisoner. De Gournay turned and fled up the platform, shoving aside screaming passengers and swinging his heavy Gladstone bag to clear the way.

Achille and Legros ran to Rousseau, with the plainclothes detectives close behind. Three officers continued pursuing de Gournay while Achille and Legros stopped to aid their fallen comrade.

Rousseau grasped his bleeding shoulder and swore. When Achille tried to help him, he exclaimed, "Damn it, Achille, I'm all right. Get after him!"

Without a moment's hesitation, Achille dashed up the platform, his strong rower's legs soon outpacing the other pursuing officers. He fixed his eyes on his quarry, running several meters ahead.

"Stop! *Sûreté!*" he cried, but only once to save his breath. As he neared the end of the train shed, his lungs and muscles ached, and he regretted his coffee-and-cigarette diet. When he reached the vast excavation through which trains entered and exited the station, a gust caught his bowler and blew it onto the tracks.

De Gournay ran on past startled switchmen and signalmen, into the brightly lit expanse of the rail yard. Far above, the light on the signal tower flashed red as a flaming star. As he gained on the fugitive, Achille wondered, *Where is he going? What's in the bag?*

Two blasts of a horn signaled an approaching train. In the near distance, on the other side of the Pont de l'Europe, an express roared out of the tunnel at forty miles per hour. Men rushed to throw switches; the light on the tower turned green. De Gournay jumped off the platform and sprinted across three lines of double track. A signalman shouted a warning.

Achille kept running toward the switching hut at the end of the platform. *Crazy bastard! He'll never make it.* He bent over next to a signalman, gasping for air as the train rushed by.

Achille caught his breath and straightened up, and turned toward the signalman. "I'm Lefebvre of the *Sûreté*. That man's a fugitive. Did he make it?"

The man pointed toward a concrete abutment on the other side of the sunken roadway. "Look over there, Monsieur."

De Gournay was standing on the abutment. He had opened the bag and set it down on the pavement. He pulled out a rope attached to a grappling hook, swung the hook around, and cast it toward the bridge's iron latticework guardrail. It bounced off the railing.

Achille grabbed his revolver. "Is it safe to cross?"

"Yes, Monsieur, if you're quick about it!"

Achille leapt off the platform and ran over the tracks, just as Legros and the three pursuing officers reached the switching hut.

The grappling hook took hold on the second try. De Gournay was climbing the masonry pier as Achille mounted the abutment.

"Give it up, de Gournay!" he cried. "I'll shoot!"

De Gournay ignored the warning; he was within reach of the girders. Achille fired a shot above the fugitive's head that ricocheted off the pier. De Gournay kept climbing. Achille's second shot ripped into de Gournay's lower back, near the spine. He screamed, dangled by one hand for a moment, and then fell backwards onto the concrete three meters below.

Smoking revolver in hand, Achille walked to his quarry and stared down into the fading eyes. De Gournay gazed up at the inspector. A tear streamed down his pale cheek; blood foamed and bubbled on quivering lips.

"Was it worth it?" Achille murmured.

Legros and the detectives ran to him. "Should we call for an ambulance?" Legros asked.

"Yes, for Inspector Rousseau," Achille replied. "As for this one, he's meat for the Morgue."

De Gournay heard these words, and nothing more.

⌘

Rousseau occupied a ward bed at the Hôtel-Dieu, the recently rebuilt hospital located conveniently near both police headquarters and the Morgue.

Curtains surrounded the cramped bed, providing a modicum of privacy, though the flimsy partitions could not screen out the occasional cries and groans of the other patients.

Achille sat on a crude wooden chair crammed between the bed and a table upon which rested a glass and pitcher, a spoon, two brown medicine bottles, and the morning newspaper.

"Are the sisters taking good care of you?" Achille inquired of Rousseau.

The inspector grimaced. "The nuns are like prison guards—cold, ugly, and efficient. They feed me swill three times a day and empty the chamber pot when the crap comes out the other end."

Achille smiled. "According to the surgeon, you won't be here much longer. The wound's clean and you're healing well."

Rousseau shifted about and scratched at his dressing. "It itches like the devil," he grumbled. "They say that's a good sign. Anyway, I'm like the great Napoleon. 'The bullet that will kill me is not yet cast.'"

Achille contemplated his former partner with mixed feelings. He questioned Rousseau's methods, especially the brutal treatment of prisoners. In addition, Rousseau's rash departure from Achille's plan to arrest de Gournay could have resulted in tragedy. On the other hand, Achille admired Rousseau's bravery and tenacity. And, as Chief Féraud indicated, the two inspectors would have to continue working together for the common good.

"I'll never question your motives or actions at the railway station," he said. "You disarmed a dangerous criminal and took a bullet in defense of the public and your brother officers. That's what I put in my report."

"That's generous of you, Achille, and well-spoken—as befits a chief of detectives. Your promotion is certain. Féraud and I go back many years. We've remained close, and he still confides in me. He's already recommended you to succeed him. Féraud has a nice pension along with his Officers' Cross. He's retiring to the country to live like a gentleman. I can see him resting beneath a willow tree on the bank of a stream, his fishing rod tucked under an arm and a jug of wine at his side, snoring away while crafty trout snatch the bait off his hook. You'll take his place in Paris, reeling in the murderers and crooks."

"As you said, you and the chief go back a long way. I suppose you know him better than anyone on the force."

"We've known each other twenty-five years, and more. He was my sergeant when I was a green kid fresh off the street. He taught me everything I know. We're nothing but old bones now, like the dinosaurs. You and Legros are the future. For what it's worth, I think Legros is a damn good man. I credit you for bringing him along."

"The prefect and Féraud consider the case closed," Achille said, changing the subject. "We were lucky with the bomb; Professor Martin defused it just in time. The prosecutor has charged Moreau and Wroblewski with the murders of Kadyshev and Boguslavsky. The *juge* is certain they'll both get the guillotine. Renard will testify against them and receive a light sentence.

"The government is suppressing the facts surrounding the attempted assassination and bombing, as the minister was here incognito. Officially, de Gournay died while resisting arrest as an accomplice to the murders.

"The Russians are pleased—as is our government. And the public is satisfied as well. People in high places will profit from the shared explosives formula and the improved relations that could lead to a Franco-Russian alliance. But I'm damned if I know why de Gournay acted as he did. Who paid him to take such a risk, and how much?

"I saw de Gournay on a slab at the Morgue. The poor devil had no penis. That's why he hid himself from Delphine. Imagine having to live as a man with something like that." Achille shook his head and sighed. "Perhaps Rossignol is one of those great mysteries we weren't meant to solve."

Rousseau rolled his eyes in the direction of the newspaper resting on the bedside table. "Have you read the latest edition of *Les Amis de la Vérité?*"

"No, I have not."

"You should, my friend. They're piping the tune and all the others are joining the dance. I read paragraph after paragraph about M. Lefebvre, France's greatest detective. I get two lines. I know them by heart: 'Inspector Rousseau received a wound in the line of duty. His doctors say he is making rapid progress toward a complete recovery.'

"I understand you and Adele will dine with the prefect when you return from Trouville. Monsieur and Madame Junot are sure to be there. Be careful, Achille. You may find the salons of the rich and powerful more treacherous than the back alleys of Montmartre."

Achille stared at his hands. After a moment, he looked up and said, "Orlovsky wants a meeting at my earliest convenience."

Rousseau screwed up his face in disgust. "Watch out for Orlovsky. He's a serpent. The Okhrana likes to divert attention from their crimes by pointing fingers at convenient scapegoats. This time it was the anarchists; tomorrow it might be the Marxists, or the Tsar's favorite villains, the Jews. Orlovsky's already scheming with the anti-Semitic journalists here in Paris."

"I'll keep that in mind."

The partition curtain stirred and then drew back, revealing a nun bearing a steaming bowl of broth on a tray. Achille rose from his chair and respectfully removed his hat.

Rousseau grinned sarcastically. "Ah, here comes Sister Clare with my afternoon dose of rat poison."

The nun pointedly ignored Rousseau. She placed the tray on the table and then turned to Achille with a smile. "We're honored by your presence, M. Lefebvre. All France is grateful for your service."

Achille flushed crimson. "Thank you, sister," he murmured.

Rousseau laughed until his wound ached.

12

Laws are spider webs through which the big
flies pass and the little ones get caught.

—Honoré de Balzac

TROUVILLE

*F**aites vos jeux, mesdames et messieurs!"*

The starter made his familiar call for bets. Adele ventured two francs on Number 4, the handsome tin jockey in green silks. She received her ticket and dropped two francs into the betting cup. The *Salle des Petits Jeux* filled with a clamor of players gathered around the tables, the most vociferous action emanating from the crowd surrounding the *Petits-Chevaux* track. Men and women reached out with their one- and two-franc

232

bets; little boys and girls jumped up and down and tugged at their parents' sleeves, begging them to place a wager on their favorite ponies.

Adele and Achille had been playing for nearly an hour and were even. "This is our last bet, Adele," Achille said. "It's a mug's game. The house always wins."

"Don't be such a stick in the mud," she teased. "We've got ten-to-one this time, and I've a good feeling about the color green."

Achille shrugged, shook his head, and clasped her hand gently.

The starter made his final call and the betting closed. He yanked the lever and the mechanical horses began whirling around the track. The players and spectators cried with excitement followed by hushed, intense observation. The casino game transported the vacationing Parisians to Longchamp, little tin horses like snorting thoroughbreds, their hooves pounding turf, and toy jockeys more like animated riders, whipping their galloping mounts.

After a few circuits of the table, the machine ran down. As the mechanical horses neared their goal, the crowd stirred and began shouting encouragement.

Adele watched intently until her horse edged out Number 5. "We won, darling! We won!" she cried and hugged Achille so tightly it hurt.

The losers ripped their stubs and dropped them on the floor. Some glared enviously at Adele as she received a twenty-franc Napoleon from the starter.

She held up the glittering gold piece for Achille's inspection. "You see, darling, I was right about green. Shall we play again?"

Achille smiled. "Twenty francs is a fortune. Let's quit while we're ahead. It's a lovely evening. We can take a walk on the pier."

"All right," she replied, and deposited the coin in her purse.

They exited the casino and walked arm in arm up the esplanade to the promenade pier. Nearby, a band played excerpts from *Mignon* by Thomas. Plangent tones of woodwinds and brass echoed over the beach, mingling with the cries of circling seabirds and rushing surf. Clouds drifted through a purple sky tinged gold from the sun lowering toward the horizon. A

mild, salty breeze ruffled capes and coattails, and sudden gusts threatened
any hat not firmly pinned.

The men, women, and children on the pier for an early-evening stroll
represented nearly all the Parisian classes one might encounter on the
boulevards and in the public parks. At Trouville, the fashionable aristo-
crats and haute bourgeoisie mingled comfortably with the lower middle
classes and an infusion of foreign tourists. As Achille glanced to his right
toward the hotels lining the esplanade, he noticed several flags fluttering
in the breeze. No matter the time or circumstances, he could never see
the tricolor without feeling a sense of pride, obligation, and a call to duty.

Achille and Adele passed up the promenade, greeted by several Parisians. Adele seemed to take this recognition in stride, but Achille felt a
keen sense of embarrassment. Regardless, with the publicity of the Hanged
Man case and Achille's impending promotion, the inspector would have
to become comfortable with it. The thought of his new responsibilities
weighed heavily on his mind, even in his happiest moments. That evening, they would dine with millionaires, a self-styled baron and his wife
who had taken them up the first day they arrived at the hotel. Adele was
flattered, but Achille sensed self-seeking personalities and a penchant for
bribery lurking behind the smiles and social graces.

Toward the end of the pier, Achille and Adele walked to the railing
and spent a few quiet minutes gazing out into the channel. Achille focused
on a trail of brown smoke drifting behind a steamer bound for England,
raising thoughts of his contacts at Scotland Yard. As soon as he returned
to headquarters, he would wire the Special Branch to obtain more information about the Okhrana's British operations.

The great nations were playing a dangerous game that would inevitably
lead to war. Could Achille manage to forestall it, somehow? He shook his
head in despair. *I'm bound to the wheel of fortune as surely as the little tin
jockey riding his mechanical horse.*

Adele broke into his thoughts with a worried frown. "Are you all right,
darling? You seem so pensive."

He turned to her. "I was taking in the seascape, that's all."

"Oh, Achille, you're crying." She stared at his face, his hidden sorrow unmasked by the intense white glow of an electric lamp.

He smiled and brushed away tears with the back of his hand. "It's nothing, my dear, just the brisk salt air. Now, I'm going to give you the first two lines of a poem and I'll bet you a franc you can't name the title and poet."

She smiled broadly at the challenge. "It's a bet!"

Achille recited the lines:

Vois, ce spectacle est beau. - Ce paysage immense
Qui toujours devant nous finit et recommence . . .

Adele laughed. "That's too easy. It's Victor Hugo, 'Au Bord de la Mer.' Pay up, Chief."

Achille dug into his pocket and pulled out the coin. She snatched it from his palm and dropped it into her purse, along with her other winnings of the evening.

"This must be my lucky day," she said.

He brushed a couple of stray hairs from her forehead and kissed her cheek. "We're both lucky, my dear. Now, shall we return to the hotel and dress for dinner?"

"If you wish, but we won't dine for hours."

"Let's go back anyway."

They strolled arm in arm, up the pier and along the esplanade in the direction of their hotel. Achille remained aware of the challenges ahead, the risk and the danger. But he also valued the moment—the ocean breeze, the sound of surf breaking on the beach, and Adele's reassuring presence.

"I know something we can do to pass the time," Achille said.

Adele drew closer, resting her cheek against his shoulder. They continued on to the hotel.

END

ACKNOWLEDGMENTS

I am grateful to Donald P. Webb, Dana M. Paramskas, Bill Bowler, and Carmen Ruggero, for reading and commenting on my early drafts of this novel. Thanks to my agent, Philip Spitzer, and his associate, Lukas Ortiz, for their outstanding representation. Thanks also to Claiborne Hancock and his staff at Pegasus, most particularly my excellent editors, Maia Larson and Katie McGuire.